TO SAVE SIR

LAYLAH ROBERTS

Laylah Roberts

To Save Sir.

Cover Design by: EDH Graphics

Editor: Eve Arroyo

❀ Created with Vellum

LET'S KEEP IN TOUCH!

Don't miss a new release, sign up to my newsletter for sneak peeks, deleted scenes and giveaways: https://landing.mailerlite.com/web-forms/landing/p7l6go

You can also join my Facebook readers group here: https://www.facebook.com/groups/386830425069911/

BOOKS BY LAYLAH ROBERTS

Doms of Decadence

Just for You, Sir

Forever Yours, Sir

For the Love of Sir

Sinfully Yours, Sir

Make me, Sir

A Taste of Sir

To Save Sir

Sir's Redemption

Reveal Me, Sir

Montana Daddies

Daddy Bear

Daddy's Little Darling

Daddy's Naughty Darling Novella

Daddy's Sweet Girl

Daddy's Lost Love

A Montana Daddies Christmas

Daring Daddy

Warrior Daddy

Daddy's Angel

Heal Me, Daddy

Daddy in Cowboy Boots

A Little Christmas Cheer

PROLOGUE

Jenna watched in horror as the ball of chocolate ice cream slipped off the cone and landed with a splat on the ground. Tears streamed down her face as she watched it melt until it was a dark blob on the white concrete patio.

"Hey there, little bit." Someone large crouched beside her, his voice deep and soothing. Locked in her misery, she couldn't pull her gaze away from the rapidly disappearing mound of ice cream. "Now there's no use crying over spilled ice cream. I'm sure we can get you another scoop."

She finally turned to look at him. He was an older boy, his dark hair long and scruffy, dressed in ripped jeans and a red T-shirt. He gave her a smile and a wink. Then he stood and reached out his hand to her. "Shall we go find some more?"

She looked at his hand. "Nancy said I'm not s'posed to go anywhere with strangers."

He nodded. "Nancy is correct. You shouldn't. Do you want to go back inside and get the ice cream yourself?"

She sighed, feeling sad. "I can't. Nancy said I could only have one scoop, 'cause otherwise Momma will get upset."

"Why would she get upset?"

She shrugged. "She don't like me eating ice cream."

"All right then. Wait here and I'll be back soon."

She watched as he disappeared into the house. Her bottom lip trembled. She'd wanted that ice cream so badly. She'd been a good girl and said please, and Nancy had actually said yes. But after two licks it had slipped off the cone, onto the ground.

"Here you are, little bit."

When she looked up, her eyes widened at the sight of a fresh cone with two large scoops of ice cream, one chocolate, one vanilla. It was the biggest ice cream she'd ever seen. And the boy held it out to her.

"For me?" She didn't dare reach out for it in case it was some kind of joke. Maybe it wasn't for her at all. Maybe he didn't want to share.

He smiled. "It's for you, little bit."

"Thank you," she said, remembering her manners as she took the cone from him and took a giant lick.

He grinned. "You're welcome. Be careful not to lick it too hard, though. Don't think I can get us a third one."

She smiled and in that moment, as she gently licked the ice cream, she knew.

She was going to marry him.

And then he'd give her as many ice cream cones as she liked.

Two years later...

She sat with her legs dangling between the banister rails of the stairs, watching all the people arrive for the party. If Nancy caught her she'd been in trouble. But her nanny was deep into her favorite TV show so Jenna knew she had a good hour before she was missed. She'd find her way back to her bed and pretend to be asleep before Nancy noticed she was gone.

She couldn't miss seeing him—her future husband.

She smiled and hugged herself. His dad came over lots to see her daddy and sometimes Curt would come with him. Then he'd push her on the swing or help her build a sandcastle in the sandbox her daddy had put in for her. Nancy and Momma didn't like when she played in the sandbox but they let her when Curt was around.

She hadn't seen him for a while 'cause he was living in the navy now. Her daddy had been in the navy. He told her stories sometimes. It sounded so exciting and when she was older she thought she'd live in the navy too, and then she and Curt could play together all the time.

Yep, that's what she'd do. She'd marry Curt and live with him.

But where was he? She'd heard Daddy say he was coming tonight, but he hadn't walked in the door yet. Maybe he'd come while she was waiting for Nancy's program to start. Could she sneak down and find him? She looked back towards Nancy's room and bit her lip. If she got caught, she'd get in trouble. Momma might even spank her. She'd threatened that a few times, although Daddy didn't like it when she said that. Then they'd start yelling. And Jenna got scared.

She stood and made her way carefully down the stairs, sneaking towards the large living room that opened out towards the pool. She wasn't allowed by the pool on her own, but there were lots of people around right now. Besides, Daddy said she was a really good swimmer. Like a fish.

Jenna thought fish were kind of slimy and smelly, but because Daddy seemed so pleased she'd always smile and nod.

She hid behind some of the indoor plants Momma was so fond of. She thought maybe some of the people would see her, but they were too busy talking. She paused a few times to stare at the pretty girls. They all looked like princesses. Momma liked buying dresses for Jenna, but she didn't really like wearing them. They just got in the way when she was climbing. She'd ripped the last one when she'd been wrestling Jonty Mason after school. He'd told everyone she slept with a teddy bear. Her feelings had been hurt, 'cause she and Jonty had been best friends last year.

And he wasn't just any teddy. He was Sergeant Teddy. Her daddy had given him to her. So, she'd had to tell his friends how he still sucked his thumb.

Then it had been on. In a rage, Jonty jumped her. She'd fought back, and it had taken two teachers to separate them. She'd ended up with a bruise on her cheek, a ripped dress, and hurt feelings.

Although Daddy said it was good to stick up for herself, he still had to ground her because you couldn't fight at school, and it wasn't nice to fight with friends.

But she and Jonty weren't friends anymore. They were mortal enemies. Not that she knew what that meant, exactly. Jonty had told her that over the fence the next day—he lived next door.

Momma hadn't been happy, but she'd later heard Daddy laugh and call her his little warrior princess.

She liked that.

When there was no one close by, she slipped outside. Where was he? Feeling sad that she wasn't going to see him, she moved further into the garden towards her sandbox.

There he was! Excitement filled her. Maybe he was looking for her and that's why he was down here. Momma didn't like her guests seeing her play area because she said it was messy. So, she'd made Daddy put it down at the end of the garden, away from the house.

"Curt, there you are."

She watched, eyes wide, as her cousin, Amelia, walked up to Curt. He turned with a wide grin then pulled her into his arms, hugging her tightly.

When he kissed her, Jenna made a gagging noise. *Ick*. That was gross. Sometimes, Daddy kissed Momma. Yuck. Suddenly, Curt turned, peering out. He was dressed all in white. His navy uniform. She didn't know how he could keep all that clean. Momma never bought her anything white 'cause she said Jenna would just get it dirty. It was just as well Curt didn't wear all that white when he came to play because he'd just get all dirty too.

"Is someone there?" he called out.

"No one's there." Amelia placed her hand on his chest and looked up at him.

What was Amelia doing touching her Curt?

Jenna knew she was supposed to love her cousin and stuff, but Amelia was so old and boring. All she cared about were clothes and makeup and boys. She never wanted to play or anything.

And she was kind of mean. She liked to pull Jenna's hair —hard.

That's why Jenna had put a frog in her handbag. How was she to know Amelia would get so upset that she'd throw her purse, which still had her cell phone in it, into the swimming pool? The poor little frog had been so scared. Jenna winced as she remembered Amelia's screams.

Probably a good thing she hadn't used a snake like she'd been planning.

She took a step back. Probably time she returned to her bedroom. Nancy's program would be over soon. A stick snapped under her foot, and Curt stilled then looked around. The lights Momma had had the gardener put in weren't very bright, but she could still his face.

He looked scary.

She whimpered.

"Jenna?" Curt called out.

Amelia let out a loud sigh. "Great. Jenna, stop playing games and get out here before I call for Aunt Lorraine and Uncle David."

She stuck out her tongue at her cousin, knowing she couldn't see her.

Then she heard a snort. As she'd been making at face at Amelia, Curt had moved closer, spotting her in her hiding place. He smiled.

"Hey, little bit. What you doin' out here on your own?"

Amelia stepped up next to Curt and frowned at her.

"She's obviously supposed to be in bed and has snuck away from that slack nanny of hers. Honestly, I don't know why Uncle David keeps that woman on. Aunty Lorraine wanted to get rid of her ages ago."

Get rid of Nancy? She felt a jolt of alarm. They couldn't get rid of Nancy. She loved Nancy. She'd looked after her since Jenna was a baby.

"Go back to bed, Jenna."

"Amelia," Curt said quietly. Amelia sighed and looked away. Then he crouched and held his arms open. "Come here, little bit."

With a final glare at Amelia, she rushed forward and let Curt pick her up. She wrapped her arms around his neck and squeezed.

"Hey, you okay?" he asked, rubbing his hand up and down her back. "No one scared you, didn't they?"

"No, I'm okay."

"I like your pajamas," he told her.

"Momma said they're boy's pajamas, but Daddy said they're warrior princess pajamas." The short pants were camouflage, the top a dark green.

He walked with her over to a bench and sat with her on his lap. "Where are your shoes?" He grabbed one foot and brushed off the dirt and leaves.

"You're such a tomboy, Jenna," Amelia told her, sitting next to Curt. "And a nuisance. What are you even doing out here?"

"I didn't see Curt come in. I wanted to see you." She looked up at him and smiled.

Amelia laughed. It wasn't a pretty sound. "I think someone has a crush on you, Curt."

Jenna glared at Amelia, but Curt gently grabbed her chin, tipping her face up. He lightly touched the bruise on the side of her face.

"Who did this?" There was something cold about his voice, and she shivered.

"Hey, don't be scared of me," he said more gently. "Did someone hit you?"

"Curt, we need to get back to the party; it's nearly time for the announcement."

"We have a few more minutes," Curt said calmly. "Jenna, I want you to answer me, now."

The firmness of his voice caught her attention. Her eyes widened. "It was Jonty the Jerk."

"Jonty the Jerk?" he queried.

"Yeah, he lives next door. We go to school together. He told everyone about Sergeant Teddy."

"It's about time you stopped sleeping with that silly bear. Honestly, aren't you, like, ten now?" Amelia flicked her long, blonde hair over her shoulder.

"She's five," Curt told her.

"And there's nothing wrong with sleeping with a teddy bear. I did until I was twelve." He winked at Jenna, and she giggled.

"Twelve? You did not!"

"Of course, he didn't," Amelia snapped impatiently. "He's just being nice. But we have better things to do than babysit you. So run along." She flicked her fingers out.

"Amelia, perhaps you should return to the party. I'll be there as soon as I take Jenna back to bed."

Amelia made an impatient noise, but she stood. Then she pointed her finger at Jenna. "I know it was you who put that frog in my handbag, by the way. Brat." Then she smiled at Curt and leaned down to kiss him. "Don't take too long."

Jenna made another gagging noise.

"Hey, what's that noise about." He tickled her, and she giggled.

"Stop! Stop!"

He pulled his hands away.

"Kissing is yucky," she told him.

"Really?"

"Yep. Jonty the Jerk tried to kiss me. I told him it was gross. Then he told everyone I sleep with Sergeant Teddy. So I told his friends he still sucks his thumb. Then he jumped me."

"He jumped you? Maybe I need to have a few words with Jonty the Jerk."

She hunched her shoulders happily. "He'd be scared of you." She bit her lip. "But his dad is real important. I heard Momma say so. She said we wouldn't be invited to their Christmas party this year. But I don't care, 'cause now I won't have to wear the stupid Christmas dress Momma bought me."

He tapped her nose and stood with her on his hip. "You know you shouldn't be out here on your own, right?"

"I know. But I wanted to see you. I haven't seen you in ages."

"Sorry about that, little bit."

"It's okay. Daddy said you've been real busy. You smell funny. All spicy."

"You don't like it?"

"No. I thought you smelled nice before. All earthy."

"Earthy, huh?"

"Yeah, like trees and grass and mud."

He laughed.

"Guess I have to go back to bed now, huh?" she asked as they drew closer to the house.

"Maybe not yet."

He came to a stop, and she turned to see her parents coming closer. Her aunt and uncle, Amelia's parents, were with them. Her momma was frowning, and her daddy looked concerned.

"Did you really put a frog in Amelia's handbag?"

"Are you gonna tell?" She peered up at him through her bangs.

His lips twitched. "Little troublemaker."

"What are you doing out here, Jenna?" Daddy asked.

"She came to find me, sir," Curt answered respectfully.

"I'm so sorry she bothered you, Curt," Momma said.

"No bother. I wondered if she could stay up for the announcement."

"Sure, I guess." Momma smiled at Curt. Then her smile widened as Amelia joined them.

"Is it time yet?" Amelia asked.

Daddy smiled too. Then he walked over to where the band had set up. He waited until the song ended then grabbed the microphone.

"Are you going to put her down, Curt?" Amelia asked, glaring at her.

"She's all right." Curt put his arm around Amelia as her daddy started talking. He introduced Uncle Justin who stepped forward and took hold of the microphone. Was Uncle Justin going to sing? Jenna winced. He was a really bad singer. But, no, he just talked.

". . . and so, I invite you all to raise your glass as a toast to the happy couple. Amelia and Curt. May their lives be filled with happiness, health, and wealth."

"Amelia and Curt!"

Everyone cheered then came up to congratulate her cousin and Curt. But she didn't understand why. When there was a quiet moment, she pulled his face towards hers.

"Curt?"

"Yeah, little bit?"

"Why is everyone so happy for you? Did you win something?"

"I sure did."

"Is it ice cream?"

He chuckled. "Even better. Your cousin and I are getting married."

She should have used the snake.

Six years later . . .

She stared across the casket at him. The wind whistled around them, the sky dark and foreboding. It was a suitable atmosphere for a burial. A sea of black surrounded her. All of the mourners who'd gathered around the grave looked up at the sky then back to the coffin worriedly.

But she just watched Curt.

He looked terrible. She guessed that was pretty typical when your wife had just died. He'd changed over the years. She remembered him with the fondness of a child who'd thought of him as her hero. But back then, he'd been softer, gentler. Now there was a harshness to him. His face was more lined, his eyes colder, his body thick with the muscle he'd lacked in his younger years. And he was more gorgeous than ever.

She'd had a crush on him since she was three. He'd always been her hero. Not that he looked like a hero now. He looked dark and dangerous. And her eleven-year-old heart beat a little faster. Immediately, she felt guilty. How could she be thinking this way when they were just about to bury her cousin—his wife.

Her heart almost broke as she thought of the pain he had to be going through. She didn't know why he wasn't standing over here with the family, instead he'd positioned himself on his own, across from them. It was just family here at the burial, although the turnout at the church had been huge. Soon they would be making their way back to her house. Hopefully, she could sneak away to her bedroom. She could use homework as an excuse. Everyone knew Jenna wanted to be a doctor someday and was working hard to achieve that goal.

And if it meant she could get away from the fake condolences, all the better. She hadn't been close to Amelia, despite their moms being sisters. And while she felt sad she was gone, most of that sadness was for Curt and what he had to be going through.

"He could have at least shaved," her mother whispered to her father over her head. Jenna was ridiculously short which had put a wrench in the works for her mother, who'd seemed to think Jenna would grow up to become some sort of super model. That had been her mother's dream, not Jenna's. Besides, even if she wasn't five feet two, the extra weight she carried kind of ruined that plan.

Jenna didn't really care what she looked like. She knew what she was going to do with her life.

"And he's barely spoken to Mary and Justin. My sister is beside herself, and he can't even show her respect by shaving."

"People grieve in different ways, Lorraine," Daddy said in a low, warning rumble. When he spoke that way, he meant business, and her mother wisely quietened.

She glanced over at Curt, and caught him staring at her. She gulped and sent him a small smile. He just looked away. A stab of hurt filled her, but she guessed she couldn't blame him. After all, they were burying his wife and unborn child today.

Daddy was right. People grieved differently.

"HEY, LITTLE BIT."

She let out a startled cry then turned, her hand going to her chest. "You scared me."

"Sorry, saw you sneak out here and thought I'd join you. What are you doing?"

He sat next to her on the bench. The same bench where he'd sat with her on his lap so many years ago when she'd snuck out to see him on the night of the announcement of his engagement to Amelia.

"That looks like a thick textbook."

"Biology," she said, showing him the cover.

"Got a test coming up?"

"No. I just like looking through it." She blushed slightly. "Probably shouldn't have told you that."

"Why is that?" He raised one dark eyebrow. Up close, he looked even harder. Almost mean. But her Curt wasn't mean.

Except she hadn't seen him for a while, and Daddy said he did a lot of top secret missions for the armed forces. Who knew what he'd seen and done.

"Because men don't like women who are smart."

"They don't?" He raised his eyebrows.

She shrugged, embarrassed.

"Let me give you some advice, little bit. Your Mom doesn't know everything about men, all right? Guys who don't like you because you're smart aren't worth knowing anyway."

"I know." But it felt better to hear it from him.

He drew her close, and she breathed in his scent. "You smell good." She immediately went red. *Lord, Jenna, why'd you have to say that?*

"I remember you telling me you liked when I smelled like mud and trees, not spicy. Amelia was the one who gave me that cologne."

She stiffened and looked up at him. "I'm really sorry, Curt."

He looked across the garden, his jaw tightening.

"I didn't know if you were going to come today," she said quietly.

"Your aunt cornered me in the parking lot. I was too scared to say no."

She snorted. "Daddy says you're the best of the best. An elite soldier. You're not scared of my aunt."

He raised one eyebrow. "No?"

She just smiled.

He tapped the book. "You like this stuff, huh?"

She nodded. "I'm going to be a doctor. I want to help people. I might even join the military."

"No, you won't."

"What?"

He shook his head then sighed. "Sorry, forget I said anything. I think it's great you're going to be a doctor, little bit." He stood.

"You're leaving?" she asked sadly, wondering what it was she'd said.

He smiled and tapped her nose like he used to when she was a kid. It annoyed her a little. She was eleven now, not a child.

"Been here long enough. Got to get back to the base."

"You're going back to work?"

"Nothing to stick around here for."

She guessed not. He glanced over the fence. "Jonty the Jerk still giving you problems?"

"No, his dad sent him to boarding school. I know you had a talk with him. You're lucky he didn't tell his dad about that."

"Just had a man-to-man chat about how to treat a lady."

"I'm no lady," she said, giving him a grin to show him she wasn't offended. "I'm a warrior princess."

He grinned and tapped her nose. "You're trouble, that's what you are."

1

Fifteen years later...

They were back. She cringed as she heard a noise at the door to the hut she was locked in. There was no source of light. No windows, no cracks in the walls, nothing except that door. Sometimes it seemed like the darkness would smother her. She couldn't even make out her hand in front of her face. It was the freakiest feeling. There were times she felt like she couldn't even tell up from down.

Light filled the dark room, making her squint and blink frantically. Someone stomped inside. She knew better than to try and talk to them. The one time she'd tried that, the man had smacked her across the face and spat on the ground next to her. Her captor emptied the slop bucket and then put down a tray of food. Food she couldn't bring herself to eat. All those years of diets her mother had put her on and all she'd needed to do was lock her in a dark room with no company, no light, and no way out.

The door slammed shut plunging the hut into darkness once more.

How long had she been here? It could have been days, even

weeks. She felt weak and ill. Her lips were dry and cracked. And she stank. If she wasn't sweating buckets from the stifling heat, she was freezing cold and shivering.

The leather cuff around her ankle chafed against her skin, digging into her. She'd attempted to pull it off several times, but that only rubbed her skin raw. A heavy chain that had been secured to a spike in the ground was attached to the cuff. It kept her on a short leash. She couldn't even reach the door.

They weren't taking any chances she might escape. Not that there was much possibility of that. Even if she could free herself, she had to get out of the camp undetected, then make her way out through the countryside. She didn't even know if they were still in Sudan anymore.

Every movement made her whimper with pain from the beating they'd inflicted. She was scared, sore, miserable. What had she been thinking? Why had she joined Doctors Without Borders?

Because you thought you could make a difference.

Yeah, that had worked out well. After a month of being in Sudan, the village she'd been working in had been raided. Everyone had been killed except her, and she was starting to wish they'd murdered her too.

Aside from a few scraps as a kid, no one had ever hit her before, deliberately causing her pain. The beating had been methodical and emotionless. She wasn't sure if that was almost worse than having them yell at her. Of course, she'd never been beaten before so she had nothing to compare it to.

They hadn't reacted to her cries, her begging. Her screams. She whimpered quietly, cringing at the memory, the terror still all too real.

Agony. Fear.

One man had held her while another beat her, everyone else looking on. She'd thought she'd be raped. Instead, they'd sat her up and taken photos of her. She didn't get it. Obviously, they were asking for a ransom, and her father did have money. But why kill everyone else in the village? Why not just take her? A cry escaped her lips, and she quickly squelched it. She could not fall apart. If she gave in to the hysteria trying to overload her system then she was letting them win.

She laid down, resting her cheek against the cool, dirt floor. It was the only way of grounding herself. Otherwise, she almost felt weightless. A bit like when she was swimming. Except then, at least, she could see. She liked to lie on the bottom of the pool and open her eyes, looking up, seeing the light glistening against the water. She remembered doing that once while Curt and Amelia were over. It was shortly after their wedding. She'd been their flower girl. She snorted at the memory. Amelia had been an absolute bridezilla. A total brat. Jenna had hated having to wear that hideous, white dress with all the bows and lace. She still shuddered at the memory. Luckily, she'd managed to keep it clean until after the ceremony.

As she'd walked down the aisle, with Curt at the other end, she'd imagined she was the bride.

God. She'd had a crush on that man for over twenty years now. That was a little sad. A case of hero worship when she was younger that had morphed into a teenage crush. And now . . . well, she hadn't seen him in years. Apparently, he'd left the navy a while back and had gone to work for some private security company.

She wondered if he thought about her at all.

Of course he doesn't, idiot. You were just a silly kid to him. He'd just been a nice guy who'd taken pity on his wife's little cousin. Eventually, he'd probably hear she'd been kidnapped and killed and he might feel a little sad, but that was it.

He certainly wouldn't come to her funeral. Or go off the rails like he had when Amelia had died. She'd heard the stories about his drinking. The bar fights. Getting into trouble with the navy.

He must have really loved Amelia. And his unborn child. She

swallowed heavily. That was one thing she never had to worry about. Losing a child. She placed her hand over her stomach. Even if she made it out of here alive, and with each passing hour it seemed less likely, she'd never get pregnant. A car accident when she was ten had damaged her uterus.

She could still remember her mother screaming at her dad in the hospital. Her dad had been driving and he still felt guilty over what had happened. He'd been driving too fast and overcorrected, sending them spinning off the road. It could have been worse. Luckily, Daddy hadn't been charged. He'd beaten himself up enough. And her mother was likely to never let him forget she'd never have grandchildren. Jenna was surprised she even wanted grandchildren. Growing old gracefully was not a term that applied to Lorraine Jasons. If there was a procedure to reverse the signs of ageing, she'd had it.

Jenna sighed as she closed her eyes. She wondered what it would be like to have a man love her as deeply as Curt had loved Amelia. Not likely to ever happen, especially since she'd barely dated over the last few years. She'd been too busy getting through medical school and then she'd taken this job with Doctors without Borders. It didn't exactly create many opportunities for romance. She snorted. Most of the time she worked fourteen or sixteen hour days, got back to her tent, washed as best she could, ate, then fell into bed. Then she got up and did the same thing again. Nope, romance was the last thing on her mind.

It didn't help that she compared every man to Curt—and found them lacking.

You have got to get over it, Jenna. He'd never be interested in you. She was nothing like Amelia. Her cousin had always looked perfect. Her clothes, her hair, her social skills. If Jenna's socks matched, it was pure luck, and she didn't give a shit about fashion or makeup. As for her social skills, yeah, she knew how to hold a dinner party. How to make small talk. Her mother had made certain of that. But when was she ever going to use those skills when she had no one to invite to dinner?

"Sad, Jenna. Really sad."

If she got out of here, she was going to make some changes in her life. She was going to stop being so damn focused on her career and try to live a little. All she'd ever wanted to be was a doctor. To make a difference. To help. And look where that had got her.

Every time the door to her hut opened she was so terrified it would be the time they dragged her out, beat her, raped and murdered her. She was so stupid. She'd been so sure she'd be fine. That nothing bad would ever happen to her. What an idiot.

Now she was paying for her naivety. Her mother had told her over and over that coming here was too dangerous. How she should leave this to other people. Jenna had just ignored her mother's dramatics, like she always did. What had surprised her, though, was that her daddy hadn't wanted her to come here either. She'd thought he would have been proud of her for doing this, but he'd asked her not to go.

And now, she really wished she'd listened to them. She'd give anything to be home. If only she was stronger, the warrior princess Daddy liked to call her then she might be able to figure a way free from this hellhole.

A loud noise made her jump and she gave a scream, huddling in on herself.

Screams. Terror. Death.

The first warnings of danger had been the gunshots. Then the screams. They'd just gone through the whole village and killed them all. Men, women, and children. All of her colleagues. She could still hear Alana begging for her life on her knees, tears streaming down her face. Then the gun had turned on her.

Nausea bubbled in her stomach, and she dry-wretched, huge sobs rocking her body.

Oh, God, please let this be over soon. She didn't know how much more she could take.

HE'D LEARNED how to control his rage, to bury it deep where it wasn't at risk of exploding out, but his defenses were down and his barriers had been chipped away, making it hard to keep the fury contained.

The icy façade had all but melted in a pool of fiery anger.

"You sure you can do this?" Travis whispered, as he crouched next to him in the bush, his night vision binoculars trained on the circle of huts below them. Black-Gray, the security company Curt worked for, had been hired by Jenna's father to come to Sudan to rescue her. He clenched his hands into fists. What the fuck was she even doing in Sudan in the first place? She should never have put herself in danger.

As Travis turned to look at him, he took a deep breath, trying to calm himself. Travis had taken lead on this rescue after Black-Gray had brought Raptor Inc. onboard. Travis owned Raptor Inc. and had overseas connections they didn't. If it hadn't been for Curt's relationship with Jenna, Black-Gray probably wouldn't have taken a job like this.

They were going to wait for the guard change then Curt, Travis, and his brother, Jace, would sneak closer, infiltrate the camp, disable the guard positioned in front of the hut where they figured Jenna was being kept, and sneak her out. Sounded easy, but it could all so easily turn to shit.

Please, let her be here—safe and sound.

He wasn't going to consider any other alternative.

Jenna's kidnappers sent photos to her father a week ago as proof of life, with demands for seven million dollars, but they hadn't yet told him how they wanted to do the exchange. That wasn't normal for a simple ransom demand. He could tell her father was hiding something but he didn't know what. And he hadn't really cared about anything except getting to Jenna.

He'd visited the village where she'd been staying, where she'd been working her ass off to help these people. The local police had already trampled over the scene and removed the bodies. Everyone had been murdered except Jenna.

She had to be so scared. Rage pounded at him as he remembered those photos of her, her eyes swollen, her nose bloody, and her clothes ripped. He was going to kill those bastards for hurting her.

"Curt? If your mind isn't in the game no one will blame you, but I need to know before I let you in there."

Before he let him? There was no way Curt was staying behind. This was Jenna. His Jenna.

But he knew he had to play the game. He'd been playing it for years, growing colder year after year as he'd buried the anger and pain deep. It had been years since he'd felt much of anything. Jenna was the only person who could bring out his emotions. The only person he truly cared about.

Oh, he cared about his team—his friends—and their women. He'd do anything for them. But what he felt for them wasn't like this.

"I'm fine. I'm focused. Just want to get in there and get her out."

He raised his own binoculars. He didn't want 'the talk". He'd heard it several times. How she could be dead already. How they might be too late. That she might not even be there.

She was here, and he was getting her out. Today.

The next shift of guards arrived, and he tensed.

"Time to rock and roll," Travis stated.

SOMETHING TOUCHED HER SHOULDER, and she hit at it angrily. She was tired. She wanted to sleep. It was the only way she had of escaping. She knew it was a bad sign. She was growing weaker the more time she spent here, not eating and barely drinking. The darkness, the loneliness, and uncertainty played with her mind.

Another touch on her shoulder.

"Go away."

"Sh, little bit, be quiet."

Oh, she was still dreaming, because she knew that voice. And there was no way Curt would be here.

"Curt."

"Quiet now, it's me." Hands ran over her body. Not rough, but not soft either.

A tremble shook her as his earthy scent filled her senses. This felt so real it was painful.

"Are you hurt?"

"This is a really good dream," she said, reaching out to pat his face with her hands, surprised by how sluggish her movements were. She opened her eyes, but she still couldn't see anything. Her fingers encountered his beard, and she ran them over it. "I always liked you with facial hair."

"Did you?"

"We're ready," a strange, male voice said, and she tensed.

"Who else is here? Tell him to go away. I'm not into ménages."

There was silence then a low chuckle. "Good to know," the stranger said.

Then why didn't he go away? She wanted to pet Curt some more. He was so pretty.

"I am not pretty," he said in a deep voice.

"Oops, didn't mean to say that out loud. Oh, well, it's my dream. Let's just pretend you never heard that."

"I'm still trying to figure out what the hell you know about ménages," he muttered.

"I'm twenty-six, not five. I know what a ménage is. Don't want one, though." She frowned over at where the other voice came from. There was another chuckle.

"Travis is just going to cut through that cuff from your ankle, then we're out of here," Curt told her.

She felt something cold against her ankle then a tugging that made her hiss with pain.

"Be careful, you're hurting her," Curt snapped.

"I'm trying to be careful," the other man said in a cool voice. "The cuff is so tight it's dug into her skin. Cover her mouth so she doesn't make a sound."

"I'll be quiet," she said, feeling panicked. This dream was taking a really weird twist. Even weirder than a possible ménage. "You don't need to keep me quiet."

"Just do it, Travis."

Curt pulled her close, and she pressed her face into his stomach, breathing in his scent as the other man pulled the cuff off her ankle. She bit down on her lip to stifle another cry of pain.

"Done. Let's go. Do you want me to sedate her? One of us is going to have to carry her since she's so weak."

"I am not weak." She scowled at the asshole who'd been talking to Curt as though she weren't even here.

"Didn't your mother ever teach you it's rude to talk about other people? Especially when they're right here."

"Nope, can't say she did. We have to go, Curt. I have the sedative."

"No. No." She grabbed Curt's arm, urgency filling her. They'd pumped her full of something when they'd transported her here, and she'd vomited for so long she'd gotten dehydrated. It was part of the reason she couldn't bring herself to eat, even now. "I can be quiet. Promise."

He stared down at her for a few seconds.

"Please, Curt." Her heart started to race. Now that she was fully awake, she realized this was no dream. He was really here. She was actually touching him. "You came for me."

He started to pull something up her legs, and she realized he was dressing her. "Of course, I did."

Relief filled her, along with happiness, elation, and something deeper.

"As soon as your father hired us, we were on a plane to find you."

Idiot. He was here because he was being paid to. There was no other reason for him to be here.

"You really have to be quiet, little bit. I have a sweatshirt for you. We have to cover up all that white skin of yours."

He helped her put on the sweatshirt; she winced a few times at the pain from her bruises. But it's warmth soon took away her shivers. It was cold here at night and stifling hot during the day. She stank from sweat, dirt, and fear, but when she put the sweatshirt on all she could smell was Curt—and safety. She always felt safe with him. As though nothing could touch her when he was around.

He tied something around her hair. A scarf.

"I'm going to carry you now. No matter what you see you can't make a noise."

He picked her up in his arms, and for the first time since she'd been taken she knew she was getting out of this alive.

Because Curt was here.

CURT NEARLY CURSED as he felt how light she was. He'd seen a recent picture of her, taken at her farewell dinner before she'd left. She'd practically shone with health. Pleasantly curvy, her skin glowing, and her face filled with happiness. No hint of fear.

The way she should always look.

He moved out behind Travis, eager to get her out of the tiny, dirty hut. Jace kept watch as they exited. Curt pressed Jenna's face against his chest as they walked past the guard, whose neck he'd broken. Not that she could probably see that in the dark. Jace quickly pulled the body into the hut and shut the door. It wouldn't take long for it to be found, but they planned to be long gone by then.

They only encountered one guard on their way out, which Jace and Travis quickly took care of. Curt pressed her face against him once more, protecting her. She shivered.

He found himself wanting to reassure her, feeling such a surge of protectiveness it took his breath away. This was Jenna, of course he was going to be protective. He'd known her since she was three. Played with her, watched over her. She was practically his cousin. Yeah, that was it. She was family. That was why he cared so much about her. Why he was so filled with rage over what had happened to her.

He'd feel the same if any other members of his family had been kidnapped and terrorized. Not that he had much left. Just a few distant cousins.

They hastily made their way towards the rendezvous point where Josh, his teammate at Black-Gray, and Gable, who was one of Travis's men, would meet with them. He tried to shelter her as best he could from the vegetation slapping at her as he moved quickly. They didn't have much time before the dead guards were spotted. When they reached the rendezvous point, they paused to wait for the others, who would be covering their backs. He set her down, crouching in front of her. It was still dark out, the moon only at half-mast. He drew his night vision goggles off. The moon provided enough light to see as Josh and Gable joined them. She let out a small gasp as she noticed the other men, then slammed her hand over her mouth and looked up at him. He gave her hand a reassuring squeeze. At least he hoped it was reassuring.

"Where are you hurt, little bit?" he asked.

"I'm just bruised," she replied. "Nothing's broken as far as I can tell."

He frowned but nodded then grabbed her ankle, examining it.

"She hurt?" Josh asked, coming closer.

"No worse than we thought," Curt said quietly. "This ankle will need to be wrapped."

Josh nodded and quickly pulled out a bandage, winding it hastily around her ankle. Curt didn't like the other man touching her, but stopped himself from snapping. This possessiveness was crazy. He needed to get himself under control.

"We can't stop long. We need to get further away from here before they spot their dead," Travis ordered.

Josh grabbed a bottle of water and a protein bar from his pack, holding them out.

Jenna just stared at the other man. Curt felt her tremble. Christ, he was an idiot. In his hurry to get her safely out of there, he hadn't taken any time to explain who these guys were.

"Take the water and bar, Jenna," he told her. "That's Josh, he works with me and he has some medical training. You met Travis, and that big guy is his brother Jace. The other one lurking around, keeping watch, is Gable. We were hired by your dad to find you."

"Oh." Her hands shook as she took the items from Josh. "Thank you."

Josh nodded and moved away.

"I'm going to carry you on my back, all right? Think you'll be okay?"

"I'll be fine."

The steadiness in her voice impressed him. He'd fully expected her to be hysterical. That they would have to sedate her. Instead she was a bit shaky but otherwise composed.

"I have something for you."

She looked on curiously as he pulled something out of the bag he had strapped to his front. Her eyes widened as she took in the worn, brown fur of the old teddy bear.

"You brought Sergeant Teddy with you?"

Embarrassment filled him and he shrugged. "Asked your father for it before we left. No big deal."

He handed it over and she pulled the old bear tight against her chest. She blinked. Oh hell, she wasn't going to cry, was she?

"Thank you," she whispered.

"I want you to drink all of that and eat every bite, understand me," he ordered in a gruff voice as he gently picked her up, and they started to move out again. "I don't want one crumb left behind or else."

"Or else what?"

"You don't want to know." He grimaced as he realized how harsh he sounded.

"Yes, sir."

He knew she was being sarcastic, but the sound of that "sir" coming from her lips made his cock stir, and his balls ache. Christ. He had to get himself under control. There was no way he could be attracted to Jenna. She was family. She was a baby compared to him, not just in years but in experience.

He'd eat her up and spit her out.

And even pushing all that other shit aside, there was no way Jenna would ever be able to handle his darker needs. No way he would want her to. She was soft and gentle and needed protection.

She definitely didn't need to be handcuffed, gagged, and whipped. Although, damned if the thought didn't send his arousal soaring. Damn, he was in trouble.

THEY HIKED for what seemed like hours in the dark. Curt carried her on his back all the way. She'd asked him a few times if he wanted her to walk, but he'd just told her to be quiet in that low, commanding voice of his. She had no idea why the gruff sound of him barking out orders turned her on.

She put her reaction down to the stress of what she'd been through.

She dozed on and off as she slumped on his back. Occasionally someone else would offer to take her, but, thankfully, he always turned them down.

When they finally stopped, she felt completely exhausted, even though all she'd done was lay against his back. He'd done all the work. And when he sat her down, crouching in front of her in the early morning light, he didn't even seem winded.

"You really are superman, aren't you?" she said tiredly as she took the bar and water he handed her, placing Sergeant Teddy on her lap. She still couldn't believe he'd done that he'd remembered how much she loved this old bear and had asked her father for it before he'd left.

It was the sweetest thing anyone had ever done for her.

He paused and raised an eyebrow. "I'm not superman, little bit."

"No? You crept in, rescued me from the bad guys, snuck out while carrying me, then hiked for hours with me on your back. You're not even winded. And you're trying to tell me you're not superman?"

"Nope, superman had a weakness. I don't."

He took the water from her numb hands, undid the top, then held it to her lips. "Drink."

She took a few sips then tried to pull back, but he just gave her a look, and she gulped until the bottle was half empty. She pushed at his hand, and he set it aside.

"You'll drink the rest soon."

She resisted the urge to salute. Barely.

He ripped open the packaging on another disgusting protein

bar. Just as she'd expected, the other had tasted like cardboard. She'd choked some of it down before slipping the rest into the pocket of her sweatpants. What he didn't know wouldn't hurt him.

He held the bar up. "Eat."

"It tastes awful," she complained. "Besides, I'm still full from the other bar." She crossed her fingers behind her back at her small lie. "And my stomach has shrunk considerably since I've been captured so I don't need to eat a lot before I feel full. I need to be careful not to eat too much too quickly or I could make myself ill. But you go ahead and eat. I'm just going to sit here for a moment and enjoy the fresh air." The sun was getting higher now and it looked beautiful as it rose against the skyline.

"That's all very interesting. Now eat."

She sighed. "You're getting even more stubborn and bossy as you get older. I'd hate to think what you'll be like when you're eighty."

"Don't plan on living that long," he told her casually. "Now either you eat this bar, or I'm going to have to get strict with you."

Hmm . . . strict, huh? Her body stirred.

Shit, what the hell was wrong with her?

"Bossy bastard, isn't he?"

The guy who'd been in the hut with them came and sat beside them. What was his name? Travis?

She nodded then yawned. "Sorry. Haven't had much sleep lately."

Travis, who was a good-looking guy and well built, gave her a concerned look. "Gonna take you a while to recover from being held captive for eight days."

"Eight days? Oh, my God. It felt like forever, but I wasn't sure how long it really was. Why did they hold me that long? What did they want? Why kill everyone else but me?"

Curt and Travis gave each other a look. "They sent your father photos of you as proof of life for ransom."

"How much? Did he pay it?"

"Seven million," Curt told her. "He was still waiting to hear details, but he didn't want to take any chances with your life so he hired us to rescue you."

She shivered and the other man gave her a small smile. "You don't have to worry about them anymore. We're going to get you home where you'll feel safe."

She nodded, although she thought it would take her a long time to feel safe anywhere again. She glanced over at Curt, who reached out and squeezed her knee. Except with Curt. She always felt safe with him. She blinked back tears. The look on his face became slightly panicked.

"Jenna?"

"I'm okay. Just feeling a bit off balance."

"Understandable. We're only a few hours from where we'll meet the chopper then we'll be airlifted out of here, and you can return home and get on with your life." Travis stood and left.

She shivered. "He makes it sound so easy. Like being kidnapped and held by extremists happens every day."

"It won't be," Curt told her bluntly. "He's trying to keep you feeling positive and happy because we can't afford to have you lose it right now. Then we'd probably have to sedate you."

Panic filled her at the thought of being helpless. "Don't. Please. I couldn't take that. I'm not going to go crazy on you."

"I know you won't. I know how strong you are."

"I don't feel very strong right now."

"Not everyone would have survived eight days in that hell hole and still come out sane. You did. Because you're strong. You remember that when you're feeling low. When you're wondering why you were taken. When you're scared. You survived. That's all you ever have to do, Jenna, survive. Because I will always come for you."

She had to glance away to hide her tears this time. These tears were for a whole other reason. Because she knew he didn't mean those words as anything more than from one friend to another, but, to her, they meant so much more.

"Here, I'll put this bar into your pocket, and you can have it later." He stuffed it into her pocket, stilling as he obviously felt the remains of the one she'd hidden there earlier. He gave her a stern look as he pulled out the half-eaten bar.

"Jenna," he said in a low, warning voice.

She shrugged. "It tastes like dry cardboard coated in artificial sweetener. It's disgusting."

His lips twitched. "It is. You're still eating it though."

"Bossy."

"Troublemaker."

2

Three months later ...

Jenna stepped out of Lacey's office feeling drained and defeated. Why couldn't she remember?

Dissociative amnesia. She knew what it was. She just never thought she'd suffer from it. She'd blocked out the memory of being kidnapped and beaten because it was so traumatic she couldn't cope. Great. So, she was weak. Too weak to remember what had happened to her.

It was the most bizarre thing she'd ever experienced. Apparently, she'd fallen asleep on the flight to the states and when she'd awoken, she had very little memory of the previous eight days.

She could recall getting up that morning, going to the temporary clinic that had been erected on the outskirts of the village. She could even remember treating people. Then nothing.

She couldn't remember anything more. Lacey had told her she had to be patient. That often memories would just return suddenly and fully, whether from a trigger or through therapy. That she shouldn't despair or stress about her lack of memory.

But she was over this. She had to know. It felt like not knowing, not remembering, was just making her more fearful. She looked around as she walked through the building that housed Black-Gray Investigations, hoping to spot Curt. She felt a little silly. He probably wasn't even here.

He's not avoiding me.

Except she couldn't help feel he was. He'd visited her a couple of times in the hospital. But once she'd been discharged all she'd received from him were a couple of texts. He couldn't even be bothered to call her.

He was probably busy.

Too busy to pick up the phone for five minutes and check on her? Maybe he just didn't care.

After she'd been cleared to leave the hospital, her parents had insisted she move back in with them. She hadn't put up an argument. She might not be able to remember what happened to her, but she'd been told the basics. And the thought of being on her own was terrifying.

Terrifying enough to make staying with her parents seem like a good idea. It hadn't taken her long to see that was a mistake. Her mother fussed over her to the point of smothering her. Daddy acted like she was fragile. An invalid.

Her mother had even hired a nurse to take care of her. Reasoning with her hadn't had any affect; Jenna should have known it wouldn't. Normally, Daddy would come to her rescue, but he'd practically locked himself in his study, claiming he had to work. She got the feeling that was just an excuse. As though he couldn't face her. After a few weeks of butting heads with her mother, which meant weeks of Jenna giving in to her demands, she'd finally told her mother to get rid of the nurse or she was leaving.

The nurse was gone the next day.

But Jenna was still stuck living with her parents. She wondered how she was ever going to get away from their good intentions.

"Hey, Jenna, how are you doing?"

She turned towards the cheerful voice with a smile. "I'm good, how are you?"

Cady looked a bit tired. There were dark circles under her eyes, and her skin was pale. Jenna wasn't sure what was going on with the other woman, and she didn't know her well enough to ask. She'd met her several times because of her therapy sessions with Lacey. Cady was married to Hunter Black, one of the owners of Black-Gray Investigations. He was one of the most intimidating men she'd ever met. Large and gruff and a little scary even though he'd never been anything but polite to her.

"All good," Cady replied. "Did you just have a session with Lacey?"

"Yeah." She bit her lip. "I'm still having trouble remembering things."

"Don't worry, it'll come."

"That's what Lacey tells me. Do you know if Curt's around?" She tried to keep her voice casual, but from the knowing look on Cady's face she hadn't quite managed that.

"He's away on a job. He should be back next week. Do you have his cell number?"

"Oh, yeah." She flicked a hand out. "It's nothing important. I might catch up with him next week. Bye."

She walked away before the other woman could question her further. Nerves danced through her stomach. She took a deep breath then let it out slowly as she stepped outside onto the pavement. Her father had wanted her to have a bodyguard. Jenna didn't like confrontation much but when she felt strongly about something she could be stubborn as hell.

And she was damned sure she didn't want some stranger following her around. She already felt like so much had been taken from her she didn't need to have her privacy intruded on as well.

But she'd compromised and agreed to a driver. Hans was more than just a driver, she knew that. She saw the way he watched their surroundings. He was always on guard, his gaze always roaming, and he was built like brick shithouse. No, he was no ordinary chauffeur, but so long as he didn't try to follow her everywhere, she'd put up with him. Because she still didn't feel safe. Not like she once had. She wondered if she ever would.

"Hey, Curt. How's it going?"

Curt looked up from his laptop as Cady walked into the office. He saved the report he'd been working on and turned to her with a smile. Petite and delicate looking, he knew her outer appearance hid a hard-as-nails attitude and a strong personality. She had to be strong to deal with Hunter.

"Am I interrupting?"

He snorted. "It's a welcome interruption, believe me. I hate report writing."

"Me too." She grinned.

He gestured to a chair, not liking how pale she appeared. "Have a seat. Can I help you with something? You feeling all right?" He turned in his chair and reached into the small fridge they kept in the office, pulling out a bottle of water and handing it to her.

She raised her eyebrows.

"You look pale."

"Can't get anything past you, can I?" she grumbled as she took a drink.

He frowned slightly. "I'm surprised Hunter allowed you come in to work when you're feeling so ill."

She raised her eyebrows. "Allowed me? Why does everyone seem to think Hunter's the boss of me?"

"Perhaps because he *is* your boss. And your Dom. And your husband. And he has been charged with your care. You need to let him look after you."

For damn sure, if she were his wife she wouldn't be working while she obviously felt poorly. She'd be at home, with her feet up, being pampered like a princess.

Of course, he never intended to marry again. So, he'd never have the bother of trying to care for a delicate wife.

She sighed, shaking her head. "This is what I get for working with a bunch of Doms. Bossy bastards, all of you."

"We try our best," he told her mildly.

"Anyway, I didn't come in here to get a lecture on my health. I saw Jenna the other day."

He tried hard to show no reaction, although he knew very little got by Cady. He didn't know if it was working as a cop or living on the streets, but she was pretty good at sizing people up. She'd taken an instant liking to Jenna.

Of course, it was hard not to like Jenna; she was like a sunny day in the middle of winter.

Christ, he was practically poetic.

But Jenna was the sort of person who made others smile. People were drawn to her friendly personality, her warmth, and the way she listened to everyone, giving them her full attention.

She was goodness and light. And she didn't belong in his world.

"Oh? She's still having sessions with Lacey, right?"

"Yes." Cady frowned. "Don't think they're going well. She's still having problems with her memory. She asked about you."

"She did? Is she all right?" He sat up a little straighter, ignoring the way Cady's gaze narrowed thoughtfully. Did she need him? Shit, why had he been avoiding her? He hadn't been around much lately, but he'd figured she was in good hands.

He'd never thought she might need him. Not when she had

her family surrounding her in love and safety. Her father had called and asked for recommendations for a bodyguard. He'd had no reservations recommending Hans for the job, even though he hadn't liked the idea of someone else being charged with her safety, but if it couldn't be him then Hans would be his next choice. Hans was a deadly bastard. Mean and capable.

He'd do whatever was necessary to protect Jenna.

Cady shrugged. "As all right as you'd expect her to be. I think it's wearing on her, not being able to remember what happened."

"What does Lacey say about that?" Maybe he needed to have a talk with Black-Gray's newest employee. See if there was something else she could be doing for Jenna.

"Lacey told her she had to be patient. I think they're going to try hypnotherapy during her next session. Just thought I'd pass on that she was asking after you. I asked her if she had your cell number, and she said she did. If she didn't contact you, it must not have been too important."

Only problem was, he wasn't certain Jenna would contact him, even if it was important. She didn't like to ask for things, even things she needed. He tapped his fingers against his desk. He could call her. Or go see her. Check on her. Or he could just ignore what Cady had told him and keep clear of her.

He let out an impatient sigh.

She was safe. He'd know if she wasn't. He'd made that clear to her father. David Jasons knew he was to contact Curt if there was any threat to her safety. Curt needed to stay away from her. It was best for everyone involved. Jenna especially.

Maybe a night at the club was what he needed. Spanking a few subs asses ought to help him forget a petite brunette with eyes too big for her face, and a smile that reached even the darkest recesses of his soul.

∽

SHE WAS GOING TO VOMIT.

The memories assaulted her. One after the other, moving so quickly through her mind she could barely keep up. Her breath sawed in and out of her lungs, the nausea bubbled as she recalled Alana on her knees, begging for her life. The images of mothers trying to shield their children. The small, dead bodies strewn about. Cries of terror and screams of disbelief and horror filled her mind.

Oh, God. Oh, God.

"Jenna, it's okay. It's Lacey. You're here with me."

No, no. She couldn't stand it. The memory of the beating she'd suffered made her catch her breath. She whimpered. She could feel each hit of his fist against her body as though it was happening to her right now.

Fear. Panic. I'm going to die.

"Jenna, you're safe. You're safe in Dallas. In my office at Black-Gray. You're safe."

You're safe, little bit.

Curt. She remembered. He'd come for her. He'd carried her on his back, brought her Sergeant Teddy, told her off for pretending to eat that horrid protein bar. She heard him telling her he'd always come for her.

I need him now.

"Jenna, open your eyes and look at me."

Lacey's calm voice broke through the memory, and she gasped, opening her eyes. She blinked, staring up at a pale Lacey.

"Jenna—"

"I'm going to be sick." Jenna rolled off the sofa she'd been lying on and stumbled, falling to her knees. She felt so weak and disorientated.

She still hadn't regained all her strength after being kidnapped. The doctor had told her she needed to eat better, develop an exercise routine . . . blah, blah, blah. She knew all that.

Everyone seemed to forget she was a doctor. They treated her like she was ill.

And right now, it felt like they were right.

Nausea bubbled in her stomach as Lacey slipped her arm around Jenna's waist and half-dragged her to the bathroom. She bent over the toilet and vomited.

Oh, God. Oh, God.

"I'll get you some water," Lacey said.

Jenna whimpered as her stomach clenched and she threw up again. When she thought she had herself more under control, she reached up with a shaking hand to flush the toilet then sat back, leaning against the wall of the small bathroom attached to Lacey's office.

Lacey entered and handed her a cold bottle of water. "Here, drink this." Then she turned towards the bathroom cabinet. "I'll get you a toothbrush and toothpaste."

"Get a lot of vomiters, do you?" Jenna tried to joke.

Lacey just sent her a small smile. "Do you want me to call someone for you? Perhaps your mom could come and get you?"

"God, no." Jenna shook her head then regretted the action as the room spun sickeningly. "That's the last thing I need."

Lacey frowned slightly. "We just had an intense session, Jenna. You're going to need support."

"I have a driver, he'll get me safely home." Not that she'd call Hans a source of support by any stretch. Hans was even more cut off emotionally than Curt was.

Curt. When was the last time she'd spoken to him? He hadn't visited her again, hadn't texted her in weeks. And yet she couldn't help but want him, miss him.

I will always come for you.

"I wasn't talking about just getting home. Although I'm glad to know you won't be driving after this."

"I'll be fine," Jenna told her. "If I need someone to talk to I've got you, right?"

Lacey looked concerned. "Aren't your parents being supportive?"

"They are. In their own way. But I-I can't tell them about this." About the horror. The fear. The pain.

Her hands shook so badly she couldn't get the top off the bottle of water. Lacey took it from her and undid the top, handing it back.

Jenna took a few sips, grateful her stomach remained calm. She leaned her head back against the wall and closed her eyes. "I hate being weak."

"I know it must feel that way, Jenna. But don't underestimate what you went through. Being afraid doesn't make you weak. It makes you smart."

"I blocked everything out to protect myself, didn't I?"

"It was the brain's way of protecting you from the trauma."

"They shot all those people. It didn't matter if they were just children. My colleague, she begged them," she sobbed, "she begged for her life, and they just shot her, but I lived. Why?"

Lacey sat on the bathroom floor with her. "I don't know that, Jenna."

"How did they know my dad had money? Did they go there for me? Why did they kill everyone?"

"I don't know. Maybe we never will."

And not knowing was going to eat away at her. How could she ever feel safe again, when she didn't have answers?

They're across the other side of the world. They're not coming for you here.

Somehow, that didn't seem to help. It was like she'd worn rose-colored glasses all her life, and now those glasses had been ripped off her and stomped into little pieces.

Nothing was the same, and adjusting to life as she now knew it was something she just wasn't certain how to do.

Fifteen minutes later, she reassured Lacey she didn't have to call someone for her, that Hans would get her safely home. She sensed the other woman was also shaken.

She walked slowly down the corridor at Black-Gray. Lacey had wanted to escort her out, but Jenna had wanted a few minutes to herself.

"Jenna? Jenna, wait."

The hand on her shoulder made her cry out in fright, and she turned, stumbling back. She saw Curt's shocked face before he took a step back, holding his hands up as though trying to appear nonthreatening.

It didn't really work. At around six feet tall, he wasn't the biggest guy she'd ever met or the most handsome. But he had a look about him that warned you he was dangerous. He could appear so cold and removed.

He could also make you feel like you were special with just one smile, one look.

She took one deep breath then another.

"I'm sorry for scaring you. I called out to you, but you seemed to be deep in thought." He studied her closely, his gaze narrowing. "Have you been crying?"

Crap. The last thing she wanted was for him to see her as weak, even though he'd seen her at her worst.

"I'm fine. I just . . . I had a session with Lacey just now. Things were a bit intense."

"I thought you couldn't remember anything."

"Well, that all changed today," she said dryly. "The hypnotherapy worked, and everything came back to me. Most of it anyway."

He frowned. "And Lacey let you just walk out on your own? Where's Hans?"

He knew about Hans?

"I assume he's waiting in the car," she said. "I've tried to tell him he should go get a coffee and something to eat while he's waiting for me. He must get so bored, but I don't think he ever does."

"In the car? How the fuck is he supposed to guard you if he's in the car?"

She jolted at the harsh note in his voice and realized this was one of the few times she'd ever heard him swear around her.

"As far as I know, he's not supposed to be guarding me." She studied him closely. "But now I think I've been an idiot; he's obviously no ordinary driver."

"You're not an idiot. Your father is. Hans has skills even the military doesn't know about, but how is he supposed to use them to protect you if he's limited to driving you around? What was your father thinking?"

"I imagine he was thinking he didn't want to upset me. I told him I didn't want a bodyguard."

"That's just tough then, isn't it? Considering that's exactly what Hans is. From now on, he accompanies you everywhere."

"No."

"No?" He gaped at her, clearly in shock.

She had to hold back a smile. "You sound like you've never heard the word before."

"Oh, I've heard it. Just not aimed at me when I give an order. Everyone usually obeys."

"Guess I'm not everyone then."

As they spoke that knot in her stomach lessened. That feeling of never being safe, of always being on guard dissipated. Around Curt, she felt like nothing could touch her. Even Hans, who was always on alert and looked like he could face down a tornado and come out unscathed, didn't induce these feelings of security in her.

"Damn it, Jenna. You're going to let Hans do his job. It's why I recommended him to your father. To keep you safe."

A feeling of happiness filled her. Maybe he'd been avoiding her. But at least he'd cared enough to send Hans to her.

"Your father wanted to hire me, but I couldn't do it. I knew Hans was coming off a job so I recommended him."

That feeling of happiness abruptly faded. He hadn't had time for her so he'd sent his friend to do the job? Because she wasn't worth his time?

Stupid. Stupid. Why did she always let herself think she was more important to him than she really was?

"If you'll excuse me, it's been a long day, and Hans will be waiting for me."

"Wait, Jenna." He reached out and touched her hand, and she had to fight to hide her reaction to his touch, the shiver that raced across her body. How was it possible for her to feel arousal after everything she'd remembered today? She felt so raw, exposed, and vulnerable.

"Come for a drink with me." There was a gentle note to his voice. As though he could tell she was near the breaking point.

"I don't know," she whispered.

"Please," he added.

She snorted. "Not sure I've heard you use that word before."

He grinned. "No, but it's a word I hear often."

"I bet. Curt, I'm not really up to being around other people."

"No other people. Just me. We'll go to my place, have a drink, and you can tell me how things are going with you."

Damn it. She should say no. But he was like a sweet treat being offered after a month of dieting. And she'd never been good at resisting temptation.

THIS HAD BEEN A BAD IDEA.

He watched as Jenna moved around his living room. It was a small, one-bedroom apartment. The living, dining, and kitchen areas were all open plan so he could easily see her as he grabbed a couple of beers out of his fridge. He grimaced as he scrounged around for any food to offer. A block of cheese and a couple of wrinkled tomatoes looked back at him.

She was still too thin. Maybe he should order a pizza. Then he could make certain she ate.

As he walked slowly towards her, he studied his apartment, trying to see it through her eyes. Sparse and cold were the two words that came to mind. At least it was clean, thanks to his next-door neighbor, who he paid to clean it once a week.

The living room held a couple of leather armchairs and a huge TV that was secured to the wall. No pictures or plants or colorful cushions to break up the white paint, gray carpet, and black furniture.

He grimaced then walked over and handed her a beer.

"Sorry, I don't have anything else to offer."

She smiled. "That's okay, I don't drink much anyway."

"I'm gonna order a pizza. Is there anything you don't like?"

She turned to look out the window. This apartment had one thing going for it and that was the view. "Wow, this is amazing." She looked out across the Dallas skyline. "Beautiful. Oh, I'm not hungry, thanks. But you go ahead."

He decided to order a couple of pizzas. She was going to eat something, even if he had to feed her himself. His cock stirred at the thought of her kneeling between his legs as he fed her.

Shit. He had to stop this. This was Jenna. Not a sub from the club. Not that he ever brought any of the subs back to his place. He never brought anyone here. He quickly ordered the pizza then turned back to find her watching him.

"You don't have any pictures of Amelia," she said with soft eyes.

He glanced away, feeling like a fraud. She probably thought it was because he was still mourning or some such shit. Truth was, he couldn't look at that bitch's face without feeling murderous.

"I get it."

"Do you?" he asked harshly.

Her eyes widened and she took a step back. Fuck. The last thing he wanted was to scare her.

"Jenna, shit. Sorry."

She shook her head. "No, I'm sorry. I shouldn't have said that. It was stupid and insensitive. I've never really lost anyone. I mean, I lost Amelia too, but I didn't love her like you did. We were never really that close, and, well, I'm sorry. That was a really stupid thing to say."

He had to turn away before he did something idiotic. Like try to shut her up by pulling her into his arms and kissing her. Or by telling her the truth, but that was something he never intended to talk about. Especially not with Jenna.

"Another beer?" he asked.

He turned back to find her staring at her still full bottle and knew he'd drunk that last one too fast. He'd gotten rid of all the hard liquor in the apartment because one scotch had soon turned into four or five. He didn't like how out of control he'd felt or how he'd come to rely on alcohol to get him to sleep so he'd thrown it all out and now when he couldn't sleep he went to the club or the gym. It was healthier, at least physically.

"No, thanks."

He sat on one of the chairs, hoping to put her more at ease. She looked wide-eyed and on edge, like she was thinking of bolting. Not that he could blame her. He was acting like an ass.

"So, what happened in your session with Lacey today?"

She shrugged. "I don't feel like talking about it." But she came over and sat in the chair next to him. She ran her finger around the rim of the bottle, not drinking from it.

"Talking can help."

"Yeah? How's that working for you?" she challenged.

He raised one eyebrow, surprised by the belligerent note in her voice.

She looked away. "Sorry, don't mean to be rude. Just a bad day."

"It's working out pretty poorly for me," he told her honestly, and she turned to him, looking surprised. "I've buried my shit deep because I think then it won't affect me."

"But that doesn't work?"

For him, it was the only way he could move forward, keep going. But it wasn't what he wanted for her. Because those problems festered and ate away at you until you became a messed-up fool like he was.

"Nope." He waved his hand around his place. "Not unless you want to end up like this. Alone, living in a crappy apartment, bitter and twisted."

"You're not bitter and twisted."

"Maybe I'm just not that way with you. Maybe everyone else thinks I'd give Ebenezer Scrooge a run for his money."

She smiled and shook her head. "If you're so awful then how come everyone at Black-Gray likes you?"

"Maybe I'm just a good actor." He winked, as though joking around. But the truth of it was, he *was* bitter, twisted, and dark.

"So, you going to tell me more about this session with Lacey? Must have been bad if you didn't hear me calling out to you. You looked so pale I was worried you'd pass out."

The door buzzed before she could say anything, and he rose, grabbing his wallet. "That's the pizza."

When he returned, she was where he'd left her. Looking

entirely too small in his large recliner. He sat the pizza box on the floor.

"Sorry, I don't have a coffee table."

"How long have you lived here?" she asked.

"Um, about three years."

"Oh."

He had to hide a grin. "You thought I'd just moved in, didn't you?"

She nodded then smiled. "You like minimalism, huh?"

"Something like that. Hawaiian or meat lovers?"

"I'm not hungry."

He just patiently waited, not saying anything. She sighed. "You're the most stubborn person I know," she grumbled, but she reached for a piece of pizza and took a bite. And he felt a ridiculous surge of satisfaction, knowing she was eating. That he'd seen to her care.

Get a grip, Curt.

He grabbed a piece of pizza to hide his surge of emotion.

They ate in silence for a moment while he thought of the best way to approach the topic of her session with Lacey. He didn't know why he felt the need to push her, to know what was going on. He could put it down to caring about a friend all he liked, but it wouldn't be the truth. At least not the full truth. He didn't care about his other friends like this.

When she'd eaten a slice then settled back into the recliner with a yawn, he placed down his piece and turned to her. He'd eaten three and hadn't tasted any of it.

"What happened in therapy today, Jenna?"

She shook her head and gave him a small smile. "You just never give up, do you?"

"Nope. So you might as well tell me."

"I finally remembered it all." She frowned slightly. "Well, maybe not all of it. I think there are bits still missing. Lacey said they might still come back to me." She rubbed her hand over her face and leaned forward resting her elbows against her knees. "I can't believe I forgot all of it. How could I forget about all those people being murdered?"

There was horror in her voice. Fear. He hated that she'd gone through all of that. That so much evil had touched her. Part of him had hoped she'd never remember any of it.

She looked over at him. "You know that saying, be careful what you wish for? I was so sure I wanted to remember. I was so frustrated that my stupid brain was blocking the memories from me. Now I realize it was probably doing me a huge favor. Not sure how I would have coped with it all when I first got back. Not sure how I'm going to cope with it now."

Those beautiful, pale blue eyes filled with tears.

Shit.

"Jenna, I'm sorry. I shouldn't have pushed you to tell me all of this."

He felt helpless to stop her pain. It wasn't something he was used to feeling.

She shook her head. "No, it's okay. I need to learn how to live with this, right? To cope with the memories without falling apart when someone mentions what happened."

"You need to cut yourself some slack. I don't know anyone who'd be coping as well as you are right now."

And why was she having to deal with it alone? Where was her family? Why weren't they accompanying her to therapy? Supporting her?

He leaned forward, clenching his hands against the need to take her into his arms. To pull her over and tuck her in against his chest and keep her safe.

"All the memories came rushing back. So fast and so real it made me ill." She placed her hand over her stomach, her gaze fixated on the wall in front of her. But he knew she wasn't really seeing the wall. "The gunshots came first. Then the screams. Oh, God." She shuddered, and he wasn't strong enough to resist. Standing, he pulled her up then settled down in the chair and drew her into his lap. He'd started this. He had to listen to whatever she wanted to tell him. No matter how much it would hurt.

He ran his hand up and down her back, feeling the tremble run through her. "You must have been terrified."

"They didn't want me to go, you know."

"Who? Where?" *The rebels? The other doctors?*

"My parents. They didn't want me to go to Sudan. My mother did her usual performance. First, she tried bribery then anger then came the guilt. It's rare for us to get to guilt because I normally give in before then and give her what she wants."

"But not this time."

"No, not this time. This time I stuck to my guns. I knew she wasn't going to like it but I wanted to do something, you know? I wanted to help. I was so naïve I actually thought I was going to make a difference. I didn't want to take some job at a private practice like my mother wanted. For some reason, she thinks the only reason I went to medical school was to find myself a rich, handsome doctor to marry. Preferably a plastic surgeon so he could help her in her fight against ageing. She's winning, by the way. She looks younger than me."

He'd seen her mother recently, and she did look youthful. But it was all fake. Everything about Lorraine Jasons was artificial, from her nails to her skin to her attitude. She'd never liked him but she always greeted him with an air kiss to the cheek and talked to him like he was her long-lost son.

How someone as genuine and sweet as Jenna had come from that woman, he had no idea.

"I don't need someone to look after me. I can take care of myself."

He disagreed but he knew better than to argue that point right now. Sometimes it paid just to stay quiet when a woman was talking. He'd learned that the hard way.

"But what really surprised me was that Daddy agreed with her." She glanced up at him. "He didn't want me to go either."

Curt got it. Had he known of her plans to join Doctors Without Borders and head into one of the most dangerous countries on the planet he'd have put his foot down and told her she wasn't going.

Okay, so she was a grown woman, but she'd been sheltered all her life. She'd grown up thinking there was good in everyone. She didn't have that hard, cynical edge to her. Not like he did. Sudan was not a place she belonged.

Again, he remained quiet. He wasn't stupid enough to incite her anger over something that had already happened. There was no question of her ever returning. It would be over his dead body.

"So, I had my mother trying to guilt me into staying, and my father practically ordering me not to go. Do you know how it felt to leave when I didn't have their support? I was so upset. But I thought I could finally make a difference, you know? What a naïve idiot I was."

He frowned, not liking her self-deprecating tone. "You are not a naïve idiot."

"Really? How did I think that anything I did would count? I was there a month, Curt. A whole freaking month before I saw everyone in that village murdered. Women, children, my colleagues. I can hear Alana begging for her life as she knelt next to me in the dirt. She was sobbing, telling them how she had a family back home, a daughter and son. A husband. And they just shot her. One minute she was there. The next she was dead. And her babies don't get to see their mother anymore."

Curt held her tightly as she started to sob, her body trembling against his. "Why did they do that? Why kill everyone? Why not kill me?"

"They wanted you for a reason."

"For the money? Then why didn't they tell Daddy how to pay the ransom?"

I'd like to know that as well.

"I guess it doesn't matter anymore. You guys rescued me. But if they came to the village for me then why kill everyone else?"

"Because they're extremists. All they care about is their cause, not how much damage they do to those around them."

She shook her head. "It's my fault."

He should have known that was coming. He tilted her face up, hating the tears that ran down her face, the sheer misery and guilt he could see. "It's not your fault. It's their fault."

"But they came to get me, right? If I hadn't been there . . . if I'd just listened to my parents. They were right to not want me to go."

Except their reasons, like his, were purely selfish. They didn't want her to go because they wanted to keep her safe. Jenna, as usual, was thinking of everyone else but herself.

"What about during the time you were held captive? Do you remember much from then?"

She wiped her face with her sleeve, the action reminding him of when he'd first met her. Only three years old with tears running down her round face, her lower lip trembling as she stared down at the melting blob of ice cream on the ground.

"A bit, I guess. Are you sure you want to hear all this?"

No, he didn't. But if there was something he'd learned it was that not talking didn't help. Not that he ever talked about his bad shit. But he didn't want Jenna making his mistakes. It was too late for him. He'd keep his issues buried until he died. She had her whole life ahead of her. She could go find that doctor to marry. Someone who'd look after her like she deserved. She'd have a big house, three kids, a crazy dog, and a husband who came home each night for dinner.

"Yes, tell me." Damn he hated this. If he thought he had any hope in hell of finding the assholes who'd taken her, he'd be searching them out now and making them pay for each bruise they'd inflicted on her, every moment of fear. But they'd scattered, and he'd be chasing his own tail.

"I knelt there in the dirt, staring down at Alana's body. She didn't move. Her eyes just stared, and I knew she was dead. But I couldn't help but reach over and touch her. I thought I was next. I thought the next gunshot was going to kill me. Someone grabbed me roughly from behind. Before I could do anything, before I could react, there was a prick on my neck. When I woke up I was in that dark hut, the one you found me in. I felt so ill. Whatever they gave me didn't agree with me, and I started vomiting. I had no idea where I was. It was so dark, I couldn't see anything in front of me, not even my own hand. I've never been somewhere so dark."

He kissed the top of her head soothingly.

"I still have to sleep with the light on," she confessed quietly.

"So do I."

She snorted and pulled back to smile up at him. "You are so full of shit. You're not afraid of anything."

"You think not?" She was right, not much scared him. Except for her. His feelings for her. He knew he had to put some distance between them. He didn't want to feel this way about anyone.

"When I finally stopped vomiting, I tried to move. I thought perhaps they'd dumped me somewhere. When I attempted to stand, I realized there was something around my ankle. I couldn't walk more than a few feet. I started to cry then. I bawled like a baby."

She sounded almost ashamed of her reaction.

"Most people would have done the same."

"Not you."

"True, but I think we established I'm superman."

"I thought you said you couldn't be superman because you didn't have a weakness."

"Jesus, that makes me sound like an arrogant ass."

"If the shoe fits . . ." She grinned at him. A real grin. He tickled her lightly, and she giggled, trying to get away from him.

"Little brat. Should have spanked you as a kid, maybe then you wouldn't be giving me this lip."

She snorted. "You wouldn't have spanked me."

Not then, but now? He pushed that thought from his head.

"What happened next?"

She stiffened. "They came for me. One of them was yelling something, but I couldn't understand him. They undid the cuff then dragged me out of the hut and into the middle of the clearing. It was late afternoon, and they all wore those bandanas over their faces, so all I could see were their eyes. I was shivering, and still trying to recover from the aftereffects of whatever they'd drugged me with. I tried to talk with them, to ask why they'd brought me there, what they wanted." She let out a sob. "But they didn't say anything. One of them just grabbed my arms, pinning them behind my back while another one beat on me. Oh, God, I've never been hurt like that. I mean, I had a few fights as a kid, but this was . . . it was . . . they never even talked, you know? They just hit me, over and over. Others stood around watching as though it was something they saw every day. No one tried to stop them. No one tried to interfere. Long after I thought I couldn't take anymore I was just dropped to the ground. I lay there, so sore I couldn't move. I could barely breathe. As I lay there I heard one of them call for a camera."

"Wait, you *heard* one of them?" He knew his voice was too tight, too low, but he could barely control the rage engulfing him.

"Yes."

"So he spoke English. The ransom demand came through via your father's email, but the address it came from was a fake account and it was pinged through so many satellites, we couldn't pin down the one used to send it. In the video, though, the person spoke very broken English with a thick accent."

"This guy he . . . he spoke really clean English. He was well-spoken. I think, maybe, he sounded British."

"Did you see him?"

"No. My eyes were swollen shut, and I was in such pain I couldn't even move. When they put me into position to take pictures, I could barely understand what was going on. After they took the photos, they dumped me back into that hut and secured the cuff on my ankle again. They pretty much ignored me after that. Just brought me food and emptied that horrible slop bucket. Sometimes I sang to myself. All I could remember were Christmas carols; it's a wonder they didn't shoot me just for that."

"Don't," he said in a low voice.

She raised her eyebrows. "Too soon to joke?"

He was pretty sure that fifty years from now would still be too soon for him to joke about what happened to her.

"And you never heard them speak again?"

"No. At least not in English. I could hear them outside talking sometimes. That was actually a relief. I worried they'd just leave me there to die from dehydration."

"Did they touch you?"

"Touch me?"

"Sexually. Did they rape you?"

She stiffened in his arms, but he wouldn't let her climb off his lap. He knew he should. He should put distance between them, but after hearing everything he couldn't let go of her. He needed her closer than ever.

"No, they didn't touch me sexually," she said in such a quiet voice he had to strain to hear her.

Thank God.

He grasped her chin, tilting her head up so he could look into her eyes. She tried to move her gaze away but he tightened his hold slightly. "Look at me."

She sighed and met his gaze, her blue eyes glistening with unshed tears.

"You're telling me the truth?" he asked in a firm voice.

"Yes."

"Good. Because you always have to tell me the truth, understand? Even if it hurts. I won't ever accept lies."

He knew by the way her eyes widened he'd spoken too harshly.

"You should have taken someone with you to therapy today."

She blinked slowly. "Like who?"

"Your mom or dad. You shouldn't try to go through this alone."

"And you think having one of my parents with me would make it better?" she asked in disbelief. "My mother would tell me she'd told me not to go to Sudan. Then she'd launch into a speech about how terrified she'd been, how horrible it had been for her wondering if I was dead or alive, imagining everything that could have happen to me. Then I'd end up apologizing to her for everything."

He knew from the way she spoke this wasn't just a guess. What the hell was her mother thinking? She should be trying to do everything she could to help her daughter through this.

"And your dad?"

"Well, let's see, if I could get him away from work to even ask him to come with me all I'd achieve would be to make him feel even guiltier than he does now."

"He's avoiding you?"

"For some reason, he thinks it's his fault I was hurt. I guess because they wanted money from him. No matter how much I try to tell him he isn't to blame, it doesn't seem to sink in."

And once again she was taking care of everyone else around her.

"I hate feeling weak, Curt."

He ran his hand over her hair. It reached past her shoulder

blades now and was filled with strands of light blonde to dark brown. The scent of strawberries hit him, making him nearly groan with need.

"You're not weak."

"Yes, I am. I can't sleep without having a light on. I wake up every night with my heart racing, feeling ill, and with no memory of what I was even dreaming about. Although maybe that won't be a problem now. I know what my nightmares are now, don't I? Do you think that will make it easier or harder? I have someone to drive me around. A chauffeur whose gaze never stops moving, who stares at everyone with suspicion and never lets his guard down. I'm living back home with my parents. Other than my therapy sessions I don't go anywhere, I don't see anyone. I'm scared. All. The. Time. Do you know what that feels like? Of course, you don't. Because you're you. If that village had been attacked when you were there, you'd probably have had those assholes disabled in under five minutes, have rescued everyone, and then just gone on with your day. All without breaking a sweat."

"I think you overestimate my abilities," he said dryly.

"I want to be more like you. Will you teach me how?"

She wanted to be an emotionally challenged asshole with no soul? At least that's what his wife had called him. Right before she'd walked out the door and died in a car crash.

"You don't want to be more like me."

"You want to know the only time I feel safe anymore? When I'm with you."

Jesus, she was killing him. This right here is why he shouldn't have played with fire and brought her home with him.

"Jenna—"

"Will you teach me how to defend myself? How to make sure no one else ever hurts me again?"

Oh, fuck.

"Jenna, I can find you—"

"No, it has to be you, don't you understand? I can't let anyone else close to me. Do you think I could sit on just anyone's lap? When everything came back to me today, when I felt physically ill with all the horror and fear, do you know what the one thought was that got me through? It was knowing that you'll always come for me. I've never felt about anyone the way I feel about you. It's always been you, Curt. Always you."

She leaned up and kissed him. And when he felt her lips against his, so gentle and unsure, he almost gave in to the urges riding him. It would have been so easy to roll her beneath him, to take from her. And take and take.

He slid his hand up her side until he encountered the underside of her breast.

"Curt, yes," she murmured, and he froze.

This was Jenna. He didn't do this with Jenna.

He pushed her back, his movement so hard and fast she almost fell from his lap. *Fuck!* This is why he stuck to subs at the club. Because they knew the score. That it was just about release. It was play. Nothing more. They knew to obey him without question. To give him their submission. There were rules they both had to follow and there were safe guards in place so that if anything went wrong, those subs were protected. From him.

Here, there was no one to watch over Jenna—just him, and he couldn't trust himself with her. He couldn't trust himself not to let the darkness inside him come out and hurt her.

He grabbed her before she fell and stood her up before stepping hastily away.

"Curt, what is it? Don't you feel the same way about me?"

"No, I fucking don't." He laughed. It wasn't a pleasant sound. He saw her wince, her face turning white. He had to do something to make her see that he wasn't her fucking knight in shining armor. He wasn't good. He wasn't her savior. He couldn't keep her safe.

"That was a mistake," he told her.

She shook her head, and he stalked close to her, grabbing her shoulders. "You know nothing about me, Jenna. You look at me and you see the man that saved you. You see the boy you knew years ago. The boy you had a crush on."

"You knew about that?"

"Of course, I knew. You followed me around with those puppy dog eyes for years."

He saw those same eyes widen with pain and he hated himself for what he was doing. But he couldn't let her go on thinking he was the good guy.

"You see me through those rose-colored glasses you said you'd lost. Well, you're still as naïve as ever if you think I'm right for you. If you think there will ever be any sort of relationship between us."

"Let go of me. I get it. You don't want me. I'm leaving."

He let her go and stepped back, running his hand through his hair. "I don't mean to hurt you."

"Good job," she said sarcastically.

"This is just an infatuation. It's common with victims and the people who help them. But I don't want you seeing me as your hero."

"No worries there," she said stiffly.

"You'll start to feel safe again, give it time. Then you can find a man who'll be good for you. But that guy won't ever be me. Believe me, you couldn't handle the needs I have. You are way too innocent and naïve to ever be someone I'd get involved with. The women I fuck know the score. And that's all I do, fuck them. Nothing more. You're the commitment type. You're also completely vanilla. When I look at you I see my cousin. Not a fuck buddy."

She snorted. "You know, all you had to say was no. I understand the word no. I'm sorry to have inconvenienced you for so long. I'll leave now." She turned towards the door, her shoulders stiff.

He felt like the absolute scum of the earth.

"Jenna." What could he say? How could he make her understand?

She didn't turn but she did pause.

"Keep Hans close, he'll protect you. And if you ever need to talk—"

"Don't come to you. I got it. Goodbye."

As the door slammed, he grabbed the bottle of beer he'd been sipping from and threw it against the wall.

Well, that went fucking well. *Shit.*

3

"Curt? Curt!"

Curt turned towards Hunter who frowned at him from the head of the table in the large meeting room at Black-Gray Investigations.

"Yeah?" he snarled.

Hunter's gaze narrowed, and Curt knew he was pushing the other man's patience. The thing was, he didn't really give a fuck. He found it hard to care about anything right now. Five months had passed since he'd seen her. Five months since that night in his apartment when she'd kissed him—and he'd driven her away.

He'd done such a good job he hadn't seen her since. For weeks afterwards he'd waited to bump into her in the corridor. He'd gone over how he would handle things. What he would say. He'd rehearsed every line in his head. Ways to smooth things over. How he'd make up for the harsh way he'd treated her. At the time, he'd thought it was for the best he didn't see her. Now, five months later, he was still haunted by the wounded look on her face—hurt he'd caused.

"Are we interrupting your midmorning nap or something?"

Hunter snapped. "Does someone want to go find Curt a blanket and a pillow? Maybe something to cuddle since I'm about to make him fucking cry."

"Oh, yeah?"

Curt stood quickly, and his chair shot backwards on its wheels, slamming against the wall. Beside him, Cady jumped, and the anger in Hunter's face grew.

"Cady, out of here. Now."

Hunter's voice had lowered in a rage that was impressive and rarely heard. Oh, he was filled with plenty of bluster, but most of it was all show. Not that he suffered fools. He only really showed his softer side when it came to his wife. But he was furious, and Curt knew it was his fault. His focus was shot to hell.

Curt placed his hand on Cady's shoulder. "Sorry, honey. Didn't mean to scare you."

"You didn't." She scowled up at Hunter. "But I do wish the two of you wouldn't yell in front of the baby. She's going to come out thinking her daddy is always angry."

"*He* won't think any such thing," but Hunter lowered his voice as he stared down at his wife and her impressive baby bump.

"The doctor said it's a girl, Hunter. You've got to get used to that fact."

"The doctor is wrong. They get things wrong all the time."

"I don't think they could miss something dangling between the baby's legs."

Curt knew Cady was trying to diffuse the heated situation with a familiar argument between her and Hunter. Hunter seemed to think denying that he was having a daughter would make it true. Curt knew a man running scared when he saw one. Bad enough to have a fragile, helpless child dependent on him for everything, but for it to be a girl added a whole other level of pressure. Pressure Curt had once welcomed, but had been taken from him in the space of minutes. He pushed that memory away.

"I think we should all just sit and take a breath for a moment, all right?" Gray said calmly. He looked at Curt then Hunter.

"I'll grab your chair," Cady offered.

"You'll stay where you are," Hunter barked. "Let him get his own damn chair."

Curt winked at her, grabbed his chair, and sat with a sigh. Fuck, what was he doing with his life? Did he want to lose the only reason he had for getting up in the morning? The only thing that stopped him from drinking too much? Because all he had left was this job and the way he was going, soon he wouldn't have that. Then what the hell would he have to live for?

"As Hunter was saying, Travis has asked for a meeting," Gray said in a low, calm voice. "He'll be here in ten minutes."

"What's it about?" Lacey asked with a frown. Travis was her cousin, but she seemed as clueless as the rest of them.

"I don't know," Gray said dryly. "He's being mysterious, as usual."

"Asshole," Hunter muttered. It was common knowledge there was no love lost between the two of them although they seemed to be playing nice ever since Lacey got involved with Gray.

"He said he has some information about an old case we might be interested in," Gray said. "I don't know what he's talking about, but it must be important for him to fly down here."

"We haven't worked on that many cases with Raptor," Josh mused. "There was that one with Lacey and another one earlier this year and the one involving Jenna Jasons."

Curt stiffened at the mention of Jenna's name. No, Travis wasn't coming here because of Jenna. That case was over. There was nothing left to talk about.

Unless Travis had a lead on who'd taken her.

"If it's about Jenna's case, I want in."

"Oh, so you *are* still awake," Hunter said sarcastically. "I was about to call a medic to check your pulse."

Curt managed not to snap back. Barely. He knew Hunter was having a hard time with Cady getting closer to her due date. Plus, he was just an asshole. He did have a point about Curt not really having his head together, though. That had to change. They talked about a few of their other jobs, nothing Curt was that interested in.

When the door to the meeting room finally opened, and Ella ushered in Travis and Jace Andrews, Curt was on edge. *Is this about Jenna's case? But why would it be?* As far as he knew that was closed. She was taken by extremists for money. End of story.

But that ache in his gut just wouldn't go away. The one that said this wasn't over.

Travis gave Ella, the new receptionist, a gentle smile. The girl blushed slightly. Curt had never seen her even smile. She was timid, jumped at shadows, and couldn't look any of them in the eye. Sometimes he wondered what had possessed Gray to hire her. Gray collected strays, as Hunter liked to say. Thank God, because otherwise half of them probably wouldn't be here. They all had their own personal shit. Gray had brought them together and made them a family of sorts. And he'd been failing his family. Too stuck in his own head to be much use to anyone.

Yeah, shit has to change.

"So, what's this about, Andrews?" Hunter barked. "Better be good, we've all got other stuff to do."

"What, you missing an appointment with your manicurist?" Travis asked.

Hunter growled.

"Oh, crap, and so it begins," Cady muttered. Then she pushed her chair back and stood. "Hey, Travis, Jace. It's good to see you again." She sent a look at Hunter.

He glared at her. "I'm not going to launch myself at them. Sit back down; the doctor wants you to rest."

Jace frowned. "Then what's she doing here? Why isn't she at home relaxing?"

"*She* is here because *she* wishes to be," Cady told him firmly.

Curt barely bit back a grin. Cady might submit to Hunter when they were playing, but that didn't mean she let him get away with ordering her around the rest of the time. Although he certainly tried. They'd butted heads many times about his tendency to be overly protective. However, on this, Curt agreed with Hunter. They all did. Cady should be at home. They all made a concerted effort to ensure she took it easy while she was here and didn't stress, but he still thought she was better off at home with her feet up.

"She keeps threatening to take the bus if I don't bring her with me."

Travis raised her eyebrows. "And you let her get away with that?"

"Travis, Jace, welcome," Gray said smoothly, walking over to shake their hands.

Lacey got up to greet her cousins, and they hugged her tightly. "Why didn't you tell me you were coming?"

"It was kind of last minute," Travis said. "We only got the info this morning and then we jumped on the first flight."

Had to be important then.

"Do you have to go back today?" Lacey asked.

"Nope," Travis said as he pulled out a laptop and sat down, plugging it into the projector on the table as though he'd worked here for years instead of having just walked in the door. "We're staying with you. Possibly for a couple of nights."

Jace gave Gray a look as he tugged Lacey in against him. "So, make sure you keep your hands to yourself while we're here. Last thing we need is to watch you mauling our cousin."

"I'll try to keep the mauling to a minimum," Gray said dryly as Lacey rolled her eyes and returned to her seat.

There was a knock on the door, and then Ella walked in with coffee. She handed out cups then went around and filled them. Hunter stood and grabbed Cady's cup before Ella could pour her any. He moved over to the small fridge in the room and returned with a bottle of water.

"Hey!" She scowled at him. "You know it pisses me off when you steal my coffee."

"And you know the doctor said to cut down on your caffeine intake."

"Got to stop taking you to those doctor visits," she muttered, scowling at the bottle of water.

"I could get some caffeine-free coffee?" Ella offered quietly, surprising Curt. She usually never spoke unless she was asked a direct question.

"No point, I don't drink it for the taste. Thanks, Ella."

She looked over at Curt's coffee longingly for a moment. "Give me some," she whispered to him.

"No way." He drew the cup out of her reach. "I've already pissed the big guy off today. Besides, if the doctor said no caffeine, then you know you're not getting any."

"Traitor." She sighed, then a wicked glint came over her eyes. *Uh-oh.*

"Oh, I feel a little ill." She rubbed her stomach.

Hunter stood abruptly, his chair crashing into the wall. If this kept up they were going to have dents in the walls. "What is it? Is it the baby?"

She sniffed then placed her hand over her mouth. "It's the coffee. The smell. Oh, I think the doctor was right. I shouldn't have caffeine. I shouldn't even smell it."

"Really? You expect him to fall for that?" Curt asked, taking a sip.

"Take all the coffee out," Hunter barked.

Cady turned and smirked at him. "You were saying?"

"You are such a brat."

"If I can't have it then I don't see why I should suffer through watching the rest of you drinking it."

"You okay, baby?" Hunter walked over and rubbed her back.

"Oh, she's fine. It's the rest of us who are suffering," Curt said. "What she needs is a good spanking."

"I agree."

What surprised him was that it was Cady that spoke not Hunter. She gave Hunter a look.

"We're at work," Hunter barked then stood and moved back to the head of the table. "Come on, Andrews, we don't have all fucking day."

Curt half-turned to look down at Cady, who stared at Hunter with a look of hunger. "He's worried about something happening to you. It's totally understandable."

Hunter's loud voice barking out demands covered their conversation.

"Yeah. This is a control freak's worst nightmare." Cady ran her hand over her stomach. "He doesn't like feeling helpless. Knowing he can't take over, that he can't do this for me; it kills him. He's worried something will go wrong with the birth, that he'll mess up at being a dad."

"He'll be a great dad."

"I know, just wish he believed it."

"A bit overprotective, of course," he added. "Poor girl probably won't go on a date until she's thirty."

"Thirty? I was thinking fifty."

They grinned at each other.

"I'm still going to get you back for taking away my coffee."

She winked.

Travis cleared his throat, and they all looked over at him. "All right, let's start."

"Finally," Hunter growled, tapping his fingers against the desk.

Travis and Jace ignored him.

Travis turned to look at him, and Curt just knew. "This is about the op we ran to rescue Jenna Jasons."

His heart beat faster, nerves on edge. He sat forward. "What about it?"

Travis met his gaze. "You know the family, right?"

Curt nodded. "You know I was married to her cousin, Amelia."

"How well do you know her dad?"

"David Jasons? He knew my dad. They served together in the marines. David got out after one tour and went to work for his father. My Dad stayed in. They kept in touch."

Even though they came from very different backgrounds, the two men had gotten along. Curt's father came from a poor family. He'd entered the marines at sixteen because he'd had seven younger siblings, and his parents were dirt poor. He'd found he liked being a marine. David Jasons had come from a wealthy family. He'd become a marine because it was a tradition. Like a rite of passage or some such shit.

"That's how I met Amelia. Why? What's he got to do with any of this?"

"He's been dealing in arms trading."

"What?" Curt couldn't have been more surprised if they'd told him he liked to dress up as a creepy clown and scare young children. "That can't be right. He wouldn't."

"According to the feds, it is. They're planning on executing a warrant to search his business and home in a few hours."

Curt stood. "Well, why the fuck didn't you say so?" He had to get over there, Jenna would need him. "Jenna will need help, I—"

Cady reached up and grabbed his hand. "Jenna's not there, Curt."

"What? What do you mean, she's not there? Where is she?"

She'd moved out? He knew things hadn't been great for her living under her parents roof but he thought she would have . . . would

He sat, feeling stunned, and realized there was some part of him that thought she would need him. That thought she would come to him again. Ask him for help.

He was such a fool. Of course, she didn't need him. Jenna was strong. She was a survivor. She'd be fine without him.

Damn that was a blow to his ego.

"If I can continue." Travis said, staring at him. Was that a hint of sympathy in his gaze?

"What evidence is there against her father?" Curt asked. "How do you know about all of this?"

"I know one of the lead investigators on his case. He called me to give me a heads up."

"Why? You've got nothing to do with Jenna," Curt said suspiciously.

Travis sat back then looked over at Jace, who was leaning against the wall. "Nothing about Jenna's kidnapping felt right to me. It seemed obvious she was targeted for a ransom demand, but why kill everyone else in the village?"

"Because that's what extremists do. They terrorize. They act without conscience," Josh said.

"Yes, exactly. So why was this done so methodically? So coldly. They just went through and shot everyone. They didn't burn the village, steal anything, or rape the women. I've got some photos." He stared over at Lacey then Cady. "Lacey, out."

His cousin sighed. "You're not my boss, Travis."

"You don't need to see this."

"I've seen bad shit before."

"So have I." Cady sent Hunter a look. "Don't even think about it."

He pointed a finger at her. "You get upset, you're out of here."

Travis snorted. "Seems getting into a relationship makes pussies out of Doms 'round here."

Hunter leaned forward. "Funny how you can't seem to find a woman to stick around more than five seconds."

Travis just shook his head.

"Can we get on with it?" Gray asked.

Travis brought up the photos.

Curt had seen some of them before, others were new. "How come I haven't seen some of these?"

Travis's jaw tightened. "The local police held some back. Had to get a friend to grease some palms."

"You have a friend?" Hunter asked. "That's a surprise."

"See that?" Travis ignored Hunter as he zoomed in on the hand of one of the doctors. A female. Jenna's friend who'd been executed beside her.

His temper stirred as he thought of everything these bastards had put her through. Jenna should never have been there. She should have been safely at home, working, hanging out with friends, her biggest problem being what to wear out on Saturday night.

"Is that a gold bracelet?" he asked. "Weren't they all told to leave jewelry at home?"

"According to her husband, this was an anniversary gift he gave her before she left. She meant to take it off and forgot. But wouldn't extremists that were after cash loot the bodies?"

"But they thought they were getting millions from Jenna's father," Lacey pointed out. "They probably didn't care about the small things."

Travis nodded. "It's a possibility. But that money could have taken a while to organize. Things like jewelry and the technology some of the doctors had could've been sold for fast cash. There were laptops, iPads, cash. None of it was touched."

Curt frowned. He hadn't really thought about any of that. His only thought had been to get to Jenna.

"For a band of extremists, they were well-organized and well-trained. They shot to kill. They didn't stray from getting their target, Jenna. And they were in and out quickly. We were damn lucky we got that intel about where she was being held. If those villagers hadn't heard the shots on their way back from a neighboring village and hidden there would be no witnesses."

"So why are you bringing this all up now?" he asked.

"And why didn't you tell us you were still looking into it?" Hunter added.

"I wasn't. Not really. I sent out a few inquiries. That feeling in my gut just wouldn't die. But I didn't think anything would come of it. Until a friend who works for the feds contacted me to ask what I knew about David Jasons. I told him what I knew. He said they had suspicions that Jasons wasn't on the up and up, although he didn't tell me what they suspected him of until today. Still, it was enough for me to send a contact I have in Sudan to talk to the local police to see if they knew anything we didn't. He came back with these photos."

"I always wondered how they knew about Jenna," Josh mused. "I mean, how did they know who she was? Who her father was? Someone had to have given them that info."

Curt remembered the guy Jenna recalled who'd spoken such clear English. The leader maybe? She'd thought he'd sounded British. Could he have been?

"Me too." Travis nodded. "And then my FBI friend tells me that they suspect David Jasons of supplying weapons to terrorists."

"I just can't believe it. He was a marine." Not that marines couldn't do shit like this. But he'd liked him. He'd always seemed like a good guy.

"A lot of evidence says he did. However, the feds are after bigger fish than Jasons. If he co-operates and gives them what he wants, they'll go easier on him."

"Poor Jenna," Cady whispered. "She loves her dad. She's going to be devastated."

"There's going to be a lot of outcry over this," Gray added. "Jenna's dad's company will suffer. He employs a lot of people. There are a lot of shareholders."

Travis looked grim. "Exactly. Which is the other reason I'm bringing this to you. Jenna and her mother could become targets for people's anger and fear over this."

Like hell. He'd . . . what? He hadn't even known that she'd moved out of her parent's place. His hands clenched into fists beneath the table.

"So, what's the connection between Jenna being kidnapped and her dad's dealings in arms trading?" Hunter asked.

"Not certain yet, but I'm working on it. Going to call in a few favors."

"Why?" Curt asked bluntly.

Travis just stared at him.

"Why are you doing this? Why do you care?"

"Because I don't like when innocents get hurt," Travis replied calmly, but Curt saw the cold, hard look in his eyes. "They shot up a whole village, killed children, murdered adults, and then kidnapped and beat up a terrified woman. And because my gut burns."

"There's a doctor a few blocks down. Pretty sure you can get something to help you with that," Hunter told him.

That coldness dropped away slightly. "Can they prescribe something to get your head out of your ass?"

"I really don't think Dallas is big enough to house both your egos." Cady looked from one to the other.

"What do you need while you're here?" Gray asked.

"Talking to Jenna would be a good start. I need to figure out if she's remembered something more."

Curt tapped his fingers against the table. Should he tell them what she'd remembered? He met Lacey's gaze across the table. She knew. But she wouldn't say. Jenna had told her in confidence. He wasn't held by the same confidence. But he would do whatever would keep her safest.

He trusted his team with this information. Question was, did he trust Travis and Jace? They'd helped rescue her. They'd risked themselves to free her. And they were Lacey's cousins. And they had come to them with this information when they didn't have to.

"There's one thing she remembered that was strange. She heard someone speak after she was beaten. In English."

"Accent?" Travis asked.

"Not a local accent. She thought if anything he sounded slightly British."

Did a look of excitement cross their faces? Travis leaned forward. "Did she see him?"

Even if she had, he wouldn't admit it now. Not after seeing their reaction. Now he was starting to wonder if he'd made the right decision telling them.

"What is it?" Hunter asked. "You obviously have some idea who this guy is."

"The Brit," Travis asked.

"The Brit?" Gray repeated. "You don't mean the guy on the FBI's most wanted list?"

"And Interpol's," Jace added. "Everyone wants this guy."

"Only no one knows what he looks like. Anyone that did hasn't lived to tell the tale."

"Genius name he's got," Hunter muttered.

"You're sure she didn't see him?" Travis asked Curt.

There was an odd note to his voice. Was this the real reason he was here? Because of this guy? After all, he barely even knew Jenna so why did this warrant more than a phone call with a friendly heads up?

He shook his head. "They all wore bandanas over their lower faces."

"Fuck. Probably just as well. If she'd seen The Brit then she'd be in a world of danger and she's already got enough problems."

Travis and Jace shared a look. Definitely something more going on there.

Curt looked over at Gray, who was staring at Travis and Jace thoughtfully.

"So, you guys going to tell us why you're really here or are we going to find out at the end after some big clusterfuck that could have been avoided if you'd been upfront?" Hunter barked.

That was Hunter. Always to the point.

Travis snorted. "Don't beat around the bush, man."

"You know me better than that."

Travis sighed. "I do. Look, I can't tell you much—"

"Course you can't. That would be too fucking easy."

Travis gave Hunter a look. "But we're interested in getting our hands on The Brit."

"You want to get hold of a guy on both Interpol and the FBI's most wanted list?" Gray asked quietly. "And you don't expect us to ask questions?"

Travis turned to look at him. "We didn't have to bring this stuff to you."

"Would have been a real jerk thing to do," Hunter drawled.

Travis glared at him. "But I probably would have called you anyway because the little I saw of Jenna, I liked. She's a fighter. And I don't want to see any harm come her way."

"But why would this guy have something to do with Jenna's kidnapping?" Lacey asked.

"The Brit supplies weapons to terrorist groups across the Middle East and Africa. His reach is far. If you have enough cash, he can get it. He's suspected of supplying arms to the group that bombed the US Embassy in Chad. It's entirely possible that he's the person that David Jasons was sending these weapons to. If Jasons crossed him, and that's the reason Jenna was kidnapped, then he could have a hell of a lot more problems than just the feds and the ATF breathing down his neck. The Brit is dangerous and he's ruthless."

"So, you think Jenna's father was sending weapons to this guy, but then something went wrong and, he took Jenna as revenge?" Cady asked. "That's a big guess based on her remembering that one of her kidnappers spoke English. It could be anybody."

"Oh, I don't think they're just guessing," Hunter said slowly. "I think they knew all along that Jasons was involved with The Brit."

Travis tensed then nodded. "The FBI think he's associated with him. But they don't know for sure that Jenna's kidnapping had anything to do with The Brit."

"But it's likely it had something to do with her dad," Gray said quietly. "If he's guilty, that is."

Jesus, that was going to kill her.

Curt swallowed.

"But this guy won't come after her now, surely," Lacey said. "It's been eight months. If he was going to do anything wouldn't he have done it by now?"

"He guards his identity ferociously," Travis told her. "If he thinks Jasons has any information that could lead to him, there's no telling what he might do."

"Like go after Jenna once again? To keep her dad quiet?" Curt stood abruptly. "I'm going to her."

"Curt wait," Gray said, standing as well.

Curt turned. "She needs me. She needs help. Protection. Whether this guy is a threat or not, there's still going to be a backlash from her father's arrest that could come back to her." There would be a lot of angry people looking for someone to blame.

His heart hammered in his chest. He had to get to her. Now. Nothing else mattered. Not the fact she'd probably rather spit on him than let her help him. Not his job or the people in this room. Nothing was as important as getting to her.

And wasn't that fucking ironic since he'd done all he could to push her away. But that had been for her own safety. Being with him wasn't in her best interest.

But just because he'd pushed her away didn't mean he would stand by while she was in danger.

"We need to think about this," Gray cautioned. "About what our next steps are."

His next step was to get to Jenna and stick so close to her she'd think he was her shadow. Impatience bit at him. "Look, I don't care what jobs I have coming up. Give them to Tiny or Josh. I'll quit if I have to, but I'm going to Jenna."

"Nobody said anything about quitting," Hunter told him. "But the fact is, no one has hired us. You might want to protect her, doesn't mean she's going to accept it."

Who cared if she accepted it or not, he'd just . . . what? Barge his way into her life? The man who'd basically crushed her to keep her away from him.

She'd as likely take a pitchfork to him as she would welcome him into her life.

"I know you probably can't spare many people at such short notice and, seeing as I'm already here, I'd be happy to speak to Jenna and convince her that she should accept Curt's protection. Or offer my own."

Curt glared at him, his hands clenching into fists. Travis just stared back at him calmly.

"Why? She didn't see this guy. You don't know it's The Brit."

"I know," Travis replied calmly. "But if it is and he comes after her you're going to need help."

"That's a small possibility," Hunter said. "People angry over the Embassy bombing and other attacks on Americans overseas, they might turn their anger against her. The shareholders in her father's company are going to be furious. Employees who might lose their jobs, too. They're likely to be more of a threat than this guy."

"I know. But it's my time. I can waste it as I see fit."

Curt?" Hunter asked. "Okay if Travis comes?"

"So long as your mind is focused on what's important," Curt told him. "Keeping Jenna safe. She comes first."

Travis nodded. "Of course. I'm certain you'll make certain nothing happens to her. I'll just be back-up."

Damn straight he was, because Curt was running the op this time. Curt started to breathe a little easier as a plan formed. And if she didn't accept their help? What then?

Then he was perfectly okay with force. Because he wasn't allowing anyone to hurt her. Never again.

4

Jenna smiled as she walked down the streets of Haven. It was a pretty town. The buildings were quaint and old, but well-kept. Flowers bloomed in planter boxes along the street. The place was clean, comforting, and friendly.

"Hey Doctor J, how are you today?"

She smiled, waving over at Mrs. Childs as she shuffled along with Daisy walking beside her on a leash. Daisy was part Great Dane, and her head reached up to Mrs. Childs's waist. She could have toppled the frail, elderly woman with one push, instead she walked patiently alongside her, stopping when Mrs. Childs had to rest, even letting the old woman lean on her. Jenna worried about what might happen to Daisy if Mrs. Childs had to go into a home.

"I'm good, thanks, Mrs. Childs. How are you?" She stopped to pat Daisy's head.

"Oh, I'm fine, dear. Nothing for me to complain about."

Jenna gave Daisy another pat and kept moving on. In a rush this morning, she'd skipped breakfast. She'd also walked out the door without her lunch, and her stomach was rumbling so she'd decided to pop into the diner. As she walked through the door, everyone turned to look, many of them smiling or waving hello before they turned back to what they'd been doing. It had taken a while for her to get used to that. She'd lived her whole life in Dallas, and small-town life was a totally different experience. Here, people didn't mind their own business. If you were new to town, they wanted to know your life story. It wasn't that they weren't accepting of strangers, but they were treated differently. At least in the beginning, until they were tested and found to measure up.

It helped that she was working at the medical center. It meant she got to meet lots of locals and it had been the perfect way to escape Dallas, her parents, and Curt.

Not that she'd worried she'd bump into him; it wasn't like they moved in the same circles. But she'd just needed some distance. Some time to regroup and get over her embarrassment.

Haven had given her the peace she'd needed to pull herself together. To build up some strength, both mentally and physically. She'd grown a lot these past few months, she'd healed and recuperated. She'd finally managed to feel safe again.

Haven was a special place where women were protected and cherished and basically coddled. Sure, it wasn't everyone's cup of tea. But for her, it was like being held in a blanket of safety without being smothered like her parents tended to do. She knew she was watched over, but it was from a distance. It wasn't stifling or condescending like Curt had been.

She snorted as she remembered him telling her how she was too young for him. Too naïve. How she'd never cope with his dark desires. Unable to suppress her curiosity, she'd asked Cady what he'd meant.

She'd been kind of shocked to hear what he'd been talking about. But not horrified or scared. Bondage and submission weren't things she'd ever explored but as she'd listened to Cady explain her experiences she'd grown curious—and aroused.

She ordered some lunch and sat at a booth. The lunch rush had been and gone, so it was quieter.

She could see herself tied down on a spanking bench, naked, while Curt did all sorts of delicious and decadent things to her. Yeah, that was something she could picture all too clearly. Too bad it was never going to happen.

When she'd learned there was a BDSM club right here in Haven, she'd decided to do some exploring. So far, she'd done little more than watch but she knew she'd have to take the next step soon, or Joel Saxon, the owner, might give her a nudge. She wasn't prepared to hand over control to him; that man scared her shitless.

"Wow, that must have been an interesting thought. Everything okay?"

She looked up with a smile at the familiar voice. "Hey, Brye. All good. You stopping to eat?"

"Just ordering a cake for Melody's birthday tomorrow." Brye Hanson slipped into the seat across from her. He was the other reason her confidence was growing. Well, the classes he taught. Soon after she'd arrived in town, Jake, Haven's sheriff had suggested she take the self-defense courses that Brye ran. She didn't know if he suggested that to all the single women in town but as she'd been considering some sort of self-defense course she'd decided to look into it. She wasn't exactly fit nor was she confident about having a man touch her, even if it was to show her some moves. However, Brye used his assistant, Melody, for most demonstrations, only touching her when he needed to adjust something. And then, he always asked her permission first.

She nodded. "We're headed to Dirty Delights this weekend to celebrate." It surprised her she'd made friends so quickly. She'd have thought most of the women would have already had their own groups of friends. That she'd be an outsider. But Hannah, the receptionist at the clinic, was close to her in age, and they'd soon become friends. She'd introduced her to Melody, Josie, and Carlie.

Brye narrowed his gaze. "Heard about that. There's a rodeo going on near Freestown this weekend, which means more strangers in town."

"Won't they all be staying in Freestown?"

He shook his head. "Not enough accommodation. Some of them like to stay here. Good for the hotel and campground, but it means our women need extra watching."

She rolled her eyes but had to smile, used to the way the men around here thought. "We'll be fine. If the bouncers and Darne can't handle whatever comes up, then Mel is a well-oiled fighting machine, remember?" Darne was one of the bartenders and he was built like a champion boxer, all muscle. But there was a kind heart beneath that rather intimidating exterior.

"She likes to think she is. She's still only five feet and a hundred pounds. Anyway, I heard Jake has put more deputies on the night shift over the weekend."

"There you go. Jake is on top of things. Stop fretting."

He scowled. "I'm a man. I don't fret."

Her food arrived, and he took off with a wave. She glanced around as she ate, staring over with a smile as she saw Logan Ferguson pull out a chair for his wife, Savannah, who smiled up at him. The tiny blonde had been through a lot in the last year, having been kidnapped and abused. Savannah's other husband, Max, walked up then and leaned down to kiss his wife's cheek. It had been a bit shocking to realize how many women around here had relationships with more than one man. Their marriage wasn't legal, of course. Savannah wasn't married to both men but she considered herself to be. Jenna had met Savannah a few times. They shared the same therapist, Molly, who was amazing. She'd helped Savannah through her fear of leaving her house. And she'd done wonders for Jenna, even though all their sessions were done via Skype.

"All good with your meal, honey?" Peggy, the owner of the diner, asked as she came and got her plate.

"Amazing, Peggy, as always." Jenna smiled up at her.

Peggy looked over as Savannah laughed and slapped Logan on the chest. "Good to see Savannah out and about and looking so happy. And Logan and Max. Been too long since they all looked so relaxed."

The older woman moved away, and Jenna watched the Fergusons for a bit longer, feeling a little sad as she saw how Logan and Max looked after their wife. She wanted that. Wanted to feel that close to someone. Wanted someone to love and take care of and have the same in return.

She thought of Curt. Recalled the cold look on his face, the slight sneer as he told her she wouldn't be able to give him what he needed.

His loss.

If he wasn't so damn closed-minded, he would've seen they could've had what the Fergusons did. Maybe she hadn't known anything about BDSM, but if that's what he needed she would have done whatever she could to give it to him. Instead, he seemed to have some picture of her being an innocent, naïve kid.

She supposed she couldn't blame him. He probably looked at her and saw that three-year-old kid crying over spilled ice cream. Or maybe he saw a victim. She stiffened at the thought. Maybe he hadn't been interested because she'd seemed too clingy, too needy. She hadn't exactly projected confidence or strength. He'd probably thought she was after his protection; she'd always felt safe with Curt.

Now, she had to work on making herself feel safe. This town helped. Her self-defense lessons helped. But there was still a part of her that was scared. She couldn't sleep without a light on, she still jumped at loud noises and she always made sure she parked as close as she could to buildings when she was out at night.

Maybe he just looked at her and saw Amelia. Not that they'd looked alike. Jenna was short and curvy, while Amelia had been tall and willowy. But perhaps she reminded him of his wife, and maybe he still wasn't ready to let go.

Jenna sighed. She'd probably never have had the guts to do what she'd done if she hadn't been so emotional that day. She blushed thinking about what a fool she'd made of herself.

The door to the diner opened and Lila Richards walk in with one of her men—she had three. Jenna wondered how the hell she managed that. Three men seemed extremely daunting to someone who'd never even had a long-term boyfriend. As she watched the way Trace looked after Lila, keeping a hand on the small of her back to guide her and pulling out a chair at the same table where Savannah sat with her two husbands, she felt that wistfulness grow.

She stood and left some cash on the table before making her way outside. Stopping for a moment, she closed her eyes and tilted her face up towards the sun. She'd never take being outside or being free for granted again.

Suddenly, she heard someone cry out. As she opened her eyes and turned, a person bounced into her, sending her flying back against the pavement. Her breath left her in a *whoosh* of air as she landed, scraping her elbows and butt painfully against the hard ground. A heavy body landed on top of her, winding her. Then the person scrambled up, stepping on her hip as they launched themselves forward. She lay there trying to catch her breath, heart racing, and body trembling. Then there was another loud yell, and she turned as tires screeched. A horn blasted as the man who'd banged into her ran in front of a car, causing it to come to a sudden stop. A man jumped from the car and raced after the guy.

"Jenna, you okay? Don't get up, you might have injured something."

She smiled up into Max Ferguson's concerned face. His wife, Savannah appeared beside him.

"Are you okay, Jenna?" she asked.

"I thought I told you to remain in the diner." Max glowered at his wife.

She just shrugged, looking unintimidated despite his firm voice. Jenna wasn't attracted to the rancher, but that tone of voice made her insides stand up and take notice. Maybe because Max reminded her of Curt. Not in looks. Curt's dirty-blond hair was always in need of a cut, and where Max was quite handsome, Curt had a harder, craggy appearance. But they both had a take-charge attitude, something that made you listen and take notice.

Max pressed his hand against her shoulder as she started to move again.

"I'm fine. I just scrapped my hands and elbow a bit." She held them up, and his frown increased. Behind him, a crowd gathered, looking down at her in concern.

Damn this is embarrassing.

"What did that kid think he was doing?" Mr. Britely, who owned the general store, asked.

"He had a purse in his hand," someone replied.

Max's face darkened with anger.

She heard a dog bark but when she looked around all she could see were people gathered around her.

"Max, I'm fine. Let me up."

"Wait for the doctor," he told her.

"I *am* the doctor."

He gave her a look. "Doc Harper is on his way."

The barking started up again. "Where is the barking coming from?"

Savannah straightened and looked over. "It's Daisy. She seems to be guarding Mrs. Childs."

"Mrs. Childs?" she asked in alarm. "Is she okay? Did he knock her over as well?"

"It was her handbag he took." This time it was Abby, the new hairdresser in town, who spoke up. "Mrs. Childs had just left the salon and was walking over to get Daisy, who was tied up beneath the oak outside the salon. This guy just bowled into her, snatched her bag, then took off."

She frowned slightly wondering why Abby wasn't helping Mrs. Childs.

The younger woman rubbed her hands together in agitation, her face pale. "I'm not good with big dogs, that's why Mrs. Childs leaves Daisy outside."

Savannah stepped back and wrapped her arm around Abby who trembled. "Don't worry, Lila and Trace are with her. And anyone would be scared of Daisy right now."

Other people nodded around her.

"Daisy is standing over Mrs. Childs, not letting anyone get close to check on her," Savannah explained.

Jenna was surprised. The big dog was always so gentle and happy.

Abby nodded. "I don't know how they're going to get Daisy to stand down."

"Let me up, Max." He shook his head. Damn, stubborn male.

"I'm not injured and I need to check on Mrs. Childs."

"No one is getting near her right now."

"Daisy likes me. She's used to me checking and touching Mrs. Childs. I need to make sure she's okay. She could have broken a hip or something."

Max didn't look happy but he nodded. Before she could move, he picked her up under the arms and set her on her feet, holding onto her for a few moments as her legs trembled, the adrenaline rush dying down. Once she was steady she gave him a nod.

He hovered close by as she moved, probably prepared to catch her if she collapsed. The crowd parted as she made her way to where Mrs. Childs lay on the ground outside the hair salon.

Daisy was standing over her, guarding her owner. She raised her lip, baring her teeth. Jenna hesitated.

Max placed his hand on the small of her back. "You okay?"

Damn it, Jenna. You've faced down armed terrorists and a big dog is going to get the best of you? Keep moving.

"Fine," she told him briskly, moving forward. She ignored the stinging pain in her arms and the ache in her butt. Jake stood next to Trace Richards, who knelt a few feet away, speaking to Daisy in a calm voice. Everyone else kept a wide circle away from where Mrs. Childs lay on the pavement. Lila was on the phone. She turned, looking tense as Jenna, Savannah and Max approached.

"Stand next to Lila, Savannah," Max ordered.

Savannah sighed but walked over to Lila, who smiled at her.

The sheriff turned with a scowl as Jenna slowly approached with Max. He walked over to them, running his gaze over her. "You okay, Jenna? I was just coming over to check on you."

"I'm fine, just a few scratches. I need to check on Mrs. Childs though."

It worried her that she hadn't seen the elderly woman move yet.

Jake looked from Daisy to her with one eyebrow raised. "Try to tell Daisy that. Colin is on his way with a tranquilizer gun."

She winced at the idea of them shooting Daisy.

"Let me have a go talking to her first. Daisy likes me."

"Daisy likes everyone," Jake said dryly, "but she's not letting anyone near."

"Just let me try. If she falls on Mrs. Childs once you tranquilize her, she could further injure her. I don't like how still she is. She might need immediate medical attention."

"Which is why I've called for an ambulance. You need to be checked over too," Jake told her firmly.

"I'm fine," she said impatiently, waving away his concerns. "Just let me try, Jake."

He sighed then nodded. "Don't get too close, and if she snaps at you then your ass is out of here, got me?"

"Fine. Fine."

"Max, help Duncan keep everyone back and quiet, will you? Got to get some more deputies," he muttered. "With Blake and Tare out with that stomach bug, we're understaffed."

"On it. You take care of Jenna."

Jake nodded, and she bit back the reply that she could take care of herself. She liked that they watched out for her, even if they could be a bit overbearing.

She moved slowly forward then knelt beside Trace, trying to hide her wince as her whole body protested. Damn, she was going to feel that hard landing tonight.

"You okay, honey?" Trace asked with concern.

"I'm fine. Worried about Mrs. Childs."

Trace nodded, his gaze turning back to the elderly woman and Daisy. "I haven't seen her move and Daisy has gone into protective mode, which is understandable but not helping at all. She's not letting me close or reacting to my voice other than to growl at me."

"Odd, considering she's the size of a small horse."

He gave her a small smile. His knowledge and skill with horses meant people brought their horses to him from all over the state.

"Let's see what happens. Daisy." She moved forward a little, hesitating when Daisy turned and snarled, showing off those impressive canines.

"What the fuck? Hey—"

have what? Told him she was leaving? Given him her new address? He hadn't spoken to her since that night he'd pushed her away. Pushed? Hell. He'd given her an almighty shove. Told her neither of them could ever be what the other one needed. What a lie that was.

He knew he could never be what she deserved. But damned if he didn't dream about that kiss every night, waking up with a hard-on. He barely slept. When he wasn't working he was at the gym or the club trying to rid himself of the memory of her soft lips pressed against him, the feel of her body, her sweet, strawberry scent surrounding him.

"She moved away a few months ago."

"Away?" He didn't like the way she said that. "Away where?"

"Small town in Texas. Has a funny name. I'd need to look back through my texts from her."

Cady was getting texts from her? He'd received nothing.

And you expected anything else, idiot?

"Haven," Lacey said quietly. "The town is called Haven."

"Haven? Really?" Travis asked.

"You know it?" Curt snapped.

"I've been there before when I was working a case," Travis replied quietly.

"Why did no one tell me any of this?"

Cady looked up at him. "Why would we? If she'd wanted you to know, she would have told you."

Fuck. She was right. She obviously hadn't wanted him to know.

"But she still needs support. It's only been eight months. What about her therapy?"

"There's an amazing therapist I referred her to who works with clients via Skype," Lacey told him. "She has a job at the local medical center. She's doing well, Curt."

Without me.

Funny, that sounded a bit like Curt. Jeez, was she now imagining his voice?

"Stay back, sir," Max stated. She pushed their voices to the background, focusing on Daisy.

"Hey, Daisy, remember me?" She held out her hand and moved a few more inches forward.

The dog let out a low woof, but she didn't get the idea she was going to attack. But maybe she was just hopeful.

"Damn it, Jenna. Get back here. Now."

Okay, that really did sound like Curt. She had to be completely losing it. He was back in Dallas, probably feeling relieved to not have to worry about her trying to jump him again.

"Daisy, I just need to check Mrs. Childs. All right? I'm not going to hurt her."

Daisy growled when she got about a foot away. Jenna paused.

"Easy, Jenna. Nice and slow."

She looked up to see Colin standing on the other side, holding a gun with a long thin barrel. She gulped.

"Don't shoot her."

"I won't unless she makes a threatening move," he promised. "I don't want to do it any more than you do."

"Damn it, shoot the—"

"Sir, no."

There was a scuffling noise behind her and Daisy looked over and snarled menacingly.

"Stay back," Jake said sharply. Daisy turned to him and growled.

"Will all of you please be quiet," she said in a calm, non-threatening voice. "The next person who upsets Daisy is getting a rectal exam during their next checkup. And I won't be gentle."

"Vicious. That's a side of you I haven't seen before. I like it." Colin winked at her, but his face remained serious, and his gaze returned quickly to Daisy.

"Come on, Daisy girl. Your owner doesn't look too well. I just want to check on her, okay?"

She drew even closer, breathing a sigh of relief when Daisy didn't snap. But she also didn't move away from where she stood. Moving slowly, her hand shaking, Jenna reached out to check Mrs. Childs's pulse.

"Okay, her pulse is steady, but she seems to be unconscious. Let me see if there's a head injury." She moved around to Mrs. Childs's head. She could feel Daisy's hot breath but she didn't dare look up. What did they say? You shouldn't look an angry dog in the eyes? Or was that wolves? Damned if she could remember what to do. She just went with whatever felt right and hoped like hell Daisy didn't bite her.

"There's a gash on the back of her head," Jenna told everyone. "She's been knocked unconscious, we need to get her to the hospital."

"Jenna, you okay?"

Jenna heard Doctor Harper call out and she turned to look at him just as Daisy started barking. Her boss came to a stop, holding his hands up.

"I think you better stay where you are," she told him.

"We need to get her to the hospital, though," Doctor Harper said. "How are we going to do that if we can't get to her?"

Good question.

Just then, a siren came blasting from up the street. The ambulance. *Shit.* Jenna forced herself to stay calm and not tense up as Daisy barked loudly.

"Damn it," Colin said over the noise. "I'm going to have to tranquilize her."

Jenna reached up and, moving on instinct, started patting Daisy. "It's okay, Daisy girl. It's just people here to help Mrs. Childs. You want to see her get better, right?"

Amazingly, Daisy stopped barking. And then, miracle of miracle, she licked her. Right, on the face. *Ick, doggy breath.*

She heard someone laugh but when she looked around with a scowl they all looked serious. Sort of.

"Well, maybe not," Colin said. "See if you can get a hold of her lead and pull her away."

Jenna nodded and she gave Daisy another scratch then grabbed her tether and stood slowly. She swayed slightly, and Daisy pushed against her, sending her crashing over. There was a yell from someone, but that noise was quickly stifled. As she lay there, Daisy gave her another lick.

Jesus. Someone needs to give that dog a breath mint.

"Jenna, you okay?" She looked over as Colin slowly approached. She sat up and hugged Daisy as she gave a rumbling warning. "I'm all right. Just getting a bit tired of being knocked over."

"Think it might be a good idea to get Daisy out of here. Hand me her lead, and I'll take her to the vet clinic."

She passed the leash to Colin, and he pulled Daisy away. The dog turned and barked, straining to get back to her. Her distress increased as paramedics rushed towards Mrs. Childs. A hand reached out towards Jenna, and she took it without thinking. Then a furious face filled her vision, and shock engulfed her.

"What the fuck did you think you were doing?" Curt demanded.

5

Curt was beside himself with worry. He still couldn't believe that everyone had just stood by and watched as Jenna approached a huge, snarling dog that had to damn near outweigh her. Even worse, when he'd tried to get to her, he'd been held back by a couple of idiot cowboys. He was still furious.

He hoped like hell he had broken the big one's nose.

He pulled Jenna up, holding her steady while she swayed. First, he'd had to watch as she'd been shoved to the ground by that asshole who'd stolen the old lady's handbag. Then, as Travis had raced off after the guy, he'd been left to park the truck and try to push through the crowd to get to her. By the time he'd reached her he'd been ready to kill someone and seeing her inch her way closer to that dog had sent his anger soaring.

"Don't you ever, ever approach an angry dog like that again, you got me?" he half-roared as he clasped her shoulders, glaring into her shocked face.

He knew he needed to rein in his anger. It had caught him by surprise, bursting through his control.

"Get your hands off her," someone ordered, and he suddenly found himself shoved back.

He snarled as he turned and saw one of the cowboys who'd held him back earlier. The one whose nose he hadn't punched. The other man gently pushed Jenna behind him, as though protecting her from Curt.

"Back for more?" Curt snarled. "Do you want what your friend got?"

"Just try it," the cowboy snapped, moving towards him.

Bring it on. Eagerness filled him. This was just what he needed to get rid of the worry and anger riding him.

Jenna stepped between them. He moved instinctively, and grasping her around the waist, turned her so his back was to the cowboy. It opened him to attack, but at least Jenna was shielded by his body.

All that mattered was protecting her. Everyone else was the enemy.

"Curt! What's going on?" she asked.

"Don't step between me and the enemy like that." He knew his voice was too cold, too dark. The way her eyes widened as she took a step back told him he'd frightened her. Something he'd never wanted to do, but if it kept her safe . . .

Then she shocked him by reaching up and cupping the side of his face. The warmth from her hand pushed away the deep chill engulfing him.

"Curt, he's not the enemy. That's Max Ferguson. I know him."

"You know this guy, Jenna?"

The cowboy, who surprisingly hadn't taken a cheap shot at him, stepped around to Jenna's side. He still frowned at Curt but his stance was less confrontational.

"Yeah, uh, he's an old family friend."

Old family friend? Really?

Curt placed his arm around her shoulders and gave the cowboy a warning look. *Mine.*

The cowboy raised his eyebrows. Good. He got the message. Then Jenna winced, and he turned to her, worried.

"You're injured."

At the same time he spoke, the other guy, Max, called out for a doctor, who turned from where he was helping the paramedics load the old lady into the back of one of the ambulances.

"Doc, can you check Jenna out?" Max asked before Curt could demand he look at her. "She fell pretty hard when that little dick pushed into her."

"I'm fine," she protested. "It's just a few scratches. How is Mrs. Childs?"

"You're still getting looked at," Curt said at the same time as Max said, "Jenna, let him check you over."

Who the hell was this guy and did he mean something to Jenna? She'd only been here a few short months, God damn it. How could she have gotten involved with another man already?

Like she owed you any sort of loyalty?

Maybe not, but he still felt jealous as hell at the idea of this backward hick touching her.

"Come over to the ambulance, Jenna. Let's see how you're doing. They're going to want to examine you anyway. Then we can get an update on Mrs. Childs."

Jenna watched them both suspiciously as the other doctor gently took hold of her forearm and led her away. Curt started walking after her but he kept the cowboy in sight, watching for any sign of an ambush. Later, he'd blame the cowboy for his inattention. Someone grabbed his arm, taking him completely by surprise. Tense and on edge, he turned, his arm already swinging out. He winced as his fist made contact with the man's nose with a *crunch*.

Too late, he noticed he was dressed in a deputy's uniform.

Oh fuck.

The guy who'd he'd punched earlier, looked on smugly as he was pushed to the ground, his arms pulled behind his back and cuffed.

"That's him, Duncan," the big cowboy said cheerfully as he held a packet of frozen peas to his nose. "That's the guy who punched me."

6

Curt paced the small cell. Back and forth. Back and forth. When the hell was someone coming to let him out of here? They couldn't keep him here long. So, he'd punched a couple of guys, there'd been extenuating circumstances. Like his woman being in danger.

Yeah, only no one knew she was his woman. Including Jenna. He ran his hand over his face. What was he thinking? She wasn't his. She couldn't be his.

She was innocence and light. And he was . . . he was the guy who went around punching people—including a deputy sheriff.

Fuck. Where the hell was Travis? He should be back by now and sorting this mess out. Curt needed to get out of here. He needed to check on Jenna. He could still hear her cry of alarm when he'd been arrested. He hadn't liked how stiffly she'd been moving or the scrapes on her hands.

He hoped she'd gone to the hospital and gotten checked out properly. If she hadn't, when he got out of here . . . *Fuck, I'll be lucky if she still wants to talk to me.* She was probably terrified after the manic way he'd acted. Getting angry at her for endangering herself one moment then punching a damn deputy sheriff the next.

He was losing it. He knew it was bound to happen at some point. He'd honestly thought it would've happened earlier than this.

He knew the sensible thing, the best thing, would be to go and leave her in Travis's hands. But he couldn't trust him with her. The man was known to have a different woman every weekend. And he was a Dom. A strict one. Something Jenna didn't need at all.

And if it wasn't Travis hitting on her then what about all the overprotective cowboys in this town, who seemed overly fond of ménage relationships? He couldn't believe it when Cady told him about this place. Was there something in the water? How could these guys want to share their woman with another man?

If Jenna were his no other man would even be able to look at her without his permission, and . . . okay, even he could hear how creepy and stalkerish that sounded.

The truth was, she wasn't his. He didn't deserve someone like her. His current predicament was a testament to that. She was injured and alone, and where was he? In jail because he hadn't been able to control himself.

But he should be with her. Taking care of her. Watching over her. Obviously, she needed it. He'd been in town only three minutes when he'd seen her knocked down by a thief, then nearly mauled by a dog before she'd pushed herself between two angry men. She was in definite need of a keeper.

And you think you're going to be that keeper? You, who let your fear morph into such anger you didn't even stop to think, you just lashed out and hit a deputy sheriff.

No, he definitely didn't deserve her. That didn't mean he didn't want her. Desperately. These last few months he'd told himself he'd forgotten about the night she'd kissed him. What she'd told him.

The only time I ever feel safe is with you, Curt.

He'd told her it had meant nothing. It was only because he'd rescued her. Hero worship.

Yeah, he'd lied to himself over and over, even as he'd spiraled into a dark, empty space. Was it any wonder he was snapping? That he'd nearly reached the point of no return? The darkness in him had grown. Denying himself her love was his punishment for all the fuckups he'd made in his life. With his wife. His child.

But he didn't know if he could do it a second time. If he could push her away again.

"Fuck." He ran his hand over his face. "Fuck, she doesn't need me in her life."

But he needed her. And maybe . . . maybe there was something he could do for her. He was tough, he was strong, and he could protect her. He could ensure shit like today never happened again because he'd watch over her. Yeah, he could do that.

And what about his need to dominate his partner? There was no way he could even think about Jenna submitting to him. Not that the idea of it wasn't hot as hell. And God only knew he'd thought about smacking her ass several times today. But that would be it.

He didn't need to tie her up, spank her, drive her to the edge again and again without letting her come. He didn't need any of that. Not if it meant he could have her. She meant everything, and he wouldn't risk losing her.

He turned as he heard footsteps, and the sheriff appeared on the other side of the bars.

"About time," he snapped. "What took you so long? Everything moves a bit slower in the country, is that it?"

The sheriff's eyes flared open and he crossed his arms over his chest. "Well, now, perhaps I should have taken my time. Seems like this wasn't long enough to cool that temper."

Curt took a deep breath in and let it out slowly. "Sorry," he forced himself to say. "I need to get out of here and check on Jenna. Do you know if she's been admitted to the hospital?"

"Not sure I should be telling you."

He ground his teeth together. "She's a friend."

The sheriff looked him up and down then sneered slightly. "Yes. That's what she said."

"You've spoken to her then? She's all right?"

"She is," was all he said, and Curt knew he said that much reluctantly. Curt hadn't won over any friends in the sheriff's department, that was for sure.

"Is she at the hospital? I need to speak to her." He wanted to get to her before she heard about her father from someone else. According to Travis's source, they'd arrested her father about an hour ago, and he'd gone quietly. Her mother, on the other hand, had thrown a fit worthy of a two-year-old. He hoped to speak to Jenna before her mother did so he could . . . what? Comfort her?

What the hell did he know about comforting a woman? He'd never been able to comfort Amelia. And after a while he'd given up. It seemed like everything he said and did angered or upset her. He couldn't win.

He hoped like hell Jenna didn't fall apart.

"Around here, we don't really take kindly to people hitting our deputy sheriffs. Or our citizens."

"Yeah, well, that upstanding citizen was holding me back from getting to Jenna."

"Because the last thing she needed was someone interfering. It was a delicate situation with Daisy and Mrs. Childs. Logan and Max were acting on my orders when they restrained you."

"Well maybe your orders were wrong."

"That so?" the sheriff drawled. "You know, I was going to play nice and let you out with a warning. Seeing as how *our Jenna* speaks so highly of you."

He didn't miss the emphasis on "our Jenna." She wasn't *their* anything. She was Curt's.

"But now I see that maybe you need a bit more time to think over your actions."

He turned to walk away, and panic filled Curt. "Wait!"

The sheriff stilled.

"Jenna was putting herself at risk. I thought this town took care of its women."

"It does." The sheriff turned back with a glare. "But she was being watched over. Colin was there to tranquilize Daisy if she went for Jenna. And Mrs. Childs desperately needed help. She's one of our women as well."

He knew they'd be here all day and still not come to an agreement. Curt would never agree to Jenna putting herself in danger. Whatever the reason.

"I have some urgent business with Jenna."

"Yeah?" the sheriff drawled. "You want to tell me what that is?"

"It's personal."

"Yeah, that's what the Travis said."

"Travis? You've spoken to him?"

"He made himself a citizen's arrest. Not really something we encourage, but his tactics were effective. He got the purse snatcher. And he managed not to punch him in the nose. There's a lot you can learn from him."

Curt knew that if he kept grinding his teeth together like this he was going to wear away all the enamel. Plus, he'd give himself one hell of a migraine.

"Look, you can keep me in here overnight, but that's just a waste of tax payers' money and your time. We both know I'm not a threat to anyone."

"Well, now, maybe I'm keeping you in here for your own protection. Got a couple of pissed off men who wouldn't mind a little chat with you."

Curt blew out a breath. "Let me talk to Jenna, and I'll be out of this town by this evening."

"Yeah? You planning on dropping this information and leaving her, are you?"

"Of course not. I'll be taking her with me."

The sheriff raised his eyebrows, smirking slightly. "That so? Seems funny, considering the life Jenna has built here, a job, a house, and friends, that she'd just up and leave. With you."

Calm. Remain calm.

"What I have to tell her concerns her parents. She needs to come back to Dallas with me."

The sheriff didn't appear to move but he seemed more alert. "They okay?"

"Not really. Now will you let me out?"

"All right. On the understanding that if you create any more trouble in my town, I'm going to come down hard on you."

Yeah, yeah, yeah. Come on. He nodded impatiently and waited for him to unlock the door.

After they went through the paperwork, and he gathered up his stuff, including his weapon, which the sheriff felt the need to lecture him about once more, he walked out into the waiting area. Around him the noise quietened, and people stared. And through that silence came her laughter.

He froze.

When was the last time he'd heard her laugh?

"Everything okay?" the sheriff asked, breaking his stillness.

"Yeah, fine." He walked around the corner, jealousy filling him. Who was causing her to laugh like that?

"Remember, you promised no trouble," the sheriff warned.

He shot him a look and then turned, seeing her sitting next to Travis. He said something else, and she laughed again then winced, as though in pain.

Curt stormed forward, worry filling him. "What are you doing here?"

"Smooth, man," Travis told him as Jenna looked up at him, her eyes filling with hurt. "Real smooth."

She slowly got to her feet, and it was obvious it took some effort. Her face was pale, her clothing rumpled and ripped from where she'd fallen. He couldn't understand what she was doing here. If she'd been discharged from the hospital she should at least be home resting.

"Don't worry, I'm going home now." That hurt look had turned into anger, her beautiful blue eyes sparkling as she gave him a withering look.

"Wait, Jenna. I didn't mean it like that."

She raised her eyebrows. "Then what did you mean? Obviously, you didn't expect to see me, you didn't want me to be here waiting for you, worrying that you were okay."

She'd worried about him? Why the hell would she worry about him when she was the one who was injured?

He took too long answering as she started shuffling her way with slow steps towards the entrance.

"Man, we need to work on your approach with the ladies, because that couldn't have gone worse."

"Not unless she punched him in the nose," the sheriff, who he'd forgotten was behind him, stated. "And then half the station would have cheered her on."

"Only half?" Travis asked.

The sheriff shrugged. "All right, the whole station."

"She should be in the hospital, obviously she's injured." He glared at Travis who held his hands up.

"Don't look at me. I chased after that asshole who knocked her over, tackled him to the ground, and dragged him all the way here, only to be told you'd been arrested. By the time I spoke to Jake here, to plead your case, Jenna was sitting in the waiting room."

"Did she even go to the hospital to get checked out?" Curt asked.

Travis shrugged. "She said she didn't need to. Something about being a doctor and knowing the difference between being injured and just dinged up."

Dinged up? Dinged up?

"That's unacceptable. She should have gotten care." Someone should have insisted she go to the hospital. What the hell were the men in this town thinking? Suddenly, he realized she'd already left. He strode after her, Travis matching his steps.

"You should have picked her up, put her in your car, and driven her to the hospital yourself."

"She's a client, not my sub," Travis said mildly. "I can't make her do something she doesn't want to do. And neither can you."

Oh yeah? Just watch me.

ARROGANT ASSHOLE. Jerk. Bastard.

Damned if she knew what she'd been doing there. As if she didn't have better things to do with her time than sit there waiting for him to be released from jail. She still couldn't believe he'd punched Logan and Duncan. And he'd been here for all of two seconds.

She had about a million other things she could be doing, including going home, getting out of her torn clothes, and having a long soak. Now *that* was just what the doctor ordered.

Nope, there was no reason for her to be waiting around on Curt Nolan to get out of jail.

So why were you there?

Because she'd been worried about him. Duncan had been furious after Curt punched him. The former linebacker was a big guy. She'd felt like she needed to vouch for him. After all, he didn't normally go around punching people. He'd just been . . . what? Worried about her?

A small tendril of warmth unfurled inside her. But then she squashed it, remembering how cold he'd just been. She sighed. This had been a hell of an afternoon. She just wanted to go home and forget all of it.

Jenna shuffled her way down the pavement, muttering about rude, arrogant men. She wished like hell her car wasn't parked back at the clinic. What had seemed like an enjoyable walk in the sunshine during her lunch hour was now an excruciatingly slow, painful shuffle.

"Jenna? Are you all right?" She looked up as Joel Saxon approached. He ran his gaze over her, his eyes widening slightly. "Who did this to you?"

"No one."

"No one? You did this to yourself?"

"I mean, I don't know who he was."

"Where is he?" His voice had taken on a cold, deadly tone, and a shiver ran down her spine. Probably just as well the purse snatcher was safely ensconced in a cell. She would not like to get on the bad side of Saxon.

"The sheriff has him locked up."

He looked over at the jail. "That so?"

"You didn't hear what happened?" she asked. Gossip tended to run rampant in most small towns, and Haven was no different. Maybe no one was game to share gossip with Saxon, although she'd be surprised if much of anything got by him.

"I've been in Freestown, just got back. I was on my way to talk to Jake about something. What happened?"

"Oh, this young kid snatched Mrs. Childs's purse and knocked her down. Then he bumped into me. Daisy went all protective over Mrs. Childs, and we had to coax her away so the paramedics could get to her."

"We?"

"There were lots of people around," she said vaguely, trying to ignore the way his cold eyes narrowed in warning. Time to get out of here. "I won't keep you. Have a nice day."

She started to shuffle off again, trying to move quicker than she had before.

"Jenna," he said in a low voice just as she heard Curt call out to her. She stiffened then winced again. Damn it, at this rate it was going to be midnight before she got to soak her aches away.

Saxon looked over her shoulder. "Who's that?"

"That's Curt."

One of Saxon's perfectly formed eyebrows rose imperiously. He had the kind of looks that made you pause and take a breath. Arresting, almost majestic. Top that with a very forceful personality, and he was a man who was used to people hanging on his every word and obeying him without question.

She was certain she'd never have the strength to go against him. Not that she ever intended to battle him.

"A friend?"

"Yeah, sort of. He was married to my cousin."

"Oh. It didn't end well?"

"She died. I don't think he's gotten over her."

He eyed her as Curt rushed over.

"Sometimes we tend to see the past through rose-colored glasses. We remember all their good points and none of what was wrong. And because we're focused on the past we don't see what's standing right in front of us." He was looking straight at her as he said that.

She blushed slightly. "There's nothing between Curt and me."

"But you'd like there to be."

"I would like for this conversation to be over," she said firmly as Curt reached them. She looked over and saw Travis walking at a more leisurely pace towards them. She hadn't recognized him when he'd first approached her. He looked different without his camouflage gear and that fierce look on his face. Wearing jeans, a shirt, and a smile he'd almost looked approachable. When she'd realized who he was, she'd felt a little uncomfortable, knowing he'd seen her at her most vulnerable. But it hadn't taken him long to have her laughing at one of his stories, which she was certain had been greatly stripped down so what had probably been a dangerous situation just sounded funny.

"Sometimes we don't get what we want."

Actually, she'd found that was pretty much always the case.

"Hello, you must be Curt," Saxon said calmly as Curt reached them. He held out his hand while Curt eyed him suspiciously.

She shot Saxon a warning look.

He smiled slightly.

Oh crap.

Saxon smiling was not a reassuring thing.

"Hey," Curt replied, shaking his hand.

"Curt, this is Joel Saxon. He's. . . um . . ."

"The owner of Saxon's," Travis said as he drew close. "The local BDSM club."

"I prefer the best BDSM club in the state," Saxon said smoothly. "Travis, how are you?"

"You two know each other?" she asked with surprise.

"I worked a case here in Haven a while back," Travis said. "Met Saxon back then. Not sure I'd call Saxon's the best, though."

Saxon narrowed his gaze. "That so?"

"Maybe you two could go somewhere and work out your differences. I need to speak to Jenna."

Jenna sighed. "I don't think there's anything to say, Curt. It's been a long day. I just want to go home, call the hospital to check on Mrs. Childs, and then soak in the tub and forget any of this happened."

"We need to talk," he replied stubbornly.

Was he completely without sympathy? He hadn't been when he was younger, but she was starting to learn this Curt was far different from the boy, and even the man she'd known before Amelia's death. Had losing his wife turned him into this hard, stubborn man before her?

She guessed so.

"Curt, I don't know why you're here, but surely whatever it is can wait until morning."

"Actually, honey, it can't."

She looked over at Travis as he gave her a sympathetic look. "What Curt was trying to say is we know this has been a rough day and we wish we could just let you rest, but the reason we came here is important. We need to talk to you. Now."

She stared at Travis then Curt, who remained quiet, although his face looked pinched and displeased.

"Wonderful. I guess my day is about to get worse, right?"

Travis grimaced. "I'm afraid so."

Yippee.

7

"You want to tell me what the hell is wrong with you?"

Curt looked down into Jenna's furious face. Her fists were jammed on her hips, her foot tapping a furious beat against the floor.

Damn, she was breathtaking.

"Well?" she asked, sparks shooting out of her gorgeous blue eyes.

"Nothing's wrong with me."

How was he going to tell her what her father had been accused of? That he could have been the reason she was kidnapped? She'd always been close to her dad, and this was going to devastate her.

"Nice place you have here," Travis said easily as he sat on the sofa and looked up at them both. There was a hint of a smile on his face, as though he was enjoying himself.

Bastard.

"Thanks," Jenna said distractedly. "I'm just renting it right now. The owner has gone into a retirement home. But her son said she might be willing to sell if I want to buy it."

"Buy it? You can't move here permanently," Curt protested.

Why would she want to live in this nothing little town forever?

Her gaze narrowed at him. "I can do whatever I like."

"You're a city girl. You'll get bored living here."

"I happen to like living here and I like these people. Although I have my doubts about how much longer I'll be welcome here if you keep going around punching people!"

Travis let out a chuckle. Curt turned to him. "Don't you have something to do? Phone calls to make?"

"Nope. I'm good."

Jenna looked over at Travis apologetically. "Sorry, I'm forgetting my manners. Can I get you anything?"

"He's fine," Curt said impatiently, annoyed with the other man. "He's not your guest."

Jenna frowned at him. "Will you stop acting like a fucking ass!"

"Don't swear."

"Why the hell not?"

"Because I don't like it."

She threw her arms up into the air then winced as the movement caused her pain.

"And whatever Curt wants, Curt gets, is that it?"

"No." There was only one thing he truly wanted, and she was standing right in front of him. Having her so close to him, her face flushed, her eyes filled with fire, filled him with a desire he could barely contain. Combine that with his overwhelming need to protect her had his possessiveness raging out of control.

She would be his. A calmness filled him at that thought.

Nothing would touch her. Nothing or no one would take her from him. He'd do whatever it took to claim her and keep her, regardless of what he had to give up.

"I'll swear if I want to swear, Curt," she said in a quiet voice. "I'm not that three-year-old kid anymore. And you're not my big brother."

"Oh, darlin' you can be damn sure I don't see you as my sister."

A flash of hurt filled her eyes, and she looked away.

Fuck. What had he said? He glanced over at Travis, who stared at Jenna with interest and concern.

"Fuck off, Travis. I need to speak to Jenna alone."

She swung back around and winced. "Damn it, Curt. Stop being such a jerk! What is wrong with you today? First, you punch Logan—"

"He deserved it," Curt muttered.

"Then Duncan, who is a deputy sheriff for goodness sake!"

"That was an accident."

"And then you were rude to Saxon."

"I wasn't rude to him."

"You told him to go away! He was just trying to be helpful by offering us a ride home."

"He was flirting with you. And he wasn't offering all of us a ride, just you."

"He was looking out for me; it's what the men around here do."

"Oh, that wasn't him looking out for you. Do you know what sort of man he is?"

She gave him a tired look. "I don't know, Curt. The sort of man who offers a tired, injured woman a lift home? Wow, what a bastard. We should have him arrested."

Travis snorted.

Curt closed his eyes and prayed for patience. He was going about this all wrong. When he opened his eyes again he saw Jenna rapidly blink back tears.

God, she was right. He really was an asshole. She'd had a horrible day, and here he was, compounding it. And he hadn't even gotten to the worst of it.

"Can whatever the two of you are doing here wait until the morning? I need to take a bath." She rubbed at her forehead. "I'm really sore and I want to soak. I should also call the hospital and check on Mrs. Childs."

Travis rose and placed his hand on the small of her back. Then he leaned down and kissed the top of her head. She kind of melted. *Damn it, why can't I get that reaction? All I seem to do is fire her up.*

Curt gave him a look, but the other man just grinned.

"I think it's best we tell you now, honey," Travis told her gently. "Before someone calls you or you hear it on the news."

"Hear what on the news?" She looked at Curt in alarm. "What is it? Is it my parents?"

"Let her sit down first," Curt grumbled and took hold of her arm, leading her to the sofa, away from Travis.

The other man gave him a knowing look. That was the problem working with Doms, they didn't miss much.

"Curt, what is it?" She gave him a frantic look, and he wished he could shield her from this, make it all okay. He knelt in front of her and reached out to clasp her hands in his. All their earlier arguments and irritations faded. She clung to him.

"Baby, it's your dad." His gut clenched, knowing the pain he was going to cause her.

"Something's happened to him? Why didn't you tell me right away?" She jumped to her feet, then groaned and swayed.

"Hey! Easy." He stood and grasped her shoulders, holding her steady. "I knew you should've gone to the hospital. Travis, get the car started, we're taking her in."

"No. I'm fine. I just stood up too quickly. I need to know, Curt. Is my dad hurt?"

Curt shook his head and pressed her onto the sofa once more. "He's not hurt. Jenna, he's been arrested."

ARRESTED? What?

No. There had to be some mistake.

"Arrested? What for? Are you certain?" Why hadn't her mother called? "Where's my phone? Oh, drat, it's still at the clinic. I forgot it. I-I need to call my mother." *Oh, God, she'll be a mess.* And without her father around it would be up to her to calm her mother down. Although, there was no chance in hell she'd achieve that.

"I'll go and get your phone for you," Travis reassured her.

"Okay, good. Thanks." She rubbed her head, trying to think. "Wait, what was he arrested for?" This had to be a mistake.

Curt shared a look with Travis, which she couldn't decipher. She tensed, knowing it wasn't going to be good. Of course, it wasn't good, her father had been arrested for God's sake.

Curt took a deep breath then tightened his hold on her. "Supplying arms to terrorists."

"What? But . . . what . . . that's ridiculous," she stumbled over her words, almost stuttering. "How could they possibly think my father is dealing in arms trading? The company he runs builds parts for airplanes. We don't make weapons."

"But his company ships things all over the world," Travis pointed out. "The FBI and ATF believe he's been shipping weapons overseas to a dealer who supplies arms to terrorist groups across the Middle East and Africa."

"That's crazy. How would he even get ahold of any weapons?"

"So, you've never heard him talk about any of this?" Travis asked, looking at her intently. "Never heard him speak of someone called The Brit?"

"The Brit? What? Who's he? I've never heard him say anything about any of this. Curt, this has to be a mistake, right?" He knew her father. He knew he wouldn't be capable of this.

"Do you know Doug Shipman?" Travis asked.

"Yes, he's a good friend of Daddy's. We often went on summer vacations together. His family owns . . ." she trailed off as it hit her.

"Shipman Arms Manufacturing," Travis finished. "The feds have also arrested Shipman on suspicion of supplying arms."

"Oh, God, I feel ill. It can't be right. Are you sure Daddy was a part of it? Maybe it was all done without his knowledge."

"Maybe," Curt told her, but she sensed his doubt. He thought this was true.

"FBI and ATF agents are currently searching the buildings and warehouses belonging to your father's company. It will take a while, but then we'll know if they find anything," Travis told her.

"He was a marine." She stared at Curt, wishing he'd tell her this was all some stupid joke. But he just watched her steadily, the look on his face resolute.

"This is no joke, is it?" she whispered.

"No, baby."

She looked up at Travis. "I need my phone. I don't have a land-line and I have to call my mother."

"You don't have a landline?" Curt asked. "What if your cell dies or you forget it like today?"

She pressed the palms of her hands against her stinging eyes. She really didn't have the energy to fight with Curt right now. She needed some time to herself to think. She just couldn't believe this of her father. She couldn't.

"Curt, maybe give her a break, huh?" Travis said.

She moved her hands away from her eyes and gave him a grateful look.

"I'll go get your phone, Jenna. Just think about whether you remember anything your father told you. Anything you might have overheard."

She shook her head, staring at Travis in amazement. "I didn't know anything about this. Is that why you're here? Because you think I'm guilty of something?"

"Nobody thinks you're guilty of anything." Curt said, glaring at Travis.

"Of course not. But if you have any information that could lead to finding The Brit we need to know."

"Travis," Curt said in a warning voice.

"Why? Do you think that would help my father?"

"Perhaps," Travis allowed. "The feds might go easier on him."

"If he did this," she said coldly. "You sound like you've found him guilty already."

Travis grimaced. "I'll go get your phone."

Once Travis was gone, she stared up at Curt. "You believe it? That he did this?"

His face shut down, becoming unreadable, and she had her answer.

"You do believe it."

"I don't know, Jenna. I've known David a long time and, at first, I thought it was preposterous, but there have been some things that didn't add up. Like why was everyone else in the village in Sudan killed except for you?"

"But . . . what has that got to do with anything? They took me because they wanted my father to pay a ransom."

"How did they know who you were? And why weren't any instructions sent to your father about how to pay the ransom? Even the ransom amount was odd."

"Do you think my kidnapping had something to do with my dad?"

He looked away for a moment.

"Curt?" she pressed.

He faced her. "We think you were kidnapped because of your father's dealings with this guy called The Brit. He's on Interpol's and the FBI's most wanted lists for supplying weapons to terrorist groups. They believe some of the weapons he shipped were used to blow up the US Embassy in Chad. The nickname is because of rumors that he has a British accent. But no one has ever seen him. No one knows who he is."

"And you really believe my father sent weapons to this guy? Weapons that Doug Shipman's company manufactured. That he sold weapons to this man who is arming terrorists?" She rubbed her stomach. "I still don't understand what this has to do with my kidnapping."

"Remember the man you said spoke perfect English and you thought he had an—"

"Accent. Oh, God, that was him? But why would he kidnap me if he was working with my father?"

"I don't know that. But the feds seem to think your father is involved with him. Perhaps your father owed him something. Or your father failed to send him something. This could all be wrong, of course."

"My father would never do anything to put me in danger."

"No. And I suspect he settled the debt when you were kidnapped. But remember how hurt you were that he didn't support you going to Sudan?"

"Yes, but he could have just been concerned for my safety. He loves me."

"I know he does. And we could be wrong about this. Your father could be innocent."

But she knew Curt didn't really think that. He thought her father was guilty and he was the reason she'd been kidnapped.

Could this day get any worse?

"So, you came here to tell me all of this in person?"

"Yes. And because you're going to need help, Jenna. Whether your father is guilty or not, there are going to be a lot of angry people over this. Your dad's company is going to suffer, the shareholders and employees will be affected. Then there are people whose loved ones have died overseas fighting terrorism or who were hurt or killed in the Embassy bombing. The Brit has been linked to several incidents across Africa and the Middle East."

"And you think these people will be angry at me?" She had nothing to do with any of this.

"You could end up as a target."

"Even if Daddy isn't guilty?" Her head pounded at the thought.

"Yes. You know how people are. Sometimes they want to believe the worst. And once this story breaks, reporters will be hounding you for an interview. You're going to need protection."

"And what? You're offering to protect me?"

"It's what I do. I work as a bodyguard and investigator. I'm here to help you, Jenna."

"You want me to hire you?"

He scowled. "I'm not after your damn money."

"But you work for Black-Gray. You can't just work for free."

"I'll take leave if that's what you're worried about."

It wasn't. She couldn't think. "Why is Travis here? He doesn't work for Black-Gray."

"Travis came to us with this information before your father was arrested. He has a contact in the FBI who wanted information about your kidnapping. He gave Travis a heads up in return."

"Why did he come to you about this?"

"He knew we were family."

Right, family. Because of Amelia.

She blew out a sigh. "I don't expect you to disrupt your life because of all of this, Curt. You should go back to Dallas. Both of you."

He shook his head. "We're not going anywhere."

Those words filled her with relief. She should be strong enough to deal with all this on her own, but right now she really didn't need to be alone.

She rubbed at her head. "I can't believe this."

"Look, this has all been a shock and you can't do anything right now. Why don't you go have that soak? Then you can call your mother and we can talk about where to go from here."

Right, because a bath was going to make everything better.

Fuck.

8

Jenna lay back in the bath, thoughts whirling around in her head. She should be attempting to relax and relieve the ache in her tight muscles, but she couldn't focus on anything except what her father must be going through right now.

Travis had returned with her phone as she'd been running the bath. She'd tried to get through to her mother without success. Eventually, she'd managed to get ahold of her aunt, who had taken her mother back to her house after she'd been interviewed by FBI and ATF agents, apparently both groups were involved in this case.

According to her aunt, her mother was an absolute mess. Jenna had figured as much. She'd been given a sedative, so she wouldn't be able to talk to her until morning.

She should go home, but just the thought of it made her stomach tighten with dread. Going back to Dallas would involve dealing with public scrutiny and condemnation. It would mean having to look after her mother and cope with her dramatics. It could also mean confronting her father about whether he was guilty.

She shouldn't have any questions in her mind. A good daughter shouldn't. She should just believe her father was innocent. But there was a little niggle in the back of her mind that wouldn't go away.

She didn't want to return to the city. She wanted to stay here in Haven where it felt like nothing bad could touch her. Out there, she'd be on her own. Well, she'd have Curt. But for how long? No matter what he said he couldn't just take time off from his job. And while she had some money, she knew hiring Black-Gray would be costly. If her father's assets were frozen, she might need to help support her mother.

Jesus, what a mess.

Finally, when the water was cooling, Jenna rose. Earlier, Curt had wanted to help her in and out of the bath. She blushed at the thought. He was completely overreacting to what had happened earlier today.

She studied herself in the mirror, wincing at the big, nasty bruise on her hip. Her elbows were scraped raw, but the cuts weren't deep. She wasn't badly injured but she looked drawn, pale, and fragile.

She clenched her hands into fists. Damn it. She'd worked long and hard to build up her strength, to find her old confidence and courage, and to ensure she wouldn't be a victim again. Yet, that's exactly what she looked like.

Not again. She wasn't going to let this push her back into that mindset where she jumped at shadows and thought everyone was out to hurt her.

Was she strong enough to return to Dallas, though? Would she feel like that victim again? But, then, how would everyone around here react once they heard about her father?

You don't know he's guilty.

At least she hadn't told anyone who her father was. Hopefully they wouldn't put two and two together. To begin with, anyway.

Eventually, she'd have to face this mess. But not yet. Maybe for a little while longer she could just be a small-town doctor.

Yeah, and what about the two great hulks hanging out in your living room? How was she going to explain them?

The knock on the door startled her, and she let out a small cry, banging her knee against the handle of the cabinet door as she suddenly turned.

Crap, as if she didn't have enough bruises? She glared at the door as she rubbed her throbbing knee.

"Jenna! Jenna, are you okay?" Curt asked through the door.

"I was until you scared me half to death!" she snapped.

The door handle turned, and she was thankful she'd thought to lock it. Normally, she didn't even shut the door. But then she wasn't used to having guests. Her parents hadn't been to visit her yet; there had always been some reason they couldn't come. It was probably a blessing. No doubt her mother would find fault with everything, and Daddy would work the whole time anyway.

"Did you hurt yourself? Damn it, why is this door locked?"

"Because I'm taking a bath and I don't want to be disturbed."

"Are you naked?"

What?

"Yes," she told him, hoping that would send him away.

"Good."

Good? What did that mean? Her body tightened, heat filling it. He wanted to see her naked?

"Don't get dressed."

Was this happening? She stared at the door, all thoughts of her sore knee fading. What would he do if she opened it and greeted him stark naked? Would he pull her into his arms and kiss her, squeeze her ass, maybe give it a few smacks? She shivered at the thought. What would it be like to be over Curt's knee as he spanked her butt? What would it be like if he ordered her to her knees then told her to suck him off? Or if he blindfolded and bound her? That thought would terrify her with someone else, but not with Curt. He was so protective that at times it was smothering, but she knew he would never do anything to harm her.

Physically, anyway. Her emotions were a whole different story.

"Just put on a robe. I have some antibacterial cream to put on your injuries and I want to check you over before you go to bed."

Right, he didn't want her naked because he had the urge to make mad, passionate love to her . . . or, hell, even to just fuck her.

He wanted to put cream on her boo-boos and put her to bed.

When would she learn not to get her hopes up? Not to wish for more than he was willing to give?

"I'm fine, Curt." She picked up the soft tracksuit pants and tank top she'd grabbed earlier and pulled them on. Despite her state of mind, the bath had helped ease the tension in her muscles, and she could move around more freely.

Still, she found her energy was quickly draining. She hoped like hell she could sleep once she closed her eyes, though she had a feeling she'd be up late, worrying.

When she opened the door, she found him standing there, arms over his chest. Sure enough, he held a tube of antibacterial cream in one hand. He scowled as he saw her.

"I told you to get into a robe."

"And I told you, I'm fine."

"You didn't get checked over properly, you could be seriously injured."

"Curt, I'm a doctor. I'd know if I was badly injured."

He shook his head. "You might not. I've heard of guys who were shot, carrying on as if they were fine then, as soon as the adrenaline crash hit them, boom, dead."

"Boom, dead? Really? Are you sure about that?" Although she

was skeptical, she was also the first to admit the human body could do amazing things.

"Yes, it's true."

"Either way, it doesn't matter because I haven't been shot. I fell over. Happens to people all the time."

"You didn't fall, you were pushed."

"Look, if it makes you feel better, you can put the damn cream on my elbows. They're not that bad." She bent her arms to show him. He studied her elbow carefully.

"Come on, I'll get them fixed up."

He gestured for her to follow him down the stairs and she walked behind him into the empty living room. "Where's Travis?"

"He went to find some dinner for us. Your phone has been buzzing. I put it over there." He nodded at the table.

"Oh, thanks." She quickly looked at the messages, all from her friends, checking in with her after today. Warmth filled her as she realized how many people cared about her.

"You might need to change your number if reporters start harassing you."

She put the phone back down and sat on the sofa, sighing as he began to gently apply cream to her elbows. She tried to ignore how her body reacted to his closeness. Honestly, she shouldn't even have the energy to get aroused.

"That's going to be a real pain."

He placed some bandages on her elbows then leaned back to look up at her. "I know. But they're persistent. You need to prepare yourself for that."

"Then I guess it doesn't matter if I keep the same number or not."

"Maybe not. Might give you some more peace, though. I'll try to keep them away from you as much as I can."

"Thanks." She smiled at him. They stared at each other for a moment before he looked away suddenly then stood.

"Got any other bruises or scrapes?"

"Nope, all good." Well, nothing he needed to know about anyway. There wasn't much that could be done for the bruise on her hip.

"You sure?"

"I'm sure, Curt." She sighed. Although it felt nice not to be alone, she knew she had to put on her big girl panties. "I appreciate you coming here to tell me in person but I'm an adult. Don't feel you have to stick around just because you were married to my cousin. We don't even know that I'm in any danger."

He studied her for a moment. "This has nothing to do with my marriage to Amelia. I've known you a long time, Jenna. Right now, you're not thinking properly. But when you are you're going to realize you need someone on your side, looking out for you. We have no idea who The Brit is or what he might do once he realizes your father has been arrested."

"You think I could be at risk?" She swallowed heavily, trying to moisten her dry mouth. Would he come after her? How was she going to be able to function knowing she could be in danger? This couldn't be happening to her. Not again.

"I don't know. Travis seems to think there's a possibility, but I think it's unlikely. However, I don't want to take any chances."

She leaned her elbows against her legs and rested her head in her hands. "What a mess."

"Does your father have someone who'll step in to take over the company?"

"Yes. The vice-president, Ron, is my dad's cousin. He'll be facing a nightmare. I should call him."

"I wouldn't worry about that right now. He's probably got a lot he's dealing with, and there won't be much you can do to help. In fact, I suggest you distance yourself from your dad's company as much as you can."

"But all those poor people whose jobs could be in jeopardy.

Share's will plummet when this gets out. People are going to lose a lot of money."

"And they'll be angry and desperate. That means they might do things they wouldn't normally do. Like attack someone who's innocent in all of this."

She sat back and looked up at him. "You really think I need protection?"

"Yes."

She rubbed her hand over her face and then she had to laugh. "Just as I'm getting my life sorted out, this happens. Why is it every time I think I have everything worked out something goes disastrously wrong? I don't think I can deal with this again, with looking over my shoulder all the time, waiting for someone to strike."

"Look at me, Jenna." He crouched before her and lifted her chin. She stared into his rich, hazel-colored eyes. A woman could get lost in those eyes. When he stared at her, she felt so important, so special, like she was his sole focus. It was no wonder Amelia had snapped him up when they were so young. She couldn't even imagine how it would feel to have him love her. Intense, all-consuming and no doubt satisfying as hell.

"I'm not going to let anyone hurt you, understand? Just do what I say, and we'll get through this."

She snorted. "You know I don't do well at following orders."

He smiled. "I know. You were always trouble."

"My middle name," she said lightly. "This feels like a dream. Well, a nightmare really."

"I know. But we'll get through it. Together."

"I have some money my grandmother left me," she told him. "I can pay you."

He gave her a look so cold she bit her lip in worry.

"You're not paying me."

"But what about Black-Gray? I know you said we're family, but if a paying client comes along they'll need to put them first. What if I hire them to look into all of this?"

"They already are."

"They are?"

"They know how important you are to me. I don't care about many people, Jenna. My team. And you. That's it. And you can believe me when I say I'm going to make damn sure nothing happens to you."

She stared at him, those gorgeous eyes, his chiseled cheeks, his full lips. He leaned forward, almost as though he were going to kiss her. Her breath caught in her throat. This was it, what she'd been waiting for, for so long.

The door suddenly opened, and Curt pulled back, almost falling on his ass in his haste to get away from her. Seeing him so uncharacteristically clumsy might have been funny under different circumstances, but the speed with which he put distance between them was more than a little insulting.

"Hey." Travis walked in holding a white bag in each hand, the scent of the food wafted in around him, making her stomach turn over sickeningly.

"Roast beef was the special at the diner," Travis said, putting the bags down on her coffee table. "I'll get us some cutlery and plates, if that's okay?"

"Oh, sure," she said, still feeling a little stunned and hurt.

As he walked away, she looked up at Curt, but he kept his gaze on the food, unable, or unwilling, to meet her gaze.

"Curt, I—"

"Do you want to eat here or at the table?" Travis asked, walking in. He came to a stop. "Everything okay?"

"Fine," Curt said. "I've just got a couple of phone calls to make. You guys start without me."

She watched him walk out. He didn't once turn to look at her.

"Sorry, did I interrupt something?"

She shook her head. "No. Or at least nothing he didn't want interrupted."

Travis pulled out some Styrofoam containers, opening two of them. She stared down at the food with no interest.

"I don't know Curt that well. I worked with him when we rescued you, though, and I figured out very quickly how much he cares for you."

She smiled, knowing it didn't reach her eyes. "He sees me as family. Like a cousin."

"Oh, I don't think his feelings for you are at all cousinly. I've seen the way he looks at you."

"Like he wants to murder me one moment and cuddle me the next?"

"Well, sort of. I would replace the word cuddle with kiss, though."

She snorted. "Curt doesn't want to kiss me. He's not attracted to me."

Except, he did just try to kiss you, right?

"No? He's very protective of you. From what I gather, since the death of his wife, he hasn't had any sort of long-term relationship with a woman. Yet, he was so frantic today when he thought you might get hurt that he punched a guy to get to you."

She wished she could believe he cared about her that much. "When Amelia died, Curt was devastated. He wasn't always like this—so cold and hard. Once, he knew how to laugh and have fun. When I was little, I thought I'd marry him when I grew up because he'd give me all the ice cream I wanted."

Travis smiled.

"But I was just a silly kid. Curt looks at me and sees someone he needs to protect, to look after. He has a white knight complex."

"Curt? While I might agree he's probably protective over anyone he cares about, I don't think he reacts this way to just anyone."

"Well, like you said, you don't know him very well. And these are special circumstances."

"True. It's not every day the woman you love is in danger. And you seem to get yourself into trouble more than most."

You are way too innocent and naïve to ever be someone I'd get involved with.

"Curt has made his feelings towards me very clear and while he cares about me, it's nothing more than that. He definitely doesn't love me." Not *that way* anyway. "And I don't go around looking for trouble, you know."

"No? If you were my woman you'd never have been allowed to go to Sudan alone. If I couldn't have gone with you, then you wouldn't have gone."

She wrinkled her nose at his arrogant announcement. "It's just as well I'm not your woman. And I'm not Curt's woman either."

Travis shook his head. "I expected him to be the stubborn one. Didn't realize you were just as bad."

"I'm not stubborn, just realistic. And can we please stop talking about this? Curt doesn't want me. I don't want him."

Liar. Liar.

"That so? You're saying I didn't interrupt a near kiss between the two you before? Sorry about that, by the way. My brothers will tell you, I have the worst timing."

"It's kind of weird talking to you about this, considering we barely know each other."

"I don't know. We were together during an intense situation. That tends to build bonds between people, don't you think? And I don't discuss ménages with just anyone, you know."

"What? We've never talked about ménages." What was he talking about?

"We have. I'm crushed you don't remember our conversation in Sudan. Of course, you were telling me you didn't want to participate in a ménage with me. Perhaps you've changed your mind? I have a brother, and we like to share."

Was he serious? There were lots of ménage relationships in Haven. They were almost the norm around here. But that didn't mean she wanted that sort of relationship. And certainly not with Travis, although, she had the feeling he was playing with her. Trying to gauge her reaction. She frowned at him. She didn't like games.

Her phone rang. Saved. Thank God.

She jumped up, ignoring the way her body protested and grabbed her phone off the table.

"Check who it is before you answer," Travis warned.

She nodded. "It's the sheriff." She answered the phone. "Hey, Jake. What's going on?"

"Jenna, just wanted to check on you. Everything okay?"

"I'm fine. Just had some dinner and I'm about to go to bed."

"Travis and that other guy with you?"

She nearly rolled her eyes when he referred to Curt as "that other guy" as though he didn't know his name.

"Yes."

"Want me to get rid of them?"

She looked over at Travis thoughtfully. "Not yet. But I'll save that as an option."

"You do that. I don't want them bothering you."

"Thanks for calling. Oh, have you heard how Mrs. Childs is? It's too late to call the hospital."

"Yeah, she's got a broken hip and a concussion. Gonna be in the hospital a while."

"Oh, no. Poor thing."

"Apparently her biggest concern is Daisy and who will take care of her. I better go. Sleep well."

She placed her phone down.

"What did the sheriff want?"

"Just checking in. Mrs. Childs has a broken hip and a concussion. I'll send her flowers tomorrow." She yawned. "I'm going to go to bed."

"You haven't answered me yet. Running away?"

She narrowed her gaze. "No. I just assumed that was a joke."

"It wasn't."

Holy hell. So, it wasn't some game?

"You make that offer to a lot of women?" Maybe it was some sort of weird pickup line. Did women actually say yes to a ménage with Travis and his brother?

Hell, yeah, of course they did. And she was probably nuts for not immediately saying yes.

But why her? He didn't seem like the type to have a different woman in his bed each night. Well, his and his brother's bed. Wasn't his brother one of the guys who'd been part of the team to rescue her? Yep, she remembered now. The big guy. What was his name? Jace?

Christ, one would be more than she could handle, but the two together would eat her alive.

"Nope," he told her. "Just the special ones."

Before she could answer, Curt returned.

"Everything all right here?" he asked, looking back and forth between them suspiciously.

Travis leaned back. "All good. Just discussing ménages."

"What?" Curt's face filled with thunder, and she glared at Travis. Was he trying to deliberately rile Curt?

"Travis is just being an idiot," she said hastily. "I'm going to bed."

Curt was still scowling as she walked past him towards the stairs. She needed some space. Now.

Reaching out, he grabbed hold of her arm.

"Did you eat some dinner?" he asked, surprising her.

"Yep."

"Not much," Travis added.

The rat.

"I'm fine. I'm not very hungry. I just want to go to bed. Before you guys leave, just lock up, will you?"

Curt looked over at Travis. "Jenna, we're staying here tonight."

"Oh, but I only have one spare bedroom. The hotel is way more comfortable than my old couch. There's really no need for you to stay."

"I'm staying," Curt said firmly. He turned to Travis. "You can stay at the hotel."

"Bit late to head out now. One of us can take the couch," Travis replied. "Means we can get an early start heading back to Dallas tomorrow."

"I'm not going back to Dallas tomorrow," she told them.

"What?" Curt looked at her in surprise. "Why not?"

"I've got commitments here. I can't just up and leave my job without notice. I have patients to see. I have things to do this weekend."

"What about your mom?" Travis asked. "Won't she need you?"

Guilt stirred inside her. "When she's not self-medicating, she'll spend her time complaining about how hard this is on her. I don't need that. Not right now."

"The feds will want to talk to you," Curt told her. "They're going to have questions."

"But I don't know anything."

"Doesn't matter," Travis said. "And staying here won't shield you from all of this. They'll find you here. Just like the reporters will."

"Look, I get that you guys need to go back. I'm not stopping you. I'll be safe here. This town looks after its own. Especially the women."

"Despite its name, this isn't some safe haven where nothing bad happens," Travis told her. "Not so long ago, I was here trying to help capture a serial killer who'd fixated on one of the women who lives here."

Was he talking about Laken?

"And didn't I hear about his girlfriend holding a gun on another one of the town's women?" he asked.

"Yes, but those were extraordinary circumstances," she said. "That doesn't happen every day."

"I'd hope not," Curt muttered. "I don't trust the men in this town."

"What? Why?"

"I'm sure they don't think much of you, either," Travis said with a grin. "I think Curt doesn't like the way some of them look at you."

What did that mean?

"They're nosy. And they act protective, but you got hurt today."

"That wasn't anyone else's fault except for that purse snatcher's," she told him. She rubbed her forehead. "I'm tired of arguing. I'm not ready to go to Dallas yet. If the two of you want to stick around, that's up to you. I'll see you both in the morning."

"Good night then."

Curt gave her a nod and Travis winked at her.

Dear Lord, help me. Maybe everyone was right. Trouble really did like to follow her around.

CURT FROWNED as he watched her walking away. He hadn't thought about the fact she might refuse to return to Dallas. Although it was typical of Jenna to worry about inconveniencing people, he'd figured she'd want to get to Dallas quickly to support her parents.

"Surprised you, didn't she? I didn't realize she was such a stubborn thing. She seemed so sweet and docile before. This is a pleasant surprise."

Curt turned to him. "What's that mean?"

"Well, you might like the obedient type, but I like a little bit of brat in my subs."

Curt gaped at him then stepped forward and pointed at Travis. "Jenna is off-limits."

"Says who?"

"Me." Just the thought of Travis setting his sights on Jenna made his blood boil. Jesus, did every man who met her want her? He guessed he couldn't blame them. Hell, yes, he could blame them. She was his.

"So, you do want her? Strange way to go about it. All you've done since you've gotten here is argue with her and upset her."

Curt ground his teeth together, although he couldn't really argue. There was something about Jenna that sent his emotions into overdrive. She brought out the caveman in him, which he acknowledged had always lurked beneath the surface, it was just that he usually had better control over himself.

"And Jenna isn't a sub."

"No? You sure about that?"

"Yes, I am." Why the hell did he get the feeling that smug bastard knew something he didn't?

"You don't have to stick around. I'm perfectly capable of looking after her myself."

Travis leaned back against the couch. "Oh, I think I'll stay for a bit. This town is kind of growing on me."

It was? Curt thought he was mad. This place would drive him crazy in a week.

"Want to toss for the couch?"

"Sure," Curt said pulling out a coin. "What'll it be?"

"Heads," Travis replied.

He flipped it. Heads. *Wonderful.*

Travis rose from the couch. "Great. Wasn't looking forward to trying to sleep on this tiny thing. Good night." He slapped Curt's shoulder as he went by. "Oh, Curt?"

"Yeah?" Curt snapped without turning, his gaze on the short, lumpy couch.

"Claim her soon. I don't think I'm the only one who's interested."

Fuck.

9

The dark was closing in around her. Suffocating her.

Something scratched at the walls of the dark hut. Rats. At least she told herself it was rats. God knows, it could be anything. She wouldn't know.

A sob worked its way out of her. She should have been all cried out by now. She couldn't afford to cry anymore, she was already dehydrated.

Sometimes she thought it would be easier to just give up and let herself fade away. What if the worst was yet to come? What if the beating she'd received was just the start of it? What if they planned on hurting her again? Or...God...raping her?

A tear made its way down her face. She closed her eyes and pulled in on herself as best she could, hugging herself. It had to be night because it was freezing cold. It was the only way she had of knowing. Every time they opened the door to drop in food and water, the sun shone through, but that was the only light she ever saw. The rest of the time she lived in darkness.

She bit down on her lip to hold in her screams of fear. She bit so hard the cracks in her lips split. She licked at the blood, not wanting to wipe it *away with her dirty hand and risk infection.*

She laughed. Jesus, why did she care? Maybe an infection would be a good thing. Kill her off quicker.

No. No, she had to live.

She had to get out of here.

HEART POUNDING, breath sawing in and out of her lungs, Jenna sat up, feeling disorientated. Sweat coated her body, making her feel sticky and gross. She looked around, getting her bearings. Not the hut in Sudan. Her bedroom in Haven. She gulped the water down. She always woke up so thirsty from these dreams. She didn't know if it was a trick of her brain, her memory making her think she was dehydrated, or whether she did something in her sleep that made her mouth so dry.

She used to think it was the screaming. For those first couple of weeks, she'd woken up night after night screaming and crying. Her mother couldn't take it. She'd end up in hysterics as well, and her poor dad would have two crazy women to calm down.

Her dad.

She set the glass back down on the bedside table and pulled her legs up against her chest, wrapping her arms around them, hugging herself. She guessed all this talk of her kidnapping today had brought on the nightmare. At least she hadn't woken anyone else. How humiliating would that have been? No doubt her screams would have brought Travis and Curt rushing into her bedroom. Then she'd be left explaining what the hell was going on, that she was still so messed up she had nightmares, panic attacks, and she couldn't sleep without the light on.

She was better. A lot better. For a while, she'd wondered if she'd ever be able to live on her own again, but here she was not only living alone but in a town where she'd known no one when she moved here. She'd made friends, she was taking self-defense lessons, and she was getting better.

But sometimes something would remind her of that time, would bring it crashing back, and she'd suffer flashbacks and nightmares.

She took a deep, shuddering breath. She felt chilled now, the sweat drying on her skin. She laid down and pulled the blankets tighter around her, even though she knew it would be nearly impossible for her to get back to sleep.

At least she hadn't dreamed about the attack on the village. That's what most of her nightmares were about. She'd hear Alana beg over and over for her life and she'd wake up in a panic, barely able to breathe. It would take her hours to recover from that.

She yawned. Maybe she would go back to sleep tonight. She was safe. She was in her little house. Curt was here.

Christ. She couldn't believe he was here. She knew he thought she needed help and protection, but she could hire someone. But could she trust them as much as she did Curt?

It was painful to see him. She was still embarrassed. Her anger had long since faded. All she had now was sorrow that she'd driven away someone she cared about so much by her foolish behavior. Of course, he didn't need to be such a jerk about it all. She understood the word no.

She sighed and rolled over. Worst of all was that as soon as she'd seen him, her body had sat up and taken notice in a way it hadn't done in a long time. She never reacted to other men the way she did to Curt. With lust, desire, and love.

Yep, it really sucked to be in love with someone who didn't feel the same. It sucked big time.

10

"Where do you think you're going?"

Jenna gasped as she crept past the couch, where she thought Curt was sleeping. She'd waited until it reached five a.m., before finally getting up and dressed in her exercise gear. If she couldn't sleep, then she might as well be doing something productive. Normally, her poison of choice when stressed was to cook, but since she didn't want to wake her houseguests, she'd decided to go for a run. Well, it would be more of a walk given how stiff she felt this morning. But moving around should take care of her tight muscles.

She stared at Curt's firm chest as he stood. Muscles rippled beneath his tight, tanned skin. Damn he was perfect. Wide-shouldered, abs that wouldn't quit, and a fine trail of hair that led down to . . . *Oh, fuck.*

"I'm . . . uh . . ."

"Jenna, are you okay? Has something happened?"

"I'm fine." She pulled herself together. "I'm going for a run."

"By yourself? I don't think so."

She sighed. She really didn't have the energy to argue with him. "Fine, I'll wait while you get ready."

"What?" He sounded surprised. She guessed he'd expected her to put up a fight. But she was all out of fight right now.

"I'll do some stretches outside while you change."

"You'll do your stretches in here, I'll use the bathroom to get changed." He studied her. "You shouldn't be running."

"I feel fine. Just a bit stiff. Although it's going to be more of a walk than a run. Hurry up. I have to get back and ready for work." She actually had plenty of time as she didn't start until ten today, but the more time she stood here, the harder it was going to be to tear her eyes off him. Combine that muscular chest with his sleep-tousled hair and the stubble on his cheeks and chin, and she was in serious trouble. Sexy Curt overload.

Ten minutes later, they set out. The sun was starting to rise as they started along the road.

"Sorry if I woke you," she said, needing to break the silence.

"I wasn't asleep." He kept his gaze on their surroundings, not looking at her.

"Oh, couch not too comfortable?"

"It's fine."

Great. So, he wasn't much of a conversationalist in the morning. He was probably a night owl. Ick.

"Is this something you do often?"

"Huh?" she asked, confused.

"Go for a walk on your own in the dark?"

"It's hardly dark. But, yeah, I go for runs in the mornings when I can."

"You should wait until it's lighter and go with a friend."

"I'll take that under advisement, Dad."

He gave her a funny look but then turned away.

"Have I done something to annoy you?" she asked.

"No. Why?"

"Because you don't even want to look at me."

He glanced down at her, looking startled. "It's not that. I'm keeping watch."

"For what? Flying saucers?"

"An attack."

She gulped then forced herself to calm down. No one was going to attack. He was being overly cautious. "Do you really expect one, or is it just force of habit?"

He glanced down at her again, a slight frown on his face. "Force of habit, mainly. But I'm here to protect you."

And she had no doubt he'd step between her and danger without a second thought. It made her feel nervous. She didn't want anything to happen to him because of her. Just the thought made her feel ill. She realized that while she was normally cautious, she was going to need to be even more so to protect them both.

"I don't usually go running this early. I wait until around eight on mornings when I start late. And my friend Melody generally comes with me."

"Good. You know it won't take long before someone figures out where you are. Someone could come looking for you here."

"I'm sure it won't make any difference to wait a day or two before heading to Dallas." Or three or four.

He clenched his jaw. "Don't you want to see your mother?"

She sighed. "I love my mother, but she and I have never really gotten along that well. She's better off with Aunt Mary. She'll look after her. Give her all the attention she needs."

She turned and walked off. She just wasn't ready to leave the safety of this place. Haven had healed her. Taught her she was stronger than she'd thought, and she was worried all that strength would disappear if she left.

Maybe it was stupid, but she needed a bit more time.

Reaching out, he grabbed hold of her forearm and turned her.

"You think your precious town will still be happy once you bring trouble to their door? Because that's what's going to happen if you stay."

They both heard footsteps approach, and, turning, she saw Saxon jogging up to them. Damn the man, he even looked sexy when he was running.

When she ran she looked like a sweaty beet.

"Everything okay here?" He gave Curt a suspicious look, staring pointedly down to where he held Jenna.

"Everything's fine," she told him, forcing a smile as she extricated herself from Curt's hold. His words sat like a lump of lead in her belly.

Saxon looked Curt up and down. "You're still here."

"I'm staying with Jenna."

"Why?"

"That's none of your business."

"Curt," she said admonishingly. She understood that he didn't like it here, but it didn't mean he had to antagonize everyone who lived here. They were her friends. Although she admitted Saxon wasn't acting much better.

"Curt was married to my cousin, remember? He came to tell me something about my family and he's decided he likes it here so much he's sticking around for a few days."

"You're a terrible liar, pet," Saxon told her.

Curt stiffened, and she saw him open his mouth. God, the last thing she needed was for him to get into another argument. She reached out and grabbed his wrist, squeezing.

"It's personal stuff I'm not ready to talk about yet, all right?"

Saxon's gaze narrowed, and a small shiver ran up her spine. She knew he wanted to press her for more, and he would have if Curt hadn't been there.

Finally, Saxon nodded. "Melody isn't joining you today?"

"No, it's her birthday, and she wanted to sleep in."

"Ah, yes. I believe the celebration is tomorrow?"

"Yep."

"Should you even be out running today considering you were injured yesterday? I'd think you'd be home resting." He gave Curt a look as though blaming him.

Jenna sighed. Dealing with a bunch of Alpha males could certainly be trying at times. She tried to hold onto her patience, knowing they only acted this way because they cared. She wasn't used to having people fuss and worry over her. For most of her life she'd been raised by Nancy, her nanny. She knew her parents loved her, and her father tried to be there for her. But he worked a lot, and her mother was so busy with her charities and social life she'd spent most of her time with Nancy.

When she'd hit twelve, her mother had dismissed Nancy, saying she didn't need a nanny anymore, and Jenna had been on her own. It had been tough being a teenager without anyone to talk to. She'd had some friends, of course. But teenage girls didn't always make the best companions. Sometimes they were your best friend, then your worst enemy. Plus, Jenna had always been a bit of a tomboy. She'd never quite fit in.

It had taken her a while to get used to the way things worked around here, but once she had, she'd discovered a place where she belonged.

And now, when she needed them most, she had to leave. It sucked. And, like a toddler, she wanted to stomp her foot and scream no.

"We're out for a walk not a run. Jenna needed to stretch her muscles. Besides, I'm pretty certain I would have had to tie her up to stop her."

"Hmm, that has possibilities." Saxon gave her a dark look that made her shiver.

"We need to go," Curt said, tugging at her hand.

She gave him an exasperated look but nodded.

Saxon took her other hand, giving it a squeeze. "If you need any help, Jenna, you know where I am."

"Thanks," she told him. He nodded and ran off.

"I don't trust that guy."

"You don't trust anyone," she told him dryly. "Saxon's a good guy." A bit scary, especially when he was in the dungeon.

"Who name's a club after themselves?"

"Really? That's the reason you don't like him?"

"He's too possessive of you. I know you don't understand what sort of man he is, but I do. You should stay away from him."

"Like you said earlier, Curt. You're not my big brother. Butt out. I'm making pancakes for breakfast. If you want any, I suggest you stop trying to run my life and remain quiet for the rest of our walk, okay?"

HER APPETITE quickly disappeared as she watched the end of the news story about her father's arrest.

"They make him sound guilty."

She looked over at Curt then Travis as they sat around her small dining table eating pancakes. The dining area and den were one long, narrow room. She'd turned the television on so they could see it from the table.

She stood and grabbed her half-full plate, chucking the remains in the garbage can. How could this be happening? This was crazy.

There was silence from the table, then Travis cleared his throat. "The news always sensationalizes things, you know that."

She nodded. Curt was silent.

"Curt, you got anything to add?" Travis prompted.

She looked over at him. She could really use a few positive words from him right now. She needed to hear that everything was going to be okay. That her dad hadn't done this. That he hadn't put her in danger. That he hadn't sold weapons to terrorist groups.

"I'm going to work with you today."

Not quite the pep talk she'd been hoping for. "What?"

"That wasn't exactly what I meant," Travis said dryly. "Any more pancakes?"

He'd already had two helpings.

"Sure, I'll get you some."

"He can get his own," Curt said with a scowl. "And he can do the dishes since you're going to work."

"Curt, you have the worst manners. That's no way to speak to a guest."

Travis winked at her. "That's okay, honey. For breakfast like this each day I'll happily do whatever chores need doing."

She smiled at him then turned to Curt. "You can't come into the exam room with me. My patients expect privacy. And confidentiality."

He looked irritated, then he nodded. "Fine, if you're still determined to go in—"

"I am." She needed some normalcy. Something to take her mind off everything. At least that news report hadn't mentioned her. It gave her a bit more time before people found out what her father had been accused of.

"Then I'll stay in the waiting room."

"Don't you think that's overkill? I wasn't even mentioned on that news clip. People have no idea who I am around here, and, even if they did, I can't see anyone here trying to hurt me."

"You never know what people might do. I'm coming with you, or you don't go."

She scowled at him, but he just crossed his arms over his chest, clearly not willing to bend.

Stubborn, arrogant male.

"We leave in twenty minutes," she told him. "I have errands to run in town first."

As she came down the stairs fifteen minutes later, feeling calmer and more in control of her temper, a vehicle pulled up outside. Travis, who'd been sitting on the sofa with his laptop out, got up and moved to look out the window. She noticed he stood to the side. Habit? Had to be.

"Sheriff just pulled up."

"Jake? Wonder what he wants."

Travis opened the door.

She pushed past Travis with a smile. "Hey, Jake. Want to come in? Want some coffee? I've even got some pancakes left over."

"What? I thought you said they were all gone?" Travis complained.

She stared down at his stomach pointedly. "You ate three servings. Any more and I'll have to roll you out of here."

"You calling me fat, woman?" he grumbled.

There wasn't an inch of fat on him.

"I'll take the coffee," Jake said with a nod, walking inside. The sheriff didn't smile much. It wasn't in his nature. He and Curt had that in common. Although she remembered Curt smiling a lot when she was younger. But perhaps she was just remembering him through the eyes of a child. Maybe he'd always been this serious and intense.

"What can I do for you, Jake?" she asked.

"Actually, I called and asked him to come over," Travis said. "If we're all staying a bit longer he'll need to know what's going on."

Oh, right.

They spent the next few minutes bringing Jake up to speed. Feeling agitated, she got up to refill everyone's coffee. After she put the coffee pot back and moved to the table, Curt grabbed hold of her hand and pulled her close to him. Warmth filled her.

"That's why the two of you came here? To tell Jenna?"

"And to protect her," Curt said.

Jake's eyes narrowed. "You think there's danger?"

"A lot of people are going to be upset when the news gets out," Travis said. "Shareholders, employees, people who will be mad over Jenna's dad's possible guilt."

"Any reason to think she's in danger from this British guy?" Jake asked.

Curt shook his head. "It's unlikely, but until we know where things stand it's best to be careful."

What if the worst was true? What if he was guilty?

"I'm sure Curt and Travis are overreacting. I don't think I'm in any real danger."

"Let's hope they are," Jake said standing and putting his empty coffee mug down. "But it's best to be prepared. When do you leave for Dallas?"

"In a day or two," Curt said, giving her a look.

"I don't want to bring trouble here," she said, remembering Curt's earlier warning.

"Don't worry about that, honey. I'd prefer you were here where we could watch out for you. I'll keep an eye out for anyone hanging around. Thanks for the heads up. Take care of our Jenna."

Warmth filled her at those words even as she saw Curt scowl.

"I better go get ready for work," she said. "Thanks for coming over so quickly, Jake."

"You sure you're ready for work after everything that happened yesterday?" he asked.

"I'm fine. Thanks for asking."

"When I asked that, you bit my head off," Curt grumbled.

"You didn't ask, you tried to tell me. There's a difference."

Travis snorted. "Good luck teaching that to him, sweetheart. Old dog, new tricks. You know how the saying goes."

∼

JENNA DROVE towards the florist shop. Because of Jake's visit she now had only about forty minutes until she had to be at the clinic, and it was going to be a push to get all her errands done.

"Slow down," Curt warned.

"Doesn't Travis need to get back to work?" she asked. They'd left him at her place, cursing the slow Wi-Fi connection.

"I told him to go. He wants to stay."

"I don't understand why. He must have better things to do. Seems like overkill to have two of you here."

"He has his reasons for being here. He's looking for leads on The Brit."

"But I don't know anything about that guy, and you said it's unlikely he'll come for me, right?"

He sighed. "I'm not taking chances with you, Jenna, and for the moment he's providing another pair of eyes and ears, which increases your safety."

She pulled into a parking space.

"Come on then, you overprotective bull dog. We haven't got much time."

She ordered a bunch of flowers to be sent to Mrs. Childs, spoke for a few minutes to Gracen, the florist, reassuring her she was okay after yesterday's excitement. Then as Curt moved out of earshot, she'd had to field questions about who he was and what he was to Jenna, and if they were dating. Gracen wanted to know if it was okay if she asked him out. By the time Jenna left the florist's shop, she was feeling irritated. As they left, Curt opened the door for her.

"You okay?"

"Fine. I wish everyone would stop asking me that."

He let out a low whistle. "Hey, that's what you get for moving to a small town. Everyone thinks they can poke their nose into your business. It would drive me nuts."

"You really couldn't live in a small town?"

"No way. I've had enough of people trying to interfere in my business. I like my privacy. I don't want to get involved in other people's lives. Their problems don't interest me, just like mine are none of their business. I'm surprised it doesn't annoy you."

"It did in the beginning. But I kind of like it now. It means I'm never alone."

He gave her a sharp look as they stepped into the bakery. She ordered some of Mel's favorite cupcakes to be delivered to the gym where Mel worked later.

"They deliver cupcakes?" he asked in surprise after she ordered.

"For locals they do," she replied as she pulled out some cash from her wallet. The elderly lady ahead of her was fumbling with her debit card.

"Oh, darn," she said, nearly in tears. "I had to change the number last week and now I've forgotten it."

"Here, let me get it, Mrs. Rogers," she said, reaching past her to hand over some cash.

"Oh, I can't let you do that, Jenna dear."

"Of course, you can. You go to the bank and figure out a new pin, though, okay?

"Yes. Yes, thank you, dear." The older woman squeezed her arm with her hand. "Are you okay after yesterday's scare?"

"I'm fine. Just a few scrapes and bruises, nothing serious."

"Good. Good. Terrible business when you're just walking down the streets and some thug attacks you. I hope the sheriff comes down hard on him. Too many things have been happening around here lately."

"I'm fine. Really. And I'm sure the sheriff has things under control."

"Thank you again, dear." The elderly woman gave Curt a look, eyeing him thoroughly. "You look like a strapping young man. I hope you're taking care of our Jenna."

"I can take care of myself, Mrs. Roberts," she said firmly.

Curt gave the woman a nod, and she nodded back.

Jenna gave him a look as they left.

"What?" he asked.

"Nothing." She shook her head. They continued to the post office before they headed to the clinic. It was the same wherever she went. There were questions about how she was. Comments on how terrible yesterday's incident must have been for her. But most of the attention was centered on Curt. She'd expected it, although she was kind of annoyed everyone seemed to assume he was taking care of her. She was also irritated by how many women looked him up and down or smiled at him. It made her want to do something crazy like get him a T-shirt that said, "back off, bitches, he's mine."

It was official. She was losing her mind.

By the end of the day she had a pounding headache. If one more person asked who her friend was, she was going to scream. All she just wanted to do was go home, crawl into bed, and sleep.

"Going home now, dear?" Doc Harper asked as he poked his head into her office after the last patient.

"Yep." She stood and gathered her stuff.

"Good. I hope you didn't work too hard after what happened yesterday."

"Not you too, Doc. I've been fielding questions all day."

He smiled. "And questions about the young man who's been sitting in the waiting room, carefully studying everyone who went into your office, I suspect. I have no doubt that if one of your patients even looked at you wrong he would have pounced like a panther."

"I think your imagination is going into overdrive," she said dryly as she moved towards the door. "I'm sorry if he intimidated anyone or made them feel uncomfortable. I told him it wasn't necessary for him to sit out there all day, but he insisted."

Doc waved his hand. "No, no, not at all. No doubt he's feeling rather protective after yesterday's occurrence. I would feel the same if it were my Bessy."

She nodded, feeling uncomfortable she hadn't told him the full truth. She was glad she'd never told anyone who her father was.

"Now, I got in contact with a locum who's on stand-by in case you need to go home suddenly. He should be able to stay all week if you need to remain in Dallas that long."

"Thanks, Doc. I hate to do this to you on such short notice." She'd told him this morning she might need to return home for a few days. She couldn't hide in Haven forever.

"Not at all. I just hope everything's okay."

"So do I." She gave him a tight smile."

"Well, go. Have fun with your young man. He's an intense one, isn't he?" Doc wandered away without waiting for a reply.

11

Jenna sat down on the sofa and looked awkwardly at Curt.

"Are you sure I can't help?" she called out to Travis, who was doing the dishes. She stood, ready to help him. She had to do something. Despite barely sleeping, working all day, then coming home to cook dinner, she felt full of energy.

"Sit down," Curt told her without looking up from his phone. Whatever he was reading seemed to upset him as he frowned, then tapped out a message. "He's fine. You've been working all day. Just rest."

Yeah, resting wasn't something she'd ever been good at. Keeping busy kept her from thinking too much.

"I'm going to do some laundry."

Curt looked up, piercing her with his hazel gaze.

"You look terrible. Did you sleep at all last night?"

She smiled at him tightly, trying to ignore the pang of hurt. When she'd gotten home, she'd put on some track pants and an old T-shirt and tied her hair up into a messy bun. Now she had the urge to race upstairs and fix her hair, maybe put on the makeup she'd just washed off. But why should she? This was her usual after work attire, if he didn't like it then he didn't have to look at her.

She tapped her foot. "I can't just sit around."

He shook his head, a small smile on his face.

"What?" she asked defensively. "What is it?"

"Just remembering you as a child. You never could sit still."

Right, because all he saw when he looked at her was a kid.

As if she hadn't gotten that message loud and clear.

"I'll be in the laundry room, if you need anything." She stormed into the small space, blinking back tears of frustration and disappointment.

She'd thought he'd been about to kiss her the other night, but obviously she'd been mistaken. She'd misread things. Again.

She shook her head as she threw a load of dirty clothes into the machine and added powder. This was all Travis's fault. He was the one going around insinuating Curt felt something for her.

She sighed and closed her eyes for a minute. She was exhausted. A headache was forming in her temples, a mix of tiredness and tension, and she still hadn't managed to talk to her mother. She should really do that now.

Walking back into the living room, she grabbed her phone then headed up the stairs to her bedroom.

"Jenna? You okay?" Curt asked.

"Fine."

She snorted. It was the question she hated most, she'd heard it so often since she'd been kidnapped. It was almost as bad as all the pitying looks. She'd gotten used to automatically telling people she was fine. It was what they expected her to say.

She'd often wondered what they'd do if she'd turned around and told them she was a mess. That she suffered from nightmares where she heard screams of terror that were quickly silenced by gunshots, that she often woke up in the middle of a panic attack that could leave her shaken and vulnerable for hours.

But she could never do it. Making someone else feel bad wouldn't help her. In fact, it would probably only make her feel worse.

"You sure know how to say the wrong thing, don't you?"

Curt glanced away from the stairs to stare up at Travis as he leaned against the entrance to the kitchen.

"What do you mean?" Although he knew exactly what the other man meant. He kept managing to upset Jenna. He always spoke without thinking first. He wasn't normally like this. He'd learned with Amelia to weigh each word first, so he didn't set her off into one of her rages or crying spells. But with Jenna, things just kept coming out wrong.

What he'd really wanted was to get her some pain relievers and a glass of water then sit on the couch with her head on his lap so he could massage away the headache he could see was annoying her. He'd wanted to tell her to talk to him, to let him take some of the load.

He'd wanted to strip off her clothes, put her in a bath, pamper her, love her, then sleep with her all night. But he couldn't say any of that. Not yet.

Irritation at himself for pushing her away, combined with sexual frustration meant he'd ended up growling at her instead.

"You're lucky I'm here to smooth things over."

"Is that what you're doing? Because from where I'm sitting it looks like you're coming on to my woman." And he was making Curt look even more like an asshole.

Travis raised an eyebrow. "Not your woman though, is she? You better get your act together fast. Because that is not a woman who will remain single long."

"So, you *do* want her?"

Travis shook her head. "Jenna's a forever girl, and I'm not looking to settle down." He turned away. "But she's special, maybe she could change my mind."

Curt ground his teeth together. Not happening. Not while he had breath in his body. He rose. It was about time he apologized for the asshole he'd been months ago. And for the way he was acting now.

JENNA STARED down at her phone as it shook in her hand. Her breath came in fast pants. A sick feeling developed in her stomach. She'd thought Curt was exaggerating. She hadn't really believed anyone would blame her for her father's actions. But the text messages were there on her phone.

How does it feel to get rich from murdering innocent people?

Murdering bitch.

Hey, bitch, die.

There were some recorded messages, but she didn't have the guts to listen to them. She sniffled. Oh, God. Her stomach lurched. The idea that strangers could hate her so much they'd send messages like this made her feel ill.

She stood, knowing she was going to vomit.

There was a knock on her door, and she half-screamed. "Jenna? You okay?" Curt pushed open the bedroom door just as a loud bang sounded.

With a screech, she dropped to the floor, the phone skittering across the floor. Sobbing hysterically, she placed her hands over her head.

THE SCREAMS SURROUNDED HER. *Terror-filled. Frightened. Babies cried. People yelled.*

She looked over at Alana in alarm. They stood frozen in the make-shift clinic. Some of the patients lying on beds in the clinic started to yell out in alarm.

The patient Jenna had been examining, a young man with a bad infection in his leg due to lack of access to antibiotics, grabbed her arm, his eyes wide.

He climbed from the bed and took off. She didn't bother to call him back. She looked over at Alana as their patients hastily left.

"What is it?" she asked the other woman, her heart racing. This was her first overseas assignment with Doctors Without Borders. Alana had been on a few, but the older, more experienced, woman looked shocked and scared.

"I don't know. I think we better get out of here."

The door to the clinic flew open, and armed men entered. They were dressed in khaki shirts and pants but they weren't military or the local police. Neither one of those groups wore bandanas on the lower half of their faces.

Fear washed over her as she saw the machine guns in their hands. Oh, God, what was going on? What were they after?

"Whatever you want, just take it," Alana told them as they advanced towards the women.

They turned their guns on them, and Alana cried out. Jenna was too scared to make a sound, her breath caught in her throat as she stared at the two men. Was this it? Was she going to die here?

Oh, God, had her parents been right?

Something wet ran down her cheek, and she realized she was crying. She wanted to wipe the tears away but she didn't dare move.

"What are you doing?" someone yelled from the doorway. "Get away from them!"

She turned, her gaze falling on Richard, one of the other doctors, walk through the doorway. One of the armed men turned, then there was a tat-tat-tat noise, and she watched in shock as Richard fell to the ground. He remained still.

They'd shot him. Shot Richard.

Alana cried out, and she turned back as the other man aimed his gun at her.

"Please, please," Alana begged, dropping to her knees. "My name is Alana. I'm forty-two. I have children. A boy and a girl. A hus—"

She was cut off mid-sentence, as the gun was fired, slumping to the ground. Her eyes staring lifelessly towards Jenna. That's when Jenna started to scream.

CURT RAN FORWARD, his heart stopping as he saw Jenna on the floor, curling in, her arms over her head as though trying to protect herself.

"Jenna! Jenna!" He knelt, reaching for her.

Her whole body shook. Her cries of fear made his gut clench.

"What's wrong? What happened?"

He turned to find Travis behind him, staring down at Jenna in concern.

"I don't know. A car backfired, and suddenly she screamed. Jenna!" He reached out and picked her up. She cried out again, the noise filled with such fear he almost dropped her.

"A flashback?" Travis asked, coming forward as Curt settled on the bed and held Jenna on his lap. "Try talking to her. She's more likely to react to your voice than mine."

He rocked her instinctively, barely aware he was doing it as she stared off into the distance, her eyes wide, tears coursing down her cheeks. She looked so pale and fragile he wanted to tuck her somewhere safe and keep her there, where he knew nothing would ever touch her again.

"Jenna, come on, baby. Come back to me now. Listen to my voice. You're safe. I'm here. Jenna, come back to me."

· · ·

JENNA.

Jenna, come back to me.

She was in the darkness again. Curt was there this time, though. Oh, no, they'd caught him too. But, no, Curt was strong. He wouldn't let anyone take him.

Jenna. I'm here. You're safe. Come back.

She blinked then gasped as she saw a man leaning over her. With a whimper, she shrank back. That wasn't Curt.

"Back off, Travis, you're scaring her."

She knew that gruff voice. Curt. She turned her head, looking up into his face. So familiar, yet different. He had more lines now. Some gray hairs. But they only made him more attractive.

"Curt."

He smiled down at her gently.

"I'll get her a glass of water," the other man said.

Her heart was racing. She felt weak and she was trembling uncontrollably. Where was she? Confusion filled her.

"Curt?" she asked, clinging to him.

Sweat coated her body, and she probably smelled less than pleasant, but there was no way she was letting him go. He'd just have to put up with the stink.

"It's okay, baby. You're safe. I have you. No one will hurt you again."

Her breath sawed in and out of her lungs. The other man returned, holding out a glass of water. She knew him. He smiled at her gently.

"Travis."

"That's me."

Slowly, reality came back. She lived in Haven now. This was her bedroom. Travis and Curt were staying with her.

"Here, baby, have a drink."

Curt held the glass of water to her lips. She tried to take it from him, but he just gave her a firm look. She dropped her hand and started to drink.

"Easy now, don't make yourself sick," he told her.

"So thirsty. Always thirsty. Never enough water."

She felt Curt tighten his hold on her. "Fuck," he muttered under his breath.

"Don't swear," she chided, remembering how he liked to scold her for doing the same.

"Sorry, baby."

He was being so gentle. He kissed the top of her head as he rocked her. She could snuggle in against that wide chest and let him take care of her forever. Let him take care of everything. It would be so easy to allow him to take charge—to give up.

But she couldn't do that. She had to fight. She was stronger than this.

"Flashback?" Travis asked, crouching in front of her.

"Yes," she answered as steadily as she could manage. There was no use denying it.

"Do you have them often?"

He kept his voice low, and his face was filled with sympathy, but there was no pity that she could see. And that gave her the courage to answer him.

"Not anymore. When I . . . when I first got home I had a hard time adjusting. Sometimes I would wake up and I wouldn't know where I was. I'd think I was back there. In that hut. Or in the village, standing next to Alana as she was shot." She gulped, resisting the urge to bury her face in Curt's chest and hide. "Sometimes things would set off a flashback. A noise or a smell." She stiffened, trying to remember what she'd been doing in the moments before the flashback. "I'm not sure what happened this time."

"A car backfired," Curt told her.

"Ah, right."

"Although you seemed on edge when I knocked on the door."

She frowned. Then she remembered. "My phone. Where is it?" She tried to push away from Curt, but he kept a tight hold. "I need to find it."

"Stay still. I need to hold you a little longer." She froze and looked up into his face, shocked by his words. He stared down at her with haunted eyes.

She cupped his face. "I'm okay, Curt. I'm fine. That wasn't even a bad one. Sometimes I'll wake up in the middle of a full-blown panic attack. I rarely get them anymore and when I do, they don't affect me as badly. Plus, this time . . ." she trailed off.

"This time what?" he asked.

Before she had to answer, to tell him she thought she was coping better because he was here, Travis had found her phone and returned it to her. "Here it is."

She opened the messages and held her phone so they could both see.

"Mother-fucking bastards," Curt swore. This time she didn't bother to scold him. She totally agreed with the sentiment.

"I'll send the phone numbers to Jace so he can trace them," Travis said. "If you don't mind me taking your phone for a bit?"

She half-laughed. "You can have it. Don't think I want it anymore."

"There are some voice messages on here, do you mind if I listen to them?" he asked, taking the phone and flicking through it.

She shook her head tiredly. "Nope, do what you like. I was going to call my mother, but I don't feel like doing that right now."

Travis nodded, patted her shoulder, then left. Leaving her and Curt alone.

She attempted to pull herself from his lap, but he held on tighter. When she looked up at him, she saw how tense his jaw was, the muscles in his neck tight. He was staring at the wall, thinking hard about something.

"Curt? What is it?"

He glanced down at her. "I thought this would happen, but seeing those messages, people threatening you, it . . . pisses me off."

She got the feeling he wanted to say something else but was holding back.

"I know. I guess part of me thought you guys were exaggerating. That this would all be fine." She shivered. "It's horrible to think perfect strangers hate me so much."

"They won't touch you. You know that, right?"

"I know," she said softly, sensing he was the one who needed reassuring now. "Thanks for being here for me just now. Usually, after one of these flashbacks it takes me hours to recover. Having you guys here helps."

Having him here helped. Having him hold her was more comforting than anything anyone else had done. But she couldn't sit here forever.

"I'm going to go take a shower now."

He didn't move.

"Curt?"

"I'm sorry if things I've said have upset you," he said stiffly. "Around you, for some reason, my mouth seems to talk before my brain catches up. I don't mean to hurt you. I never have."

"I know."

He stared down at her, and she nearly gasped at the pain she saw in his eyes. "I acted like a jerk. I shouldn't have said what I did to you that night in my apartment."

"It's okay, Curt. I get it." And it was. Because no matter what hurt he'd put her through, he'd also helped her move on. "If it wasn't for you, I might still be stuck living in my parents' house, letting them coddle me. I don't think I would have come here and made a life for myself like I have. You helped me heal. So, you see, I owe you for rejecting me. I don't know what I was thinking, like we would have worked as a couple. We're much better off with as friends."

WE'RE MUCH BETTER *off as friends.*

Christ, he'd really screwed this up. He sat on the bed, listening to her shower. He'd pushed her away, not ready for a relationship, thinking it was better for her. And now that he'd decided he wanted her, she'd decided it was better they just be friends. She'd thanked him for turning her down.

Was he too late? Had he ruined any chance of having her? Could she really love living here?

He ran his hand over his face. There was still something there. He was certain of it. They'd nearly kissed last night before Travis had interrupted them. No, there was something there. The question was, what exactly was it? He knew what he wanted. Her. All of her.

But what if she just felt a sexual attraction and nothing more? What if she didn't want a relationship with him? What if this town was really where she truly wanted to be? Would she move to be with him? Curt couldn't live here.

Fuck.

What was he going to do?

12

_____

Everyone turned to stare as she entered the gym the next morning. Not that people were looking at her. No, the looks were for the two men walking in behind her.

The two testosterone-laden, muscular men whose work-out gear only served to highlight their firm bodies. Not that she'd looked at Travis's body. Well, not much anyway. She wasn't a saint after all.

After last night's embarrassing flashback, plus receiving those horrible messages on her phone, she'd expected she wouldn't have been able to sleep. But she'd had an amazing rest and had woken up full of energy and ready for this morning's class.

Travis' brother had traced some of the numbers; they belonged to some people with mental health issues. She was amazed by how people had discovered her phone number so quickly, but apparently, very little was private nowadays. Most of the recorded messages were from reporters.

Brye walked toward them, looking Travis and Curt over as though sizing them up.

"Jenna."

"Brye, hi," she said cheerfully. "Meet Travis and Curt. They're staying with me for a few days. Curt was married to my cousin."

Brye held out his hand and shook theirs. He was a little shorter but just as muscular. Brye had been Special Forces before he'd retired and moved to Haven.

"Is it okay if Travis and Curt use the gym equipment?" she asked.

"Sure. Any friends of yours are welcome here."

"I'm going to the class with you," Curt told her.

She gave him an exasperated look.

"We don't allow men in our self-defense classes," Brye told him.

Curt turned to her, giving her a thoughtful look.

"It makes the women nervous to have someone watch. I'm sure you understand." Brye raised his eyebrows at her as if questioning Curt's overly protective behavior.

Curt sighed. He pointed at her. "Fine. Stay here, though."

"Got nowhere else to go."

He was being ridiculous. After those messages last night, he'd become even more protective.

As soon as Curt and Travis left, her friends surrounded her. She gave Mel a hug for her birthday yesterday.

"Whoa, girl, don't tell me you're sleeping with both of those hunks of spunk," Mel said.

Jenna blushed. "Of course not."

"Just one of them then?" Josie asked. "Which one? Because I call dibs on the other."

Hannah whacked their friend on the head. "Josie, you can't just call dibs."

"Thank you, Hannah," Jenna said.

"Not when I saw them first."

Melody rolled her eyes. "Guys, give Jenna a break. Well?"

"I'm not sleeping with either of them. They're just here

because they had to deliver some news in person. They're leaving soon."

Around her, faces dropped.

"But they're coming out tonight, right?" Melody asked.

"Um, I don't know. But I can ask."

Brye called them all over for their lesson.

Suddenly, she regretted she hadn't left for Dallas already.

AFTER THEIR WORKOUT, Curt followed Jenna out to her car. He kept his gaze on their surroundings. Mostly. The sight of her ass in those Lycra pants was not something to be missed, that was for damn sure.

He wanted nothing more than to pull her into his arms, place his hand firmly on that tight ass, and make sure all the assholes hanging around knew exactly who she belonged to.

A bit caveman-like, but he was feeling like a Neanderthal right now.

Travis had driven his own car to the gym so he could talk to Jake about the messages and phone calls Jenna had received. After listening to a couple of the sick voice mails, Curt had been so filled with rage he'd had to go for a run to clear his head. He and Travis had agreed that Travis would handle the messages on her phone. Curt didn't trust himself not to call the bastards back and threaten them with bodily harm.

As Jenna drove them back to her place, Curt's phone rang. Looking at the screen, he saw it was Travis.

"Yeah?"

"Just answered a call from Colin Richards on Jenna's phone. He's the vet. He's been taking care of that old woman's dog. Anyway, the dog isn't very happy, and he wants Jenna to stop by the vet clinic to see it."

"All right." He ended the call then relayed the message to Jenna.

"Oh, no, poor Daisy. Okay, the vet clinic is just a few minutes away. We'll head over and see Colin."

When they arrived, the door to the clinic opened, and Curt saw the guy from the other day step outside. He'd been the one waiting with a tranquilizer gun.

"Colin, how are you?"

He smiled. "I'm good, Jenna. You still sore?"

"Bruises are still a bit tender, but I'm okay."

She hadn't told him any of that. Curt scowled. She shouldn't have been participating in that self-defense class this morning if she was still in pain. But he made certain he removed the frown when she turned to look at him. He wasn't doing anything to ruin the truce they'd come to. This morning, she hadn't fought when he'd told her they were coming to the gym with her, and that was a step in the right direction.

"Sorry to call you like this on a Saturday morning but I'm worried about Daisy. She's not eating and she appears to be moping."

"Oh, poor baby. She's probably missing Mrs. Childs."

"I've been to see Mrs. Childs. She's going to be in the hospital a while," Colin said as he led them down a hallway and into a large back room. Daisy sat in a big pen. She had a large bed and blanket as well as dishes filled with food and water. She simply lay there, her head resting on her paws as she watched them approach. The vet was right, she did appear to be moping.

Jenna crouched down. "Oh, Daisy, you poor girl. Are you missing Mrs. Childs?"

"The thing is, I don't think Daisy can go back to living with Mrs. Childs. We could be talking months by the time she's recovered enough to look after Daisy, and, even then, Mrs. Childs has told me she's thinking about going into a home. As much as it pains her to do it, she's decided that the best idea would be to rehome Daisy."

Jenna turned to look at Colin, her face filled with sadness. "Oh, no, that's terrible. She must be so upset."

"She is. She really wants Daisy to go to someone who will love and take care of her. Someone the dog loves."

Curt could see where this was going even if Jenna couldn't and he didn't like it. Not that he had anything against dogs, although this dog was more the size of a small horse. How much would she eat? If Jenna had a dog this size she might not be inclined to rely on Curt for protection, and, right now, that's all he had to tie himself to her.

"What are you going to do?"

"Well, both Mrs. Childs and I put our heads together and we came up with someone we thought would be perfect."

Colin was silent for a moment, obviously waiting for Jenna to figure out who he meant. But Jenna was busy patting Daisy. Curt resisted the urge to snatch her hand back, remembering the way the dog had stood over Mrs. Childs, snapping and snarling at everyone. A dog this big could do a lot of damage to someone Jenna's size. How the hell could she be expected to take care of her?

Curt gave the other man a warning look. The vet just smiled and shrugged. Then he pointed down at Daisy as her tail started wagging when Jenna patted her head. The dog stared up at Jenna with such hope in her eyes.

"That's the first time I've seen her tail wag since I brought her back here. We definitely made the right choice."

Jenna stood, and Daisy followed her with her gaze, a look of doggy devotion on her face. "What do you mean?"

"Daisy loves you, Jenna. It's clear to see you'd be the perfect person to look after her."

"I can't."

Exactly his thoughts. He gave the vet a triumphant look. The other man just looked patiently at Jenna and waited. Jenna bit her lip, looked at Daisy then back at Colin. "You really think I'm the best person to take her in? I work all day. Won't she be lonely?"

"She's a pretty easygoing dog. She's well-trained, and if you exercise her a lot, I think she'll be okay. You could pay someone to walk her. I'm also certain you could arrange something with Doc so you could take her to the clinic. I could take her out to the ranch, but she definitely doesn't react to me like she does you."

Jenna bit her lip a little longer then stared over at Curt. "I might need to go back to Dallas for a bit. Some family stuff is going on."

"She can come with us," Curt told her in a gruff voice. Clearly, she wanted the dog. Damn dog was going to take up most of the backseat. Although the look on Travis's face when he told him the dog was going to ride in his brand-new truck with its leather upholstery would be worth it.

Her eyes lit up. She smiled at him like she'd won the lottery.

It was also worth it to see her face.

Colin opened the pen. "Come on, Daisy girl, looks like you've got a new home."

Daisy shocked them all by bounding out of the space and bowling into Jenna, who would have gone flying if Curt hadn't caught her.

"I thought you said she was well-trained," he snapped at the vet.

"She is," Colin said, looking surprised. "She never once jumped on Mrs. Childs."

They both looked over as Jenna giggled; Daisy was licking her hands. "It's okay, I think she's just excited, aren't you, Daisy girl?" She ruffled her fur. "We're going to have so much fun together, aren't we?"

He'd now hit a new low; he was jealous of a damn dog.

13

"You're not going."

"Yes. I am."

"It's a bar filled with people. I can't protect you properly there."

"Curt, you're overreacting. I know you take this whole bodyguard thing seriously, but I'm not in any danger."

"You've received death threats!" he yelled. And each one filled him with mindless fury. He couldn't stand that he had no way of stopping these people from hurting her.

"It's Mel's birthday. I said I'd go. I want to go. I'm going. With or without you."

He ground his teeth together.

"Does anyone else think this feels like déjà vu?" Travis asked, looking up from his laptop as he sat on the sofa.

Curt just growled at him.

"Curt, it will be fine. You can come if you like."

"Like you'd be allowed to go without me."

She rolled her eyes at him. His palm itched with the need to pull her over his lap, tug up that ridiculously short skirt she was wearing, pull down the panties she wouldn't be allowed to wear once she was his, and paddle her ass.

She was in sore need of discipline.

"And what about Daisy?" he asked, pointing at the dog, who sat on her bed in the corner, chewing on a new toy Jenna had bought for the mutt. As if sensing the attention on her, she looked up and gave a doggy smile.

"Daisy will be fine, it's just a few hours. We're going."

"Good, it's settled." Travis stood and stretched. "I could use a drink."

"No drinking on the job," Curt told him then he turned back to Jenna. "And you have to promise not to go anywhere without one of us."

"Last time I looked you haven't got the bits to allow you entrance to the women's bathroom."

"You've been looking at my bits?" Travis asked with a grin. "I'm flattered."

Jenna blushed, and Curt scowled at the other man. Travis held up his hands in surrender, although it was clear he was trying hard not to laugh. "I'm going to go get ready. It's been a long time since I had a good night out."

"It's not a night out," Curt told him. "We're working."

"Yeah, yeah."

"I should probably warn you that my friends might hit on you," she told Travis.

His grin grew. "Even better."

Curt let out a deep breath. He knew when he was outnumbered.

"Fine, we're going. But I want your promise."

She threw her hands up into the air. "Whatever will make you feel better. I promise, okay?"

It wasn't okay. Not at all. He didn't like that she was being threatened and he didn't like that she wasn't his to command.

Because if she were, she certainly wouldn't be going anywhere but his bed, where she'd spend the night under him, pleasing him, pleasuring him.

The thought made his cock stir.

He needed to claim her. Soon.

"DOES he ever take his gaze off you?" Mel asked her as she pressed close to her at the bar.

Dirty Delights was pumping, the rodeo over in Freestown meant there were lots of visitors here tonight. Plenty of cowboys looking for a good time. She looked around for their other friends and found Hannah flirting with a blond cowboy dressed in a button-down shirt, jeans, and cowboy boots. Carlie was talking with a few of the other girls who attended the self-defense lessons at the gym.

Josie hadn't stopped talking to Travis all night, although Jenna got the feeling he wasn't as interested in her as she was in him. He seemed to be more indulgent than anything else. She watched as her friend stumbled over nothing, wincing. Travis caught her with a look of concern.

"I think Josie has drunk too much."

Melody looked over with a worried glance. "I'll get Darne to call Bert."

Bert was the local taxi driver. Actually, the only taxi driver.

Mel waved down Darne, one of the bartenders, and spoke to him across the bar, pointing to Josie. Darne nodded and moved towards the back of the bar where the phone was located.

"Don't try to change the subject. What's going on with you and Mr. Intense over there?"

Almost as though he heard them speaking about him, Curt turned to look at her questioningly. She smiled, letting him know she was okay. He was only a few feet away, but it was so noisy she knew she could talk without him overhearing.

"Nothing."

"Nothing? Honey, I've been watching the two of you all night. I've seen the way he keeps checking in with you to make sure you're okay. How you keep tabs on when his drink is getting low and send Bella over with a fresh one."

She shrugged. "We've known each other for years. I care about him."

"Oh, no, it's more than that. There's heat in his gaze as he watches you. When you're not looking he totally checks you out, and you do the same to him."

"Do not."

"Do too."

"And he's scared off every man who's approached us. Maybe I should stand away from you. I might have a chance of getting laid then."

"Oh, shut up. We both know there's only one man you're interested in."

Everyone in their circle of friends knew about Melody's feelings for Brye.

"Yeah, well, he thinks of me as a little sister so maybe it's time to move on."

"I know how that feels."

"Girl, that man does not see you as his sister. Are you going to tell me why he's really here? And don't give me that bullshit that he came to tell you something. That's what phones are for."

A new song came on, and Melody grabbed her hand. "Hey, it's our song! Come on!"

Whew. Saved from having to answer that question.

She dragged Jenna over to the dance floor. Mel was spontaneous and fun, although she didn't always think things through. Jenna knew Curt wouldn't like her just taking off but she wasn't out of his sight and as she danced to the beat she felt some of her tension drain away.

She threw her arms up into the air, jiggling her hips. Arms wrapped around her from behind. For one crazy moment she thought it was Curt, but the scent was off, and this guy was smaller. She pushed at his arms, but he didn't move.

"Hey, let go of her," Mel said, moving closer.

"Let go! Now!" Jenna yelled, feeling the panic rise. Old fears swamped her. Being restrained. Hurt. No. She wouldn't let him hurt her.

Then her training took over and she slammed her foot down on the top of his. Then as he loosened his grip with a shout, she turned and rammed her knee into his balls, quickly following up with a punch to his nose.

As he crumpled to the ground with a cry, she stood there breathing heavily. Someone touched her shoulder, and she turned, her fists raised. Brye took a step back, holding his hands up.

"Hey, Jenna, it's okay. You got him."

Around them people had stopped dancing and were pointing and staring. She heard a shout then saw Curt push his way through the last of the crowd. His face was like thunder as he approached.

Suddenly, reality flooded in and mortification filled her.

"Oh, God, what did I do?" Tears filled her eyes.

"Are you all right? Did he hurt you?" Curt asked as he grabbed hold of her shoulders. He ran his gaze over her as though checking for injuries.

"I'm fine. He didn't hurt me. Shit, I can't believe I did that. Is he okay?" she asked Brye, who was checking the guy over.

"Who cares?" Mel said. "You told him to let go, and he didn't. You were a total bad ass."

She didn't feel like a bad ass. She felt shaken and unsure. She looked up at Curt, who still held her. He pulled her closer, wrapping his arm around her waist as two of the bouncers helped the guy limp off. She shook, and he ran his hand up and down her back.

"It's okay. You're all right," he spoke against her ear so no one else could hear.

"Jenna, are you okay?" She looked over as Devon, the owner of Dirty Delights, approached.

"She's fine," Curt snapped. "You might think about getting more bouncers, though. A woman should be able to dance without getting mauled."

Devon narrowed his gaze. "You're the guy that punched Logan and Duncan, right? I have extra bouncers on, but there are a lot of strangers in town. Are you girls out on your own?"

Melody nodded.

"I'm keeping an eye on them," Brye said.

Mel turned to give him a look, and he just raised an eyebrow.

"I think I want to go home," Jenna said, feeling a little ill.

Curt nodded and began to steer her through the crowd, which had mostly, gone back to ignoring them. She hated being the center of attention.

"Wait, I have to say good night to Mel." She gave her friend a hug and reassured her that she'd be fine. The other woman said good night, and Jenna let Curt lead her away.

When they finally reached her car, he opened her door and helped her in before doing up her seatbelt. She was quiet as he drove her home, but when they entered her cottage, instead of going to bed like she knew she should, she grabbed a bottle of tequila from her liquor cabinet. "Want a shot?"

CURT HATED TEQUILA, but he nodded. He didn't like the look on her face. She seemed shell-shocked, shaken. He guessed it could be just a reaction to what had happened, but it felt like more. She grabbed some salt and cut up some limes and then placed everything on the coffee table. She did the first shot with barely a grimace. He looked at her in surprise.

"This was my poison of choice during college. Medical school was intense, we needed a way of unwinding."

"I can think of another way of unwinding," he said, surprising himself. He didn't usually flirt. Didn't like to take part in anything that smacked of a game. He'd played too many of those with Amelia during their marriage. Bitterness filled him. So many years wasted with that viper.

"Yeah, well, we did plenty of that too."

Did she? Jealousy twisted in his stomach, and he had to tamp it down. He did take the shot, though, then reached out to let her pour him another. He wondered how he could get her to open up about what was bothering her.

"I thought I was back there."

"What? Where? Back in the bar?"

"No, when I was in Dirty Delights. When that guy wouldn't let me go, I started to panic. I thought he was going to hurt me. Or hold me down while someone else harmed me, like they did—"

"When you were kidnapped. Jesus, Jenna—"

"I know it's silly. I was safe. I was surrounded by people, my friends, you. Nothing bad was going to happen to me."

She looked over at him, her eyes haunted.

"You fought back, darlin'. You got yourself free. Without help from anyone else."

Huh, she had, hadn't she?

"And even if you hadn't, I wasn't far away. Nothing would ever have harmed you while I was there." Although, he was still pissed at how long it had taken him to get through the crowd to her. He should never have let her get so far away from him. When she'd taken off to the dance floor, he'd started to follow but he'd paused for a moment, captivated by her dancing. But he wouldn't have forgiven himself if something had happened to her.

She smiled. "I know. My knight in shining armor."

He snorted. "You are the only person who would ever call me that."

"I thought I was getting stronger."

"You are one of the strongest people I know."

"I still sleep with the light on."

"So do I."

She rolled her eyes. "No, you don't."

"What happened to you was terrifying, traumatizing. You had every reason to hide from the world and feel sorry for yourself. Instead, you fought back. You moved here on your own, found yourself a job, you've been taking self-defense classes, made some good friends. I don't think I know anyone stronger."

She shook her head. "I moved here to get away from everything."

"To get away from what?"

"My parents. You."

He stilled. "Jenna—"

She stood, shaking her head. "Forget I said that. I'm going to bed."

He reached up and grabbed her hand, tumbling her onto his lap. "I'm sorry, baby. I'm sorry you had to come here to get away from me. I was such an asshole."

"Let me up."

He stared down into her beautiful face, remembering the way she'd stared at him with hurt and anger.

"I made mistakes. Said things I still regret and I drove you away. You're the best thing in my world, and I pushed you away." Then leaning in, he kissed her.

Jenna couldn't believe this was happening. Curt was kissing her. Actually kissing her. And, damn, it was fucking good.

He cupped her breast, and she whimpered. The sensations were almost too much. Her whole body stiffened, needing him, hardly daring to believe this was happening. At any moment now, she knew he'd pull back and tell her this had all been a horrible mistake. But she was going to take as much as he would give. He rubbed her hard nipple with his thumb, and she wished there weren't two layers of clothing between their bodies.

"Curt, please."

If he rejected her now, it would hurt so much.

"Sh, baby. It's going to be okay. I'm going to take care of you."

"Don't start something you won't finish." She was surprised she could even speak in full sentences as he lightly pinched her nipple. Sparks of arousal shot straight to her clit, making the bundle of nerves throb.

"I won't. I want you, Jenna. So much I can barely sleep at night, imagining you next to me, under me, surrounding me with your heat."

He shifted her off his lap and stood suddenly, the loss of his body against hers chilled her. She bit back a cry of denial. He'd changed his mind. He didn't really want her. Then he leaned in and picked her up, cradling her against his chest.

"Curt!"

"We're moving this upstairs. I'm not going to risk that bastard, Travis, interrupting us. And there's no way I'm letting him see your naked body."

"I thought Doms liked to show off their subs," she whispered.

He stopped, staring down at her in shock. *Fuck, why did I say that?* It wasn't like she was his sub.

"And what would you know about that?" he asked in a low voice.

She swallowed heavily then raised her chin. She wouldn't let him intimidate her.

"Jenna? What do you know about BDSM? Did someone tell

you I was a Dom?" He shook his head then continued to climb the stairs, not even looking strained as he carried her. Laying her on the bed, he ran his hand down her cheek with a smile so filled with condescension she stiffened. "I don't know who told you that, but it's nothing to worry about, sweetheart. No doubt you think it's all whips and chains. You're probably scared by the idea of me dominating you, but I'm not going to do anything like that."

"That so?" she drawled. "How . . . disappointing."

She watched as his eyes flared at her words then narrowed thoughtfully. "You want me to dominate you?"

She snorted. "You attempt to boss me around in every aspect of my life, but when it comes to sex you decide to take a step back? What's with that?"

"If I'm bossy the rest of the time, it's only because I want to keep you safe. You find trouble wherever you go."

"Jesus." She sat up. "You have this idea that I'm this sweet, innocent girl. I'm not a virgin, Curt."

He glowered. "I don't want to talk about your past lovers."

"Well, too bad. I may not have the experience you do, but that doesn't mean I'm wet behind the ears. Curt, I know about BDSM."

He waved his hand, pacing impatiently. "Movies and books—"

"Because I'm a member of a BDSM club," she spoke over him.

He stopped his pacing. "What?" His voice was low, cold.

She swallowed heavily, not quite prepared for that reaction. But she gave him a firm look, not wanting him to see her nerves. "I belong to Saxons."

"Why?"

Tell him the truth? Or just part of it?

"Cady told me about BDSM, and the idea intrigued me." Made her hot, was more like it. Only, once she'd gotten to the club, it hadn't felt right.

Because Curt wasn't there.

"That's a big step, going from feeling a bit intrigued to

becoming a member of a BDSM club." He sat on the bed, looming over her. Her breath caught at the coldness in his eyes. The intensity in his face. "I can't believe you went into a BDSM club alone. Damn, I bet they circled you like sharks moving in on fresh prey. You really want this? For me to dominate you?"

She nodded, feeling a little hesitant now. He looked so fierce. Crap, where had all her courage fled to?

"Stand and strip for me," he ordered.

Oh, hell. Even as her body reacted to his words, nervousness filled her. "Curt—"

"Now, sub."

No. Too fast. Too much. She wasn't just going to be just some faceless sub to him. She almost caved, wanting to please him. But this was important.

"No."

His eyes widened. "Just how useless are the Doms at that club? Or do you want to be punished?"

No. Yes. Maybe. Later. Right now, she needed to make him understand.

"When I went to Saxon's, I only watched."

"I find that hard to believe. What honey is to a bee, you'd be to a Dom. Soft, sweet, and irresistible." He reached for her top, pulling it off over her head.

Her eyes widened, her breath coming faster. "I didn't participate, Curt."

He stilled. "What? Ever?"

She shook her head.

"Why not?"

"I guess because even though there are safeguards in place, and I knew it didn't have to be anything sexual, I just didn't trust anyone enough to let go. To allow them any control over me. I didn't want to be with just anyone. I wanted to be with someone who cared about me."

He was silent for a moment, and she stared up at him. "But you trust me, don't you, Jenna?"

She could have denied it, but what would have been the point? It was obvious she trusted him. Maybe more than she trusted anyone.

"Yes," she whispered.

"And you know that I care about you?"

God, she hoped he did.

She nodded.

He studied her then smiled. "Don't look so scared, little bit. When have you ever known me to be anything but protective of you?"

"Never. You're usually too protective." So why was she feeling so apprehensive? Maybe because she'd wanted this for so long and now she was scared she was fucking it all up.

He ran a thumb over her cheek. "Then all you have to do is what feels good. Tonight, we'll take things slow. Ease into it."

He took her mouth with his, kissing her, possessing her.

"Not promising I won't get a bit bossy, though," he muttered as he reached around and unclipped her bra.

The tightness in her stomach eased. This was Curt. Her Curt. "You wouldn't be Curt otherwise."

"Sassy brat." He drew her bra away then stared down at her breasts for a moment. She resisted the urge to cover herself, but her breath caught in her throat as she waited for him to say something.

"Even better than I'd hoped for." He lightly pushed her back then dropped his head, taking her right nipple into his mouth, sucking strongly.

"Oh, my God!"

He nipped at the tight nub gently, that bite of pain making everything feel more intense. The pleasure rose, and she brushed her hands over his short hair, down to his wide shoulders, holding on as he moved his mouth to her other breast, giving it the same treatment. He bit then sucked on her nipple until it felt so sensitive she thought she might scream. Her whole body was on fire and filled with such longing she couldn't stop the whimpers from escaping.

"Damn, you're responsive. I'm going to have a hard time training you to hold off your orgasm.

What? Why would he want to do that?

And why did he want to talk when she was so close to coming?

"Please, Curt," she begged as he kissed down her stomach. He pulled back and drew off her skirt. Kneeling on the bed between her spread legs, he ran his finger over her panty-clad slit.

"So wet. So much need. Poor darlin'."

She cried out as he flicked her clit.

"You need to come, don't you, baby?"

She curled her hands into the covers beneath her. She'd never been with someone who liked to talk during sex. Normally, they just liked to get straight down to it. A bit of boob work, a few swipes over her clit, then a wham, a bam and a thank you before they headed out the door. But not Curt. Who'd have known he'd turn into a chatterbox during sex?

His gaze narrowed, and he lightly smacked his hand down over her clit. She cried out, the sensation wavering between pleasure and pain.

"When I ask you a question, I expect an answer."

Oh, God. What the hell had he asked her?

As if sensing her memory lapse, he cupped her mound, the heat of his palm searing her. "Do you need to come, Jenna?"

Why was he asking such a stupid question? Of course, she needed to come.

"Here's a tip, sweetheart. Until you answer me, you don't get to come."

Oh, fuck. "Yes," she gritted out.

"Yes, what?" He slowly ran his finger up and down her clit. Oh, God, she wanted to feel him touch her. Truly touch her.

"Yes, I want to come."

He grinned at her. "That wasn't so hard, now, was it?"

Actually, it had been pretty fucking difficult. But his look of approval warmed the part of her that was constantly in search of praise. She found herself smiling back at him.

He tugged at her panties then suddenly grabbed the waistband and ripped them in two.

"Hey!" She reached for the pieces of material only to find he'd flung them away and was now studying her pussy. Her freshly waxed pussy. Even though she might not have played at Saxons, she'd kept herself groomed. Just in case.

Now, she was grateful she had.

"You ripped my panties."

He gave the bit of material now lying on the floor a disparaging look. "I hate those things. Just another layer of clothing that hides you from me. If you're in a skirt or dress I want to be able to bend you over whatever piece of furniture is close and take you. To push you up against a wall and lick and suck your pussy until you scream as you come. I want access to you when I want. How I want."

She didn't wear many skirts, tonight had been a rarity, but she thought, perhaps, she'd be doing some shopping very soon.

He ran a finger over the top of her mound. "Very nice."

More approval. That starved part of her sat up and took notice. From the way his gaze narrowed, she thought he might be aware of how much his praise meant to her.

"You're beautiful, Jenna."

"I'm not. I'm short and chubby."

He snorted. "I don't know why women think they have to be

tall and willowy. That might be what some men like, but, person-ally, I like curves. Sweet, sweet curves." And as he studied her with admiration, she believed him.

"I want to look after you. Pull your legs apart and raise them. Hold them back."

Oh, hell.

She hesitated for a moment, and he gave her a firm look.

Time to be brave, Jenna. You wanted this. You knew who he was before you got into this.

She pulled her legs back, knowing he could see everything. She was completely vulnerable, and if it had been anyone but Curt there was no way she could have done this.

He drew the lips of her pussy apart, as though inspecting her. She almost forgot to breathe as he ran a finger over her inner lips, down and up, circling her clit. He drew his finger to his mouth and sucked.

A low sound escaped from her as shock filled her. He closed his eyes for a moment before opening them and pinning her with a look so hot her pulse raced.

"Delicious."

Oh, fuck. She was so out of her depth it wasn't funny. But there was no way she was turning back. No way in hell.

"Keep those legs where they are. I want to explore."

Explore? He didn't mean . . . As he laid down and took a long lick of her juices, she groaned. Yep, he meant just that. He spread her lips apart and feasted. Driving his tongue inside her, before flicking at her swollen clit. He played, he teased, never quite giving her enough to send her crashing over. Then he pushed two fingers deep, and she cried out as he firmly tapped her clit. He drove his fingers in and out until she fell over into bliss, screaming out his name. Shudders rocked her as she lay, gasping for breath. He kissed her mound gently, as though attempting to help her calm down.

"Curt. Curt."

"Easy, baby. You're safe. I'm here."

It was almost too much. The sensations rocking her so powerful and all-consuming, like nothing she'd felt before. While she was still trying to recover from the most explosive orgasm she'd ever experienced, he prodded her asshole with his wet finger. Jenna dropped her legs in shock, trying to close him out.

He stilled then stared up at her.

"Has anyone ever taken you here, Jenna?"

"N-no." She'd dreamed about it, seen some anal play at the club, but no one had ever touched her there. He drew his fingers away, and she bit her lip, upset. She'd disappointed him.

"We'll save that for another day," he promised. "Damn, sweetheart, I want to pick you up and carry you around with me, keeping you safe, but at the same time I want to ravage you until you scream and beg, calling my name."

"I'll take number two," she told him.

He chuckled. "Oh, don't worry. That is exactly what you're going to get."

WHAT WAS GOING on with him? He didn't usually talk this much during sex. But then, when was the last time he'd fucked anyone who actually meant something to him? A long time ago. Amelia. Before he'd realized her true colors.

He shook his head. She didn't belong here. In this bed with Jenna. Not with the woman he loved.

Fuck. When had he fallen in love with her? He could tell himself it was the sex talking, but it wasn't. He hadn't even fucked her yet. This wasn't about sex. It wasn't about the need to dominate her, although that was strong. And even though he'd told her they'd take things slow, he couldn't stop himself from taking command. That was just a part of who he was.

Looking down at her, he wanted to promise her everything. But he couldn't. However, he would do whatever he had to for her to be happy and safe.

Thankfully, she'd reacted well to his orders. She'd joined a BDSM club, for fucks sake. He still couldn't believe that. He didn't like that she'd been to Saxons without him.

Never again.

He'd be accompanying her whenever she went to a club. And there would be no doubts who she belonged to. Him. Forever.

But now wasn't the time to tell her that. To claim her fully. Not when she had so much shit going on.

"I wish I had my gear here. I'd put a spreader bar between your feet then pin them back to the headboard."

She stiffened.

"What is it?" he asked.

"I'm not sure I could be tied down, at least not my feet, not after…"

"Oh baby, of course that's a trigger for you." Regret filled his face. "I'm sorry. No bonds. Not until you're ready."

He leaned over, taking his weight on his hands as he kissed her, sweeping his tongue into her mouth, taking command of the kiss. Of her. Moving down her neck, he nipped at her skin. Not too hard, not enough to mark her, but enough to satisfy that primal need inside him to claim her.

Despite her orgasm, she was already breathing hard again, her desire clear. Fuck, she was amazing. He leaned to the side and cupped the breast closest to him, squeezing gently, watching her for any signs of discomfort. Although her breath caught, she didn't look scared or unsure. She looked like she wanted to demand more.

Then that's what he'd give her. He flicked his tongue over her nub, smiling as he heard her make an irritated noise. His little sub needed to learn how to be patient.

Fuck. My sub. That was more than he could have hoped for. He pinched her nipple and heard her gasp.

"Curt!"

He scraped his teeth across it, and she cried out. Quickly, he surrounded the bud with the heat of his mouth, soothing it even as he reached down and lightly tugged at her clit. His cock throbbed in reaction, pressing painfully against his jeans.

Standing, he quickly stripped, aware of the way she watched him. He didn't have the prettiest of bodies. He had scars. He'd led a hard life. He stood for a moment, letting her take him in. If she rejected him now . . .

What was wrong with him? He'd never felt this vulnerable before. Not even with Amelia. Just as well. She would have pounced on any weakness and used it to her advantage.

But he needn't have worried. Jenna's eyes were filled with longing, with heat. She sat up and reached for him, tracing her hands over his shoulders, running them over a scar on his bicep.

"Knife," he told her, then regretted being so honest as her eyes widened. But then she leaned in and kissed his scar.

He grinned. "Bit old to have my boo-boos kissed, aren't I?"

"Hush. Let me. I don't like the idea of you being hurt."

Yeah, well, he knew how that felt. She touched a scar on his side.

"Bullet."

She took in a sharp breath but didn't say anything, moving down, onto her knees on the floor in front of him. It was his turn to take a deep breath as she positioned herself at eye level with his hard cock. But she didn't stare at his groin, instead she just gave it a quick glance then gently ran her fingers over an old scar on his upper thigh.

"Barbed wire."

She winced, glancing up at him. He grinned. "Yeah, wasn't pretty. I was about ten. Ripped my skin up good."

"Ouch." She moved behind him, going through all the scars she could find. Finally, he turned and pulled her up, drawing her against him, loving the feel of her skin against his.

"Enough," he told her.

Her eyes were filled with sorrow. Empathy. God, she was killing him. How could she still be so gentle and good considering everything that had happened to her?

He cupped her face in his hands, kissing her lightly before grabbing her around the waist and lifting her, placing her back on the bed. Then he knelt beside her, staring down at her.

"I can't wait any longer. I have to be inside you."

She looked down at his cock then reached out with one hand, hesitating before she touched him, looking up at him. A ridiculous surge of pleasure filled him at the way she looked at him, waiting for his lead. He nodded. "Touch me."

He hadn't quite anticipated how good it would feel to have her soft hand surround him... as fuck...she ran her hand up and down his cock, and he had to grit his teeth not to come like a teenager.

He wasn't going to last long if she kept this up. Her touch might be a little hesitant and clumsy, but that didn't mean he was any less aroused. When she flicked her thumb over the head of his dick, he knew he couldn't last any longer.

"Holy hell," he groaned. "You're killing me."

"I am?"

Her delight made him smile. She was too cute.

He drew her hand away and practically fell on her. His movements were a little hurried and rough, but her murmurs of pleasure told him she was just as turned on as he was. He ran a finger through her folds, discovering she was still wet. When he flicked her clit, she arched up, pressing her hips against him.

"Curt! Please!"

He lined himself up and thrust deeply. Too late, he remembered he wasn't sheathed.

"Fuck. Condom."

"It's okay. I'm clean," she told him. "I was tested before I went to Sudan. There's been no one since."

"I'm clean too. Pregnancy?"

Not that the thought of her growing round with his baby wasn't a pleasant one, but they had a way to go before they got to that point.

"It's okay. It won't happen."

She was covered then. Satisfaction filled him at the idea he got to take her with nothing between them. He drew back then thrust forward. Although he wanted to savor the moment, his body had other ideas. He spread her legs wide, rubbing his thumb against her clit until he felt her shudder beneath him, then she cried out her release. His balls tightened before he exploded and fell over into fucking goddamn bliss.

14

Jenna rolled over, coming fully awake as she bumped into a hard, warm body. She turned onto her back and placed her hand over her eyes. "Shit."

So, last night hadn't been a dream. She'd slept with Curt.

"Fuck."

"Watch your swearing," Curt muttered in a husky voice.

"I'm not a child anymore, Curt," she snapped. Damn, her head was throbbing. She really shouldn't have had those last few shots. Then maybe she wouldn't have ended up fucking Curt.

Oh, hell, who was she kidding? It wasn't the alcohol's fault she'd ended up in bed with him, having the hottest night of sex she could ever have imagined. She'd wanted him for forever, and now that she'd had him, no one else would ever come close. He'd ruined her.

She wasn't even sure what had changed. She'd thought he saw her as a cousin, not a lover.

He suddenly rolled toward her, leaning up so he loomed over her. Her breath caught in her throat. Oh, hell, he really needed to shave because he looked way too hot with that sexy stubble on his face.

"I think we've established that I in no way see you as a child." He pulled the sheet down, revealing one of her breasts, the nipple already puckered and hard, ready for him. Crap, it was so embarrassing how easily she became turned on around him.

He circled her areola with his finger. "Doesn't mean I want to hear you swearing like a sailor."

"I hardly ever swear."

"Exactly my point. And if you notice, I try to clean up my language around you."

She had noticed that. When he tugged at her nipple lightly, she reached down and grabbed his hand.

He gave her a look. One that made her still and take notice of him immediately.

"Put your hands above your head and keep them there."

"Curt."

They needed to slow things down. To talk about this. He twisted her nipple, and the sting of pain made her gasp even as her clit throbbed.

"I suggest you do as I say immediately, Jenna. Unless you want to start off the morning with some discipline. Doesn't bother me, I've been dying to put you over my knee and spank that delectable ass. But I bet you don't want a throbbing butt to match your throbbing head."

He was right. Much as the idea of a spanking intrigued her, she knew there was a difference between one given for pleasure and one for punishment. She'd seen both types of spankings delivered at the club and she knew which she'd rather experience. And right at this moment, with her head as delicate as it was, she didn't want either sort applied to her rear.

She raised her arms above her head.

"Good girl."

A shiver of pleasure raced through her. He cupped her breast then leaned down and licked at the nipple he'd just pinched, lapping at it delicately then taking it into his mouth and sucking.

A groan escaped her, and she shifted around on the bed, pressing her legs together in search of some sort of relief for her aching clit.

"Lie still."

She whimpered. That was going to be nearly impossible. Her desire for him hadn't waned one iota, despite the several orgasms he'd given her throughout the night.

Several amazing, scorching orgasms. She'd never experienced pleasure like it before.

"You know what they say the best thing for a headache is?" he murmured between trailing kisses down her stomach.

"Painkillers and sleep?" she said, knowing where he was going with this.

"Tut-tut, and you call yourself a medical professional. Open your legs."

She shouldn't do it. She should insist they talk. She needed to know what the hell was going on here.

She must have waited too long because he quickly flipped her over and delivered half a dozen sharp smacks to her rear. They came so hard and fast, she didn't even have time to think about protecting herself. Before she knew it, she was lying on her back once more with him leaning over her, his hazel-colored eyes cool and stern.

"Do I need to ask you again?"

Her breath came in sharp pants, her butt throbbing from just those few strikes. God, she didn't want to think about how a long punishment spanking would feel—she parted her legs.

"Now, don't you think it would have been simpler to do that in the first place?" he asked her as he cupped her mound with his hand. "Much less painful and more pleasurable for you. After all, I'm doing this to help you, Jenna."

"Uh-huh, is that how you're trying to justify it?"

His gaze narrowed, and he flicked his finger over her full clit, making her arch up.

"I didn't realize I had to justify giving you pleasure."

He lightly touched her clit and just left his finger there, not moving, not pressing harder. Oh, God, she couldn't take it. Already, she needed him so badly she could barely think.

"Curt, please," she begged.

"Lie still," he ordered as she started writhing, trying to create some sort of pressure against that digit. "I can see that training you is going to be a test of my patience."

"You don't have any patience."

"Actually, I have plenty of patience. It just seems to dissipate around you."

"Guess I'm just special, huh?"

"Yes. You are."

Those words sent an ache through her that had nothing to do with him pressing a single finger deep inside her wet passage.

"What is it we're doing here, Curt?"

"Well, I thought I was about to give you a mind-blowing orgasm, but if you think it's something else, please tell me."

"I don't mean that. Ohhh," she moaned as he pushed a second finger inside her and started pumping them in and out. He paused and flicked her clit with his thumb. Her hips rose, almost of their own volition.

"Keep still, Jenna."

"I'm trying."

He sighed. "You are sadly lacking in discipline."

She stared up at him, confused. "I don't understand any of this, Curt. You rejected me a few months ago, remember?"

"Of course I do. And I've regretted it ever since."

He had? Then why had he waited so long to come for her? Why wait until now?

"I told myself that keeping away from you was the right thing to do. That you deserved better. I still think that."

"That's a crock. It's just an excuse to make you feel better."

His eyes flared open.

"If you'd wanted a relationship with me you wouldn't have waited this long just because you thought I deserved better. Better than what? A man who puts me first? My protection? My needs? My wants? A man who's loyal and strong and kind. A man who'd always be there for me, no matter what shit goes down. Is that the sort of man I don't deserve?"

"You're putting me up on a pedestal I don't deserve. I'm not a good man."

"I remember your spiel from last time, Curt. Are you telling me you'd betray me? That you'd put me at risk? That you'd abandon me when things got rough?"

"No, of course not."

"Then what? Because if this is just sex then you don't have to come up with some excuse about how I deserve better, just tell me now. I'm not the person I was a year ago, hell, a few months ago. I'm harder. I can take care of myself now. I no longer look at the world through rose-colored glasses. I'm not that stupid kid who thought she could actually make a difference. If you're foolish and naïve and think everyone is good deep down, then you get chewed up and spit out. I don't need you to protect me from the world. Not anymore."

"That's not you."

"It is now."

He shook his head. "You might think it is, but I've seen how you are. I'm sorry I hurt you, Jenna. I was wrong. I was blind, and stupid. I thought I could forget about you, let you move on with your life and find a nice man to settle down with, have kids, and live a normal life."

"A normal life? What's that?"

"You know what I mean. I have needs I thought would scare you."

"So, once you found out I was a member of Saxon's club that changed things for you? I suddenly became someone you could see yourself being with?"

"No, if you remember, things had already gotten hot and heavy before I found that out. But it certainly makes things easier. Jenna, you're sweet and kind. Your first thought is always of other people. You put everyone before yourself—even me, which is going to stop, by the way." He gave her a firm look even though she had no idea what he was talking about.

"When I was in jail, instead of going to the hospital, you came to check on me. Your first thought when you saw that injured woman was her, not your own safety. You paid for that other lady's stuff in the bakery when she couldn't remember her pin number. You're always thinking about others. And if you're not watched closely, you'll burn yourself out taking care of everyone else instead of yourself."

She didn't know what to say to that.

"This isn't just sex, Jenna. It's not about me wanting to fuck you, although, believe me, I do. This is a relationship. You and I belong to each other, understand? You're mine."

She couldn't believe this was happening. Was it for real?

"And in case you don't realize it, I'm not asking, Jenna. I'm not going to take the risk of you saying no. From now on, you're my woman, my lover, my submissive."

He kissed his way down her neck, and she closed her eyes, reveling in the sensation of his lips against her skin.

"It goes both ways," she managed to say.

He leaned up. "Of course it does. I'm yours as much as you're mine. But hear me now, Jenna. I'm a possessive bastard. And a bossy one. I won't be easy to deal with."

She snorted. "Like I didn't know that already."

"You're probably going to regret this," he told her.

"Oh, shut up and kiss me."

He raised his eyebrows. "Do you really think you get to give orders?"

She grinned. "Well, it's not fair if you're always in charge. Don't you want to swap once in a while? Let me take command?"

"No," he told her darkly. "Now, make sure those hands stay above your head. I'm going to feast on my woman."

There was a knock on the bedroom door as he started kissing his way down her stomach.

"Go away," Curt snarled.

She tightened up with a blush. God, now Travis would know Curt had slept with her. Not that he probably hadn't guessed. She didn't know when he'd gotten home, but he would have seen that Curt hadn't been sleeping on the couch.

"Sorry to interrupt," Travis said through the door, sounding amused. "But we've got incoming."

"They can piss off."

"Well, I can surely tell them that, but feds tend to be tenacious bastards."

"Shit," Curt said, then pulled back to stare down at her.

"They're here to speak to me." She felt a little ill. She'd thought she'd have more time but she realized now she'd procrastinated too long.

It was time to go back. Not home. Dallas was no longer home. Haven was, but she needed to face reality.

The doorbell rang.

"Go tell them we'll be there soon," Curt snarled. He looked down at Jenna. "Ready for this?"

"No." How did one ready themselves for this?

"I'll be with you the whole time. You don't have to be scared, all right?"

She nodded. She could do this. She didn't really have much choice.

"All right."

SHE DECIDED she didn't like Paul Hendricks very much. The older FBI agent was arrogant and demanding. And he kept asking her the same questions over and over until she wanted to scream.

Finally, she snapped. "Have you got a memory problem, Agent Hendricks?"

He looked surprised, but his partner, Agent Mike Marshal, just looked resigned, and a little bored. "What? No."

"Well, I'm beginning to think you must, since you keep asking me the same questions over and over. Maybe you need to get one of those recording devices so you can tape our interview. Your phone will even do it. Would you like me to show you how?"

He narrowed his gaze at her. "This is no laughing matter, young lady."

She hadn't been called a young lady in a while. Nancy used to call her that when she got into trouble. She certainly felt like she'd done something wrong from the way Hendricks was treating her.

"I can assure you, I'm not laughing. I also think I'm done answering your questions. I don't know anything about my dad's *alleged* arms trading. I never heard him mention anything to do with shipping weapons to the Middle East or Africa. I never over-heard any conversations with Doug about it. And I never heard him mention The Brit. Now, if that's all, I've got things to do."

"We may have more questions."

"You know where to find us," Curt said as he stood.

"Actually," Jenna said, rising as well and leaving the agents no recourse but to stand. Travis lounged over by the door but he straightened as they stood. "I think we'll be going back to Dallas today. I need to see my mother and make sure she's not traumatized after being interrogated and harassed by the two of you."

"This wasn't an interrogation, Ms. Jasons. I can assure you that if it were, you would certainly know it. And we didn't harass her. She was too drugged up to be of much use."

They moved towards the door and left without saying goodbye.

"Bye-bye," Jenna called through the doorway, waving, then slammed the door behind them. "Asses."

"That's what everyone says when they meet Hendricks," Travis said with amusement. "You handled them well."

She didn't feel like she had. She felt shaken and ill.

Curt turned her towards him, brushing the hair back from her face. "Look at me."

She glanced up at him.

"You sure you're ready to go back to Dallas?"

"I'll be fine," she said bravely.

"If we're leaving, I need to go pack my stuff," Travis said hastily and left.

"Jenna, I know you haven't been in a relationship with a Dom before and we haven't spoken about what we expect from each other but as my sub, there's going to be rules for you to follow."

Funny, she'd never have guessed.

"BDSM almost became a necessity for me after Amelia and the baby died. I found myself in a downward spiral. I was drinking heavily, getting into fights, I was furious at the world. I guess part of me didn't want to keep going."

Sorrow filled her at his obvious pain. "You really loved her, huh?"

A strange look crossed over his face, and he sighed. "There are some things I probably need to tell you about my relationship with Amelia, but not right now. But I will tell you I don't know where I would have ended up if Gray hadn't found me. I knew him from my time in the navy. He helped me get sober, got me back on track, and gave me a purpose. And he introduced me to BDSM. I needed it. Needed that feeling of being in control. Even though it appeared I'd pulled myself together, inside I still felt like a mess and I didn't really trust myself."

"What do you mean? You didn't trust yourself not to hurt someone?"

"Yeah., I still had a lot of anger over what happened with Amelia. I was worried I'd take that out on a sub. Being at the Twisted Thorn gave me a sense of security. There were monitors and rules, and I could lay everything out first so there were no misunderstandings. I found that dominating my partner was what I needed, it made me feel more centered and in control."

"You could never harm an innocent, Curt."

He just stared at her. "You remember me as the man you used to know. That boy who thought the world was his to conquer. I'm a different person now, Jenna. You sure you want this with me? Because there's no going back. I'm possessive, what I have, stays mine. I'm pig-headed. I'll probably piss you off several times a day with my demands and stubbornness. I'll try to listen to you. I'll try to give you what you need. And I'll always protect you."

"Well, at least you know most of your faults. Although you forgot a couple. You're over-protective and you always think you're right."

He snorted. "Yeah, those too."

"Curt, there are things about you I don't know. Just like there're parts of me you don't know. We've both changed. But at your core is the man I've always admired. The man I've always wanted. And if you get too demanding or stubborn I'll just have to learn ways to handle you."

"Handle me, huh?" he drawled, pulling her against him. "We'll just see about that." He kissed her, hot and hard.

When he allowed her to pull back, she was breathing heavily. "I joined Saxon's because I wanted to learn about BDSM. I wanted to experience it. Cady had explained some parts of it, and I was intrigued. But I never played with those other Doms because they weren't you. It's always been you."

He cupped her face between his hands. "I'll try to make certain you don't regret it." He kissed her lightly again. "First lesson as my sub, don't ever lie to me, understand?" There was a deep note of command in his voice, and she nodded.

"So, when I ask you how you feel about something, you answer me honestly. You don't brush me off by telling me you're fine."

She knew what he was talking about and she glanced away, feeling guilty.

"Look at me."

She stared up into his eyes. "I don't want to go. I don't want to see my parents. I know that makes me a terrible daughter—"

He shook his head. "It doesn't. It just makes you human."

"But I know I have to return. My mother needs me, and I need to talk to my dad if I can. I need to understand."

"Then we'll go back. And know that I'm here for you. Whatever you need, understand? You've gifted me your submission, and I'm going to take care of that gift and you."

Those were just about the sweetest words she'd ever heard.

PAUL HENDRICKS SLAMMED his fist down on the steering wheel as he drove out of the hellhole town Jenna Jasons had decided to hide in. "She has to know something."

"I don't think she does," Marshall said mildly. "There's no reason to assume she does."

"What about that incident in Sudan? That had to have something to do with The Brit." He knew capturing The Brit would skyrocket his career. He was determined to get to the top and since he was now past forty, he had to work quickly to get there. Arresting David Jasons had been his first big break. Only the bastard wasn't talking. But, what if The Brit thought he was? He smiled.

"What are you thinking?" Marshall asked suspiciously.

"What do you think The Brit would do if he thought Jasons was spilling his guts?"

"Have him killed."

"Not if he couldn't get to him. What would stop Jasons from talking? What could he threaten Jasons with to keep him quiet?"

"I don't like where this is going."

Marshall was a wimp. But he knew how to keep his mouth shut.

"He'd come after Jasons's family. We let it be known that Jasons is talking, and my guess is The Brit will come after the wife or daughter. Probably the daughter since the wife is holed up in her sister's house."

"You're talking about putting an innocent woman in danger in an attempt to catch this guy?" Marshall stared at him in disbelief.

Hendricks waved his hand in the air. "And how many innocent people has this guy killed? How many more will he murder?" Not that Hendricks really cared. All he wanted was what this capture would do for him. "Besides, I'll have eyes on the daughter. She'll be perfectly safe. She's going to lead us straight to him."

"Yeah? You going to tell the ATF agents about this?"

"Oh, I think we'll keep this our little secret. This is going to put us on the map, Marshall. Stick with me, I'm going places."

15

She looked around Curt's apartment, feeling lost. They'd packed up without much drama. She'd called Doc, as well as Jake and Melody, to let them know she was leaving for a few days. Then she'd thrown a few things in a bag, and, along with Daisy, they'd driven to Dallas. She'd insisted on bringing her car. She didn't know why, exactly. She just felt better having it. As though she needed a means of escape.

It was now mid-afternoon. She could use the lateness of the day as an excuse not to visit her mother, but she knew it wasn't really a good one.

Travis had followed them to Dallas before heading off to stay with Lacey and Gray. He was going to come with them to the court house tomorrow for her dad's bail hearing. She'd told him it wasn't necessary, but Travis had just smiled and shrugged, saying he had nothing better to do. She knew his reason for wanting The Brit was personal, but she didn't think he was going to get any leads from sticking close to her and she was starting to think he'd realized that as well. He certainly hadn't pushed to stay at Curt's place. Mind you, Curt telling him to go away had probably played a part in that. She really had to work on his bluntness.

"You ready to go?"

"No," she replied honestly. "But I have to. I need to see her before tomorrow."

"You don't need to go to court, you know," he told her as they made their way, with Daisy in tow, down to the garage beneath Curt's building. It was well-secured. She noticed the cameras in the corridor then in the garage as they entered. Funny, she'd never looked for those things before. How her life had changed.

Daisy hopped into the back as though she'd done it all her life.

Curt opened her door and waited for her to climb in before moving around to the driver's side of his truck. Her car was parked in his guest parking space.

She clasped her hands tightly in her lap. She could already feel a tension headache brewing.

"Easy, baby," Curt told her. He reached over and squeezed her hands. "I can feel how stressed you are from here."

"Kind of hard not to be when dealing with my mother. I'll apologize for her now. In fact, I'll understand if you don't want to come inside." She hadn't thought about how this would be for him. "I know you haven't seen Aunt Mary and Uncle Justin since Amelia died."

And she was dying to know what he'd meant when he'd said he had something to explain about his marriage.

His jaw tightened as he stared out at the road. "They blame me for her death."

"I know." She sighed. "They're hurting and they want someone to blame. Guess we're both scapegoats for people's anger and hurt, huh? They don't really mean it."

"Oh, I think they do." He turned into the driveway of her aunt and uncle's place. Their house wasn't as large as Jenna's parents' place or in such a wealthy neighborhood, but it was still big by most people's standards. And it was private, surrounded by a large yard and tall fence.

She undid her belt.

"Wait for me to come around and get you," Curt told her fiercely. She waited until he opened her door.

"Does opening my door for me have something to do with guarding me?" she asked curiously.

He leaned in and brushed a kiss over her ear. "A little. But it also has everything to do with you being mine to take care of. In every way. Remember, it's not all whips and chains. You take care of everyone else, you need someone to look at for you. That someone is me." A shiver ran through her at his words. She opened the back door and gave Daisy a pat. "Stay here, girl."

Daisy whined as she shut the door. She turned towards the house and took a deep breath.

"Here goes nothing."

Walking up the wide stairs, her trepidation grew. She knocked on the door before she lost her nerve. Suddenly, she realized they hadn't talked about what to tell her family about the two of them.

Curt placed his hand on the small of her back. "Stop worrying." Yeah, that really wasn't going to happen.

"Just remember, I'm here with you. You're not on your own."

And that meant more to her than she was willing to admit.

She took a deep, steadying breath. "Do you want them to know about us? I understand if you don't."

He turned her to face him. Placing two fingers under her chin, he lifted her face up. "I want the world to know. And screw what they think."

He kissed her just as the door opened.

"What the hell is going on here?" her uncle boomed.

～

JENNA'S HEADACHE was getting worse.

Her uncle paced up and down the living room as she perched nervously on the hard sofa. Curt stood behind her. When she snuck a look back at him, he looked almost bored, but she could see the close way he watched uncle.

"Uncle Justin, Curt is here to support me. Not that it's really any of your business what Curt and I do."

"What is going on in here, Justin?" Her aunt stepped through the door, looking tired and worried. She came to a stop as she saw Jenna.

"Jenna, good you're here. Your mother has been waiting to..." her aunt trailed off, her mouth dropping open as she saw Curt. "What is he doing here?" She pointed at Curt, as though there were any doubt who she was talking about.

"That's why I want to know," her uncle growled, stilling to glare down at Jenna. "He came with Jenna."

"Jenna? What? How?"

"He's here to help me, Aunty," Jenna said with as much patience as she could muster. "We're seeing each other." It seemed an inadequate description for what he meant to her.

"This is unacceptable, Jenna," her uncle yelled, his face flushed and sweaty. "You're fucking the man who killed my daughter!"

"That's enough," Curt said in a low voice, making her uncle pause. Her aunt looked up at him fearfully. Were they afraid of Curt? "You say what you like to me but you speak to Jenna with respect."

Uncle Justin glared at Curt. "She has betrayed her family."

Aunt Mary looked close to tears as she stared at Jenna with sorrow. Jenna felt terrible they were so hurt by her decision to be with Curt, but they were acting so strangely, so out of character it was shocking. She knew they blamed Curt for Amelia's death, but she'd thought that was just a reaction to the pain of losing her.

She'd hoped they'd come to see he had nothing to do with her death.

"Oh, Justin. It's not Jenna's fault. She's always had a crush on him, poor thing. Amelia used to laugh about it. She thought it was so cute."

Amelia thought it was cute? That was hard to believe.

"Amelia's death was an accident. She took a corner too fast and flipped her car. That wasn't Curt's fault," she said firmly. Enough was enough. He might be fine with them spouting these lies about him, but she wouldn't just sit there and take it.

Her uncle turned to Curt, his gaze narrowed in fury. "Is that what he told you, Jenna?"

"She was driving so fast because she was trying to get away from him," Aunt Mary told her. "Because she thought he was going to hurt her."

"Curt wouldn't hurt Amelia and he definitely wouldn't do anything to harm his child." Her gut clenched at the idea of Curt's baby. Something she'd never have. She knew she needed to talk to him about that, although he had to know about her accident and the hysterectomy.

"Lies," her uncle snarled. "And I won't have him in my house any longer."

She stood. "Then I guess we'll be leaving. Do you know if Mother is up to going to the bail hearing tomorrow? We'd be happy to take her with us."

"Wait, no, they can't leave without seeing Lorraine, Justin," Aunt Mary said in alarm. "I'll take you up. Then you have to leave."

With her uncle glaring at them, they left the room and followed her aunt upstairs. She knocked on her mother's door then walked in. "She's been sleeping a lot. Best thing for her, I suppose. You know she doesn't do well with any sort of crisis."

And sleeping through everything was the best way she could

cope? Jenna shared a look with Curt then shrugged. She didn't know how to help her mother. When she walked into the large bedroom, she came to a stop, shocked by the sight of her usually made-up and composed mother. Lorraine Jasons didn't leave the house without a full face of makeup and a designer outfit on. This wasn't her mother. This woman looked sickly. She was washed out, her face naked, her hair spread about her in a tangled web. She blinked as she looked up at Jenna.

"Jenna?"

"Hello, Mother." She gave Curt an alarmed look, noticing how he studied her mother closely.

"Oh, Jenna, I'm so glad you're here." She clung to Jenna's arm with a strength that surprised her. "The things they've accused your father of, they're terrible. You know he's innocent, but no one will believe that. We've been vilified. I've had to leave my home, it's not safe there. Everyone has turned their backs on me, except for my sister. Even you didn't come for me. This has been such a trying, awful time for me, and where have you been? In some little town, helping people who aren't even related to you. Family comes first, Jenna."

And there was her mother. Obviously not as ill as she looked.

Jenna sat on the side of the bed, knowing the routine.

"I'm sorry, Mother."

"Why, I was truly terrified when those awful FBI agents came to the door. They just pushed their way through, messed up my house, and dragged your father away. Who knows what's happening to him in jail. What if someone tries to kill him?"

"I'm sure they're watching him closely, Mrs. Jasons," Curt said.

Her mother looked over at Curt as though seeing him for the first time. "Curt. What are you doing here?"

"He's with me, Mother."

"Oh, David hired you to look after us? Just as well, there have been some terrible threats made against me. Just ghastly. I can't believe people would say such horrible things."

"There have been messages on her cell phone," her aunt explained. "Justin gave it to the police."

"They don't care. They think David's guilty. Nobody believes he's innocent," her mother wailed. "It's so dreadful. They spray painted our gates. Someone even tried to break in."

"What?" Jenna asked, alarmed.

Her mother nodded, looking satisfied at her reaction. "Probably after my jewelry. I couldn't pack it all, and Mary didn't know the code to the safe. Would you go back and get the rest of it for me, darling?"

Jenna looked up at Curt. He just shook his head.

"I can't, Mother."

"But it's your inheritance. Some of those things came from your grandmother, they're irreplaceable."

"It's not safe," Curt told her. "Jenna has had threats too."

"Maybe we need to hire someone to guard the house," Jenna said, biting at her lip.

"That will be a huge expense," her aunt complained. "All of your father's accounts are frozen. Your mother has nothing."

"I'm destitute." Tears dripped down her mother's cheeks.

Jenna barely bit back a sigh. "Mother, you have your own accounts. Money from Grandma."

"But that won't last forever, Jenna," her aunt said. "You're going to have to figure out some way of supporting your mother through this. What if David never gets that money back? What about his legal fees?"

"I'll take care of the lawyer's bills," Jenna said, thinking of her inheritance from her grandmother, which she'd invested.

"But what about me?" her mother asked.

"You could get a job," Curt suggested.

Her mother and aunt just gaped at him. Jenna had to turn away to hide a smile at their reaction.

"It will work out, Mother. One step at a time. I'll hire someone to guard the house, and once things become calmer, I'll get your jewelry for you. Make a list." Jenna didn't like leaving her grandmother's jewelry in the house any more than her mother did. It wasn't the monetary value, though it wasn't insignificant; it was what the pieces meant to her.

"Hunter already hired a guard," Curt said.

"He did? Why didn't you tell me?"

"I didn't want you to worry."

She gave him an exasperated look. They'd need to have a little chat about that later. He wanted her to share everything but he got to hold back if he thought it would worry her? Nope. Not the way things were going to happen.

"Please, Jenna. Get your grandma's jewelry. For me and your aunt."

Jenna sighed.

Daisy gave a happy bark as they climbed back into the truck, and Jenna laughed as the dog licked her ear.

"Sit down, dog," Curt stated firmly, although she saw his quick smile.

She turned to him. "So, that was fun."

He grunted.

"Much like getting a tooth pulled. I'm sorry about the way they reacted. They had no right to speak to you like that or blame you for Amelia's death."

"I knew they felt that way. They're not entirely wrong, you know."

She stared at him in surprise. "You didn't have anything to do with Amelia's death. It was her fault."

He just looked over at her for a moment, his face impossible to read.

She decided on a change of subject. "I need to go to the house."

"No."

"Curt—"

"No."

"Will you just listen to me?" she asked with exasperation.

"I'm not taking you there. End of story."

CURT HAD to work hard to suppress his fury at the look of sadness on her face as she took in the words spray-painted on the locked gates in front of her house.

Murderer.

Die.

Traitor.

He waited for her to say something. To get mad, scared, sad. Nothing.

Amelia would never have remained silent. She'd have vented her every emotion and then she would have found some way to blame him for everything. Jenna was the opposite. Getting her to open up was difficult and he would have to watch that she didn't try to take everything on herself.

He spoke briefly to the guard that worked for the firm Hunter had hired. Curt intended to reimburse him for the cost. Over the years, he'd built up a nice portfolio. He wasn't rich like Jenna's father, but he certainly had enough to support her, and probably her mother as well.

As he drove down the driveway, he couldn't believe he'd agreed to bring her here. He'd had no intention of giving in until she'd begged him. And when those big, blue eyes looked at him with such pleading and sorrow, there wasn't much he wouldn't do. He'd seen the way her mother's reaction had affected her. Damn the woman for not being able to see past her own pain. He'd known there had always been some strain between Jenna and her mother but hadn't known the cause. But now he knew—her mother was a selfish bitch.

Not that he could say that to Jenna. How someone as sweet-natured and caring as she was had come from that viper, he had no idea. But he knew Jenna wouldn't appreciate him talking badly about her mother, so he kept his mouth shut.

"We're doing this quickly," he told her, still feeling like it was a bad idea. "I don't want anyone seeing you here."

She nodded tensely as she unlocked the house and turned off the alarm. She walked into the large house, which had always seemed so cold to him. Not that his place was much to speak of. But many hours of thought and money had gone into designing this house, and its interior, and it still felt lifeless.

Growing up, he hadn't had much. His dad had retired early from the navy due to a back injury and hadn't been able to work much. His mom had died when he was young. Still, home had been warm, lived in, and happy.

He followed Jenna into David's office. This was the one place in the house, other than the backyard, where he felt comfortable. Done in rich tones with lots of wood, it felt real and welcoming. He could see Jenna felt the same as she stood for a moment and took a deep breath. She turned away from him, but not before he saw a glitter of tears in her eyes.

Damn it. Enough was enough. He reached for her, but she was already moving forward. She pulled on a fake book and part of the book shelf opened up. He winced at how obvious that was for hiding a safe. This place needed a security upgrade. Not that it mattered much now.

She opened the safe and quickly pulled out some jewelry boxes and put them in her bag before shutting the door and pushing the bookshelf back into place.

She straightened her shoulders and gave him a small smile that didn't reach her eyes. "Right, let's go. What do you want for dinner?"

Oh, no. That wasn't how things were going to go. But now wasn't the time for a little talk about sharing with your Dom. He wrapped his arm around her waist as they left the house.

"We're having a chat when we get home," he murmured.

She stared up at him. "About Amelia?"

That stab in the gut wasn't as sharp as it used to be, the surge of betrayal not as deep. Talking about Amelia wasn't his favorite thing to do. But she deserved to know the truth.

"That too," he told her, settling her into the truck.

She looked at him with puzzlement, but he didn't elaborate.

"Put your belt on," he ordered before he started the truck.

She sighed but did as ordered, unusually quiet. He hated the stress she was under and that he couldn't do much to relieve it. As they left, the gates shut automatically behind them. He frowned when he didn't see the guard. As he braked to wait for an oncoming car, he spotted someone exit a vehicle parked further up and race towards them. Daisy growled then started to bark furiously, her paws scrambling against the window.

"Get down," he yelled at Jenna, pushing her head down as he swerved onto the road, right in front of the approaching car, which sounded its horn as something landed against the passenger window. Eggs. *Fuck.*

He looked in the rearview mirror to see some crazy idiot standing in the middle of the road shaking his fist.

"Where's the God damn guard!" He thumped his fist against the steering wheel. "Daisy, quiet!"

The dog quietened immediately.

"Good girl."

"Curt?"

He glanced down at Jenna who was still bent over, her eyes wide as she stared up at him. His gut clenched.

"It's okay, baby." He made certain he softened his voice. "You can get up now."

She rose, staring at the egg splattered against the window. Curt grew even more grim. He grabbed his phone. "Call Hunter. Put it on speaker."

"Don't you have Bluetooth?"

He snorted. "No. Then I'd have no excuse for not answering calls."

She attempted a smile. She was trying so hard to be brave and he wished he could hug her and reassure her it was going to be all right. But he didn't want to pull over until they were safely at his place.

Damn it, what if whoever threw those eggs had had a gun or a grenade?

"You could have been killed."

"It was some eggs, Curt. No big deal."

He turned to gape at her, but she was concentrating on his phone and not looking at him.

No big deal?

Oh, this was a very big deal.

Jenna looked over at Daisy. "You okay, girl?"

The dog panted, her tail wagging so Jenna figured she was all right."

"Hunter," the man answered his phone abruptly.

"What kind of fucking idiot security company did you hire," Curt spat out.

"Curt!" Jenna scolded.

But he was too far gone for niceties right now.

"What happened?" Hunter's voice was surprisingly calm.

"As we were pulling out of the Jasons' driveway, some maniac egged the car on Jenna's side."

There was a pause. Hunter would know what Curt was thinking. That it could have been so much worse than a bit of egg on his truck.

"I'll find someone new. What were you doing there anyway?"

"We went there to get some jewelry for Jenna's mother. I knew we shouldn't have gone. I won't make a mistake like that again."

"It's just some eggs, guys."

"Not the point," Hunter replied. "They got close enough to throw something at you." He didn't elaborate, and Curt was thankful. He didn't want to upset Jenna more than necessary.

"You headed to your place?"

"Yeah. Almost there. We're going to court tomorrow for the bail hearing."

"Want some extra bodies?"

"Travis is coming."

Hunter snorted. "Still hanging around like a bad smell, huh? We need to arrange a meet for Tuesday. How about eleven?"

"We'll be there."

Curt nodded at Jenna to end the call as they entered his parking garage. He got out then went around to grab Daisy before opening Jenna's door. He quickly handed her Daisy's lead. He kept a watch on their surroundings while they made their way to his apartment.

He shut and locked the door then set the alarm. "Come on, Daisy, let's do a little check." Having the dog around had its advantages. He took her leash from Jenna and walked with her through the apartment.

"All clear," he told her when he returned.

Jenna reached out a hand, placing it on his arm. "Curt, are you okay? You're kind of acting . . . crazy."

Crazy? Really? "You could have been hurt."

She placed her hands on her hips. "It was eggs."

He cupped her face. "It could have been a weapon, bullets."

She could have been seriously harmed. The thought of her being hurt, of losing her...he took in a deep breath. He needed to be in charge right now. Needed that control. To reassure himself she was all right. She was everything to him. He knew it seemed like he was overreacting and, yeah, maybe he was. But he couldn't stand the idea of her being harmed. He took hold of her hand and drew her further into the apartment before stopping and taking a step back.

"Strip," he ordered her.

She studied him, and he didn't know how he'd react if she rejected him right now. But a small smile crossed her lips, and she started to pull off her clothes.

Thank you, God.

HER HANDS TREMBLED SLIGHTLY, but she tried to hide that from Curt. He was already on edge. He didn't need to see how much what happened had spooked her. It was just stupid eggs.

She'd faced far worse. She wasn't sure why it had upset her so much.

Maybe because it happened just outside her house. Maybe because for that moment, she'd been utterly terrified that man was going to kill her. And Curt too.

If anything happened to Curt because of her . . . She took in a deep breath.

"Jenna?"

She looked over at Curt and realized she'd only gotten as far as stripping off her T-shirt.

"We don't have to do this," he told her.

Only, they did. He needed it, that much was obvious. And she did too. She looked over at the window. It was early evening but not yet dark, and only someone with binoculars would be able to see them, but still.

"Come." He turned and walked into his bedroom, not once looking back, knowing she wouldn't disobey.

When she reached the bedroom, he'd already pulled the blinds and was dimming the lights. He pointed at Daisy, who sat on the other side of the door. "Sorry, dog, you're on your own for a bit." He closed the door then turned to her, pointing to a spot in front of the bed. He sat down and stared at her. "Continue."

Jeez, would it hurt him to give her a word of encouragement? She was unused to this, after all. But as she pulled her clothes off, she saw the way his gaze heated, how his hands clenched into fists. Her nakedness affected him. He found her attractive.

Her insecurity lessened. He wanted her.

Even if he wasn't the best communicator, she could tell a lot from his body language. Maybe his reaction today was more than just from her being in danger. Maybe it had deeper roots. He'd lost Amelia. Was he scared of losing her too?

That revelation surprised her. But he didn't care for her as deeply as he had Amelia, right?

"Turn around. I want to see all of you," he said gruffly.

She spun slowly until she faced him once again.

"Very nice. You are so beautiful."

She blushed. "I'm short and chubby."

He lowered his eyebrows, giving her a stern look. "Here is another rule. Never disparage yourself. This body is perfect. You are perfect." He stood and removed his clothes, shaking his head as she reached for him. Instead he walked behind her, slapping her ass. "Speak badly about yourself and you're going to end up with a hot, sore ass. No moving without permission, Jenna. Put your hands on your head."

She bit her lip against an objection. She could tell he needed control right now. He ran his hand down her side then over one buttock, cupping it then giving it a sharp slap. She gasped and dropped her hands, and he delivered a few more smacks until she realized what he wanted and raised her hands once more to her head.

"Good girl."

Those words sent shocks of heat straight to her clit.

He squeezed her butt, and she squealed. "I can tell you're going to spend a lot of time with a hot butt. Such a naughty girl."

"No, I'm not."

More hard smacks.

"Ouch. Ouch. Stop!"

"You don't get to say stop, baby. The only thing that stops everything is your safeword."

She swallowed heavily. Damn why did the thought of giving him all the control turn her on so much?

"I don't have one."

"Red. Your safeword is red. That stops everything."

She shivered as he ran a finger down the crack of her ass. "Spread your legs and bend over. I wish to inspect what is mine."

Oh, holy hell. Face blushing furiously, she bent over. He pushed a finger against her puckered entrance, and she took a deep breath as just that touch made her clit ache. "I think I'll plug this asshole today."

Plug? Oh, God.

"Something small, don't worry. For now, anyway. Stay where you are."

He stepped away. She heard a rustling noise then something being squirted, and then a firm, wet finger pressed against her back entrance. "Breathe in. Then out, slowly."

As she breathed out, he pressed his finger inside her.

Shit. It was a stretch, and there was a slight burn, but the pleasure was what really blew her away. It shouldn't feel as good as it did. A new set of nerves were waking up, filling her with undeniable bliss.

"Good girl. Nice and relaxed for me." He moved his finger in and out before adding a second. Then he paused, and she gasped for breath. "Now, what were we talking about before? Oh, yes, how naughty you are."

"What?" Did he seriously want to have this conversation now?

"What is your number one rule?"

Huh? Oh, God, was this some sort of test? "I can't think."

"You can. Or you'll find yourself getting a spanking with a plug inside your asshole. That's a very different experience."

That thought both terrified and aroused her.

"No lying," she said hastily, glad her brain had kicked into a gear. "But I haven't lied to you."

"But you're keeping your true feelings from me. Trying to pretend you're all right, when I can tell the meeting with your mother upset you. Not to mention what happened earlier at your parents' place. That had to have terrified you, but you're acting as though it was nothing."

"That wasn't me lying to you." It was her trying to help him. She'd seen how deeply upset he'd been and she'd thought one of them needed to keep calm. "Getting upset doesn't help." Especially when it came to her mother.

"But speaking to your Dom can. That's what I'm here for, baby. It's not all about sex and spankings. It's much more. It's me being there for you. For anything."

"And what about me being there for you?" Damn, she wished she could see his face. Kind of hard to do, bent over with her ass in the air. This had to be the weirdest way to have a conversation.

"You are always there for me, Jenna. Same way you are for

everyone else. Your parents, your friends, little old ladies. Now it's your turn to let someone be there for you. Me." He removed his fingers and she groaned in protest. But then something hard pressed against her asshole.

"Breathe in. Out now."

As she slowly let out her breath, he pushed the plug deep inside her. Oh, the burn was intense, and she nearly said her safeword, it was verging on too much. But once the plug was inside her, and she could breathe more normally, she knew she could stand it. And as he moved his hand down to her pussy, running a finger up and down her slick folds, she guessed she could more than stand it. She might even like it.

He circled her clit. "As my sub, I expect you to lean on me, come to me, tell me when something worries or scares you. If something upsets you, I want to know. If you're in pain, you better fucking tell me. And if you're ever in danger, I'm your next call after the police. Not that you will be, because I intend to keep you very, very safe. You're everything to me." He smacked a hand down on her ass at the same time as he flicked his finger over her clit, and she groaned at the contrast of pleasure and pain. She clenched down around the plug, and it added another layer.

She was already completely turned on, and he'd barely done anything.

"Straighten."

He helped her, holding her steady, and she raised her hands up to her head like before. He nodded with satisfaction, and a small thrill went through her.

"You look so sexy. You are precious to me. Nothing will happen to you."

"Like what happened to Amelia?" she asked gently.

. . .

CURT TOOK A STEP BACK. He saw a flash of hurt in Jenna's eyes and forced himself to take a deep breath in, letting it out slowly—his exact instructions to her just a few seconds ago.

He didn't want to talk about Amelia. Not here, not now, while Jenna was naked in his bedroom, with her face flushed, her pussy wet, and looking so submissive and sexy it was all he could do not to bend her over the bed and take her.

But the way she watched him, with that mix of trepidation and sorrow, he knew he had to tell her the full truth. Looking away, he clenched his jaw at the memories, something he didn't like to think about much. Jenna shifted slightly, and he cursed himself for forgetting about her arms.

"Lower your arms and come here, baby." He sat and patted his lap.

Her eyes widened with surprise as she dropped her arms. Then she bit at her lip. "I ruined things, didn't I? I'm sorry."

Nope. He wasn't having that. Standing, he grasped hold of her chin, tilted her face up and kissed her. Hard. With all the heat he had building inside him.

"You didn't ruin a thing," he told her. "This needs to be said and it ain't gonna be pretty. But after, if you still want me, I'm going to bend you over this bed and fuck you until we both forget how to breathe."

Not the prettiest of declarations but it was the God damn truth. She gave him a surprised look. "Why wouldn't I want you?"

"Like I said, it ain't pretty."

She grimaced. "You forget I knew Amelia. I knew all her faults, even though my aunt and uncle might think she was a saint and you're the devil, I know that isn't the case. And I know you didn't kill Amelia."

"I didn't kill her but I did drive her out that night. I knew she was upset and I let her get in that car. With my baby inside her."

He clenched his hands into fists, barely noting the look of

sorrow on Jenna's face. She sat beside him gingerly, taking his hand in hers. Sweet, little subbie, always caring for other people. He bet it wasn't easy sitting with that plug in her ass, either, but she didn't make a word of complaint.

"You sure you want to hear this?"

"Yes. You loved her?"

"In the beginning, yes. Or I thought I did. I was young. She was beautiful, and I thought she was everything I could want in a woman. Graceful and delicate, like something out of a movie or a picture."

JENNA WINCED AT THAT DESCRIPTION, graceful and delicate she was not. But she'd been compared to Amelia her whole life. She was used to it.

"Took a while for me to figure out those things were all superficial. The trappings might be pretty, but that didn't matter if the inside was poisonous."

Harsh words.

"I know she was your cousin, Jenna. If you don't want to hear this—"

"When I was thirteen, I developed breasts," she interrupted him. He frowned, looking puzzled. "They're quite big." She looked down at her generous bosom, feeling a little embarrassed by her nudity when they were having such a heavy conversation. And she hadn't forgotten that plug in her ass. Be pretty damn hard to forget it. "Amelia told me I could make big money as a prostitute if only I wasn't so fat. Then she told me I'd better get a better bra as they'd be down round my waist like Great-Grandma Jean by the time I turned twenty."

She'd been horrified by that and had spent years wishing she was flat-chested.

"Bitch," he spat out then cupped her breast. "You know they're beautiful, right? Everything a man could hope for. And you are not fat."

She'd spent a long time coming to terms with her body, trying to be happy with it, but it didn't hurt to hear his compliments.

"What happened, Curt?"

"Amelia wasn't happy being the wife of a Navy Seal. She didn't like how often I went away. She seemed to have some ideal about what her life would be. Unfortunately, reality was a bitter disappointment. She was a master manipulator. Early in our marriage, before I learned what she was truly like, she had me so tied up in knots trying to please her that I almost fucked up a mission."

She winced, knowing how that would have upset him.

"Nothing ever pleased her. Even when I tried to do what she wanted. I grew tired of the complaints. About where we lived, how we never had any money, and how she couldn't buy the things she wanted without going to her daddy, which I'd forbidden her to do."

"She listened to you?"

He snorted. "She didn't. She liked to involve other people in our lives, but I didn't realize how much she told other people about our private life until I attended one of those god-awful dinner parties at her parents. Every fight, every imagined slight she'd tell her friends, her parents, probably her damn hairdresser as well."

Was that part of the reason he didn't like the idea of living in a small town? She had to admit that gossip was rife in Haven, but there were limits to what people revealed about their private lives.

"Took me a while to figure out that the clothes she was wearing weren't cheap knockoffs as she'd told me. The lies didn't stop there, though. I could've dealt with a few lies about money. But . . ." He looked down at his clenched hands. She covered his hand with hers, and he grabbed onto it with his other, holding on tightly.

"She was cheating on me. For months, I think. The thing was, I had decided to leave the navy when I found out she was pregnant. I'd just returned home from a mission and I was going to tell her my decision when I found them together. In our bed."

"Oh, that bitch!"

He startled then grinned slightly. "Yeah, that's what I said. Along with a few other things. Got rid of him and told her to get out. Told her it was over. She cried, asked me how I could kick out the mother of her baby. At that stage I wasn't even sure it was mine. But she told me she'd get a DNA test done that would prove it was. I told her she was still leaving. That if the child was mine, I'd take care of it, but, right then, I didn't want to see her face. I heard her on the phone to her mother as she packed some things, telling her all sorts of lies. Can't blame them for believing her, she sounded hysterical. You know, I'm not even sure why she married me in the first place."

"Her friends thought it was so cool she was married to a Navy Seal," she told him gently, hurting for him and furious at her selfish cousin. "It was a status thing."

He nodded. "Figures. I shouldn't have driven her out that night. She was upset. I should have insisted she stay while I left. Then maybe . . . maybe they wouldn't have died."

"Oh, Curt." She hugged him tightly.

He turned to look at her. "My feelings for Amelia were just a young man's lust. My feelings for you are much deeper. If anything happened to you . . ."

She knew then that she loved him. Not a child's love or an infatuation. She loved him deeply. And she had a feeling he felt the same. God, it was going to hurt so much if he didn't feel the same way, but she had to tell him how she felt.

"I love you, Curt. I always have."

Pleasure filled his face. "I love you too, Jenna."

Thank you, God. That knot inside her unraveled as elation filled her. He loved her. "Nothing is going to happen to me."

His gaze turned fierce. "No, it won't. I'll see to that."

He kissed her, and the sorrow was soon flushed away by deep lust. He cupped her breast, pinching her nipple lightly. She gasped, pulling back. She glanced down at his body, itching to explore him. She'd never taken a man into her mouth before, had never seen the appeal, but with Curt everything was different.

"Curt, please, can I?" She pointed at his cock, unable to say it.

He raised both eyebrows. "What do you call me?"

Her nipples hardened further at his hard tone. "Sir, may I?"

"May you what?"

Crap. He was going to make her say it. "May I suck your cock?"

He grinned. "You may."

She knelt in front of him, and he parted his legs as she laid kisses on them. She cupped his balls gently, delicately.

"You can be firmer than that, sweetheart," he told her.

Glancing up uncertainly, she bit her lip. "Will you tell me what to do?"

His eyes flared. "You've never done this before?"

She shook her head, blushing slightly. How many twenty-seven-year-olds hadn't given a blow job for God's sake.

He smiled, and this time it reached his eyes. "Aren't you full of surprises? First of all, there's little you can do I won't like, so long as you don't use your teeth or grab hold of my balls too hard. Take hold of the base of my cock with your other hand and take the head into your mouth."

OH, fuck, he'd died and gone to heaven. Her mouth was a little clumsy, her hold on him uncertain, but he didn't think he'd ever felt so turned on by a blow job in his life. Her mouth was warm and wet and those little noises she was making were almost his undoing.

"That's it, darlin', now take my balls in your other hand and squeeze them lightly."

He shut his eyes. Fuck! Had anything ever felt so good. She carefully caressed his balls while running her hand up and down his dick.

And unless he wanted to come in her mouth, he knew he needed to pull her back. He grasped her chin.

"Easy, baby, let me go."

She drew away, frowning. "Did I do something wrong?"

"God, no, that was too good."

"Then why stop?"

"Because I'm not as young as I once was, and it takes me a while to recover."

She tipped her head to one side, looking sweetly confused.

"I want to be inside you when I come, baby. Now, come here." He drew her up onto his lap so she straddled him, her heat against his dick. Was he trying to torture himself tonight?

He kissed her, taking his time to savor her, to build her arousal. By the time he was finished, she was squirming on his lap, making those little sounds of need he loved.

"Damn, you're good at kissing," she told him.

He smacked his hand on her ass. "No swearing."

Her gaze narrowed. "I'm pretty sure you made that rule just so you get to spank my bottom."

He hid his smile at her disgruntlement.

He rubbed her nipples with his thumbs, enjoying the way her breath caught.

"Sir, please."

He was certain hearing her call him Sir would never grow old.

"What do you need?"

"You. Inside me. Now. Well, once you take the plug out." She shifted around on his lap again.

"Who said it's coming out?"

She stilled. "You're going to take me while it's inside me?"

He nipped her neck. "Yes."

"Oh, God."

He moved her so she knelt at the edge of the bed, her body spread over the mattress. Pushing her legs apart, he knelt between her thighs. Grabbing the base of the plug, he twirled it, pulling it out then pushing it deep.

She cried out, her hands twisting in the bed covers. Knowing he was near the end of his control, he inched his way inside her, moving slowly so he could judge whether she was finding it too much.

The way she pressed back at him, those small whimpers of need, told him everything he needed to know.

"Stay still, little sub."

"I can't."

"You will. Unless you want me to take my pleasure without giving you any."

She stilled at those words, and he was glad she was facing away from him as he grinned.

"You wouldn't."

"Wouldn't I?"

"Bastard."

Slap. Slap.

Damn, that was a definite turn on. She was right, that no swearing rule he'd made was really just an excuse to turn her ass pink.

"You going to be still? Or are you going to sleep with a red ass and a needy pussy?"

"I'll be still. I'll be still," she promised hastily.

"Good girl." He drew back and drove himself deeply inside

her. His movements grew faster, harder. She was tight because of the plug, and it wasn't long until he was at the edge, ready to come. He reached around and flicked her clit, feeling how slick she was, how much she needed him.

"Come, baby," he ordered, giving her clit a final few flicks.

As she came, pulsating around his dick. He let go and flew over the edge with her.

16

"I can't believe he pleaded guilty."

Jenna lay on the bed, staring up at the ceiling. She felt a little numb. She'd been back in Dallas a week now and she felt even less in control than before. Her whole world had shifted. Some changes were good. Some not.

"It's my guess he didn't want to draw things out and put your mother and you through more than he had to. This way, things should die down more quickly. The media will soon move on to something else. People will forget."

She stiffened. She wouldn't. She wouldn't forget that her dad had made stupid decisions that had landed them all in this huge mess. She wouldn't forget that everything she'd thought she'd known about her life was a lie.

"I don't understand why he won't see me." His refusal to talk to her hurt more than anything. Was he worried she'd be angry with him? She was. How could she not be after what he had done? But just because she detested what he'd done, didn't mean that she still didn't have feelings for him. She still remembered the man who'd taught her to ride her bike, who'd picked her up when she'd fallen and bandaged her scraped knees. That was the man she missed.

"Maybe he's trying to shield you. Or maybe it's guilt. I know it's hard to think about your dad in jail, but at least you and your mother can move on with your lives."

Move on? Without knowing all the answers? Was that possible?

He pulled her against him, and she snuggled in tightly, her head resting on his chest. He was her only constant in this whirlwind, and she was damn glad to have him by her side.

"I don't know how my mother will cope. She's lost everything." She wasn't just talking about money. Her mother had money from her parents she could use, but she'd lost her husband, most of their friends, and her place in society. All things she truly cared about. And what about Jenna? What would she do now?

"She'll be okay. She's stronger than you think. And she'll have you to help her, which will be easier with you in Dallas now."

She had to work hard not to stiffen up. They hadn't talked about what would happen after this was over. Not that it was over, exactly. But, like Curt said, things should die down now that her father had pleaded guilty. The threats should hopefully go away, and she could move forward.

But did that mean moving to Dallas? She'd always figured she'd return to Haven. But what about Curt?

"You can move in here. Or, if you don't like it here, we can find somewhere else to live."

"You want me to move in?" He hadn't asked her. But then, that was Curt. He didn't ask, he told. He ordered.

He leaned up on one elbow. "Of course I want you to move in here." He brushed her hair away from her face. "I love you, Jenna. I want you with me, always. Don't you feel the same?"

That vulnerable look on such a tough guy got her every time. She cupped his face. "I love you, of course I want to be with you."

He smiled. "It's settled then. Quit your job back in Haven and move in with me. When you're ready, you can look for a job here. Or not, whatever you like. I have enough money to take care of you."

An uneasy feeling filled her. Nothing felt settled to her. He kissed her forehead then lay down. A few minutes later he was asleep.

While Jenna lay there for most of the night, worrying.

17

Jenna patted Daisy's head as she sat at the table and stared down at the scrambled eggs and toast on her plate. She didn't really want any of it, her stomach too tied in knots to eat. It had been two weeks since her father had pleaded guilty, and his sentencing was today.

She looked up as Curt entered the room. He was going into work this morning then he'd come back for her before they went to court.

"Hey, have you seen my watch?" he asked, walking up to her, placing a kiss on the top of her head.

"Yep, it's by the sink. You took it off last night to wash the dishes."

"Oh, good, thanks, baby. You made breakfast." He grimaced. "I'm so sorry; I have to get going."

"It's okay, it's nothing elaborate. Just eggs and toast."

"If I wasn't leaving work early today for the sentencing I could stay and eat with you." He pulled her up and kissed her properly. "I appreciate everything you do, you know that, right?"

She smiled at him, her heart melting a little. "I do." And he always made certain she knew it.

"And you'll be okay? You don't want to come into the office with me?" He'd only returned to work a few days ago, wanting to make certain the threats against her had died down. But there had been another disaster in the news, and people seemed to have moved on.

She wrinkled her nose. "And watch you do paperwork all day? No, thanks. I get enough of that in my job."

Well, she had.

"Speaking of your job, have you called Doctor Harper?"

No, because she was a wimp. She wasn't ready to say goodbye to that part of her life yet.

"I thought I'd wait until after the sentencing."

He frowned slightly then nodded. "I guess that's a good idea. Then you can concentrate on everything that needs to be done like getting out of your lease and having your stuff packed and sent here. If you need any help arranging it, let me know. I don't want you getting stressed out."

Right. Nope. No stress here.

She forced herself to smile and nod. God, if he knew everything she was hiding from him, he'd have a fit. Then he'd probably turn her over his knee and spank her ass until his arm tired. Maybe that would be a good thing. A long, hard spanking to make her forget everything else for a while, to release some of the tension building inside her.

She knew she should tell him how she felt. But she didn't want him to feel bad. He hated Haven. Jenna had lived in Dallas her whole life, she'd only lived in Haven a few months. It made no sense for her to be homesick. For Curt to be the one to up and move. She'd get used to being back here. She had friends here, she could find a job.

And Curt had enough on his mind without her worrying him

with her foolishness. She wasn't a child. As long as she had Curt she didn't need anything else.

Right?

～

"Hey, Curt."

He glanced up as Cady walked into the room. Everyone else was out, and he was on his own, trying to get through as much paperwork as possible so he could get home early to Jenna. He knew she was putting on a brave face for him with all this stuff with her dad.

"How's Jenna holding up? The sentencing is today, right?"

"Yeah, this afternoon. She's trying to keep it all together and be strong for her mom, but it's hard for her."

"I can only imagine. Any more threats?"

He shook his head. "We've dealt with the worst offenders, and things seem to have died down." Otherwise he wouldn't feel safe leaving her like he had. Although he'd still had a few moments of hesitation. But no one knew where she was, and she didn't really leave the apartment.

"What's she going to do after the sentencing? Has she made a decision about whether to stay in Dallas or go back to Haven?"

"She's staying." Of course she was staying. She was moving in with him. Doubts swirled through him as he remembered that she hadn't yet quit her job or gotten out of her lease. But she'd had a lot going on, it would take her time to adjust.

"That's good. I'm sure she'll find a job here easy enough. Although I suppose that's something she doesn't want to think about yet. It would be difficult to go back into the world after all of this."

"There's no hurry for her to get a job." He'd take care of her. Always.

Cady stood. "Just let her know we're here for her. If she wants a girls' night or something, Lacey and I are happy to come over or go out."

Except he didn't like the idea of her going out without him. Was he too possessive? No, it wasn't that he didn't trust her. She wasn't like Amelia, who'd played games. But he knew he'd spend the whole time worrying about her. What if she drank too much, and some asshole came on to her, and she couldn't fight him off?

"Relax, Curt. We all know at least one of you guys will be with us. As long as you keep your distance and don't interrupt, we'll let you or Hunter or Gray tag along."

Right. He should have known Hunter and Gray would have this stuff figured out. Funny, he'd never been this possessive with Amelia. Not even with all her taunts about finding herself a real man.

As Cady left him on his own, his worry increased. Jenna wasn't one to play games, but he knew she was holding something back and he couldn't help but wonder why.

∽

Eighteen years without parole.

Oh, God. Jenna felt ill as she walked into Curt's apartment. She sat on one of his chairs. Daisy came up to her with a whimper as though sensing Jenna's pain and laid her head on her lap. She rubbed the big dog's head.

"That was harsher than I expected," Curt said as he walked in. He leaned against the wall, looking down at her. "Arms trafficking penalties aren't usually that high, but they threw everything at him they could. Still, he had no priors and he pleaded guilty."

"They're not happy because he wouldn't tell them anything about The Brit," Jenna said numbly. "Probably because he wants to protect my mother and me."

"Jenna, I—"

"Will you take control tonight?" she interrupted him.

"What?" He looked down at her in surprise.

"I want . . . I need you to take control. Okay? I can't think. I don't want to think. Curt, I—" she broke off on a sob. Please let him do this for her.

"Get up, sub," he said in a low voice.

Oh, thank you, God.

She stood.

"Come here."

She walked towards him, her body trembling. She stopped in front of him.

"Look up at me."

She stared up into his stern eyes. She didn't know what was coming next but she knew Curt would look after her. All she had to do was please him, and there would be nothing else but him. Everything else would disappear.

"Daisy—" She looked over at the dog.

Curt delivered a hard smack to her ass, and she jumped, rubbing at the sting. She glared up at him. "Did I say you could look away from me?"

"No, but I thought—"

"Your job isn't to think right now. Your job is to do exactly what I say. Your job is to please me, is it not?"

"Yes, Sir," she said in a low whisper. "I'm sorry."

He cupped her chin, and his gaze softened. "You're sure this is what you need, Jenna?"

She blinked back tears. He always took the time to make certain she was okay.

"Yes. I need this right now, Curt. Please."

He kissed her gently on the lips then turned her, delivering another hard smack to her ass. "Get into the bedroom, strip and sit on the side of the bed. I'm going to take care of Daisy then I'll be in."

When he entered, her nerves were jangling, and she was almost ready to call it all off. He came straight to her and picked her up, carrying her out of the bedroom and into the bathroom, where he'd filled the bath with scented water.

"Curt, what is this?"

"It's a bath. It's good for relaxation, and you're too tense."

"But I wanted . . . this isn't what I . . ." As he slipped her into the water she sighed. Bliss. Maybe it wasn't what she'd anticipated, but, damn, it felt good.

He grabbed some soap and a cloth and started to wash her shoulders.

"Uh, I can do that." She grabbed for the cloth, and he pulled it back, frowning at her.

"I'm in charge right now, remember?"

"But I—"

"Being your Dom isn't just about sex, whips, and chains, remember?" His lips quirked up on one side. "It's also me making sure you have everything you need."

Warmth filled her. God, he was so good to her, better than she deserved.

She was crazy to think it mattered where she lived or what she did. What mattered was him. She loved him. She lay there as he washed her. Thoroughly. He even made her spread her legs and place them on the sides of the tub so he could wash her pussy and ass. By the time he finished, she was so turned on, her pussy throbbing relentlessly.

He pulled her up and wrapped her in a fluffy towel. He dried her quickly then picked her up and carried her into the bedroom.

"You're so good to me," she told him.

"You deserve it, baby. I know you've been through a lot these past few weeks. So much has happened, it's got to be hard to catch your breath. To realize it's over."

Tears filled her eyes at his understanding. "It is. I feel like I've been in an emotional rollercoaster, only it never stops and there's no way off."

He laid her on the bed and opened the towel. Then he clasped her face between his hands. "Talk to me. I'm here for you. I'm not the greatest communicator, I know. But you're the one person I will drop everything for to talk about whatever you need to. Understand?"

He was right. She'd been stupid to hold back "Yes."

"And, God willing, that's the end of everything. From now on, we can concentrate on us." He ran a finger over her lower lip, and she opened her mouth, taking the digit into her mouth and sucking.

His breathing increased, but then he drew back. Disappointment filled her. She sat. "Curt—"

"Lie on your stomach," he ordered in a gruff voice. He stood, moving stiffly, and she knew he wasn't as unaffected as he was acting. He pulled open the bedside drawer as she lay on her front and watched as he grabbed a bottle of lube and oil.

She shivered. He'd been working increasingly bigger plugs into her ass. Was tonight the night he took her ass? He poured oil onto his hands and rubbed them together before giving her a massage to end all massages. He worked on her back until all the knots melted, her body growing into a pile of goo.

"Roll over," he told her, helping her move to her back. This time, his massage was slower, more sensual, and he paid an awful lot attention to her breasts, swirling his hands around the mounds then plucking at the nipples.

She moaned, trying hard not to wriggle. He moved lower, over her stomach before dropping to her feet. That might have been disappointing if he didn't give the best foot massage. Ever.

By the time he ran his hands up her legs, she swore she'd died and gone to heaven. He spread her thighs and rubbed the oil into the lips of her pussy, not that she needed extra lubrication. He massaged her inner lips, swirling his finger around her clit until her whole body shook with the need to come.

He flipped her, drawing her up onto her knees, her upper body resting against the mattress. She could barely keep herself in place, she felt so boneless and relaxed.

Curt chuckled. "Maybe I should give you a massage more often if this is the result. I've never seen you so obedient."

"I'll do whatever you want to get massages like that."

His chuckle grew into an all-out belly laugh, and she smiled at the sound. She liked making him laugh. Then he spread her ass cheeks, and all humor faded. He ran a wet finger over her asshole, and she clenched reflexively. He smacked the side of her ass.

"No clenching. I'm taking this ass tonight."

"Oh, fuck."

"Uh-uh," he scolded. Slaps landed hard and fast on her butt. The sting quickly turning into a deep burn. Her heart raced, arousal flooding her, chasing away the last bit of lethargy. By the time he stopped spanking her, she was on fire. This time, when he pulled her ass cheeks apart, she didn't tighten, instead she welcomed the finger he thrust inside her. In and out. Slow then fast. There was no pattern and it kept her on the edge. Another finger joined the first, then a third. It burned slightly but it was a good kind of pain.

Reaching around with his other hand, he played with her clit, teasing her until she was just at the edge. "No coming without permission, baby."

Oh, damn it.

He'd been teaching her to delay her orgasms, and she didn't want to repeat the last punishment she'd been given after coming without permission. She bit down on her lip and concentrated on not slipping over. Her legs shook with the effort, and, just as she knew she couldn't take much more, he withdrew his fingers from her asshole and nestled the head of his cock against her puckered entrance.

As she breathed out, the head slipped past her tight ring of muscle.

Oh, it burned so good.

Inch by staggering inch, he pushed inside her, his cock, slick with lube, filling her completely. So full. So hot. So good.

"You may come when you like, baby," he told her, swiping at her clit as he drove himself deep then pulled back. In fast, out slow. Again and again. Then a powerful wave hit her, sweeping her away. It was so hard and deep and all-consuming that she barely heard his own cry of satisfaction as he followed her over.

Curt cuddled into her from behind and kissed her neck. "All right, baby?"

"Oh yeah." She smiled as she snuggled into his embrace. This was where she belonged. With him.

Curt placed his hand over her belly. "I can't believe you're really here. That you're mine. I know I've fucked up in the past, but nothing is more important to me than you."

Her doubts faded a little more. Maybe all she needed was time. Tomorrow she should call Doctor Harper and officially give her notice.

He rubbed his hand up and down her stomach. "You're everything I could have hoped for. Although, you can be a bit bratty and stubborn."

"Hey!" She turned to glare at him over her shoulder.

He grinned and winked. Then reaching over her, he turned off the light "You're also kind, compassionate, and loving. You're going to be an amazing mom, Jenna."

She stiffened. Oh, God. They hadn't spoken about this. They should have. She knew that. But when in the middle of all this crap was she supposed to have talked to him about this?

"Uh, Curt—"

"Not right now," he said, kissing her ear as he snuggled in behind her, holding her belly once more. "I know you're young. You have your career. But one day. You and the babies we'll make will mean everything to me, Jenna. I promise to look after all of you. I know I can be a hard bastard and, I don't always say the right thing, I'm domineering and possessive, but I'll always love you. And I'll love the children we create as well. How many do you want? Two? Three? I thought four might be a nice number."

"Four?" she asked faintly. Was this the same man? Somehow, she'd never seen Curt wanting children. But, no, that wasn't true. The Curt she'd known before Amelia had adored children. He'd have made an amazing father. So would this Curt. He'd be a bit more protective—okay, a lot more, and she'd have to get him to ease up on that to let their children breathe and learn and. . . Who was she kidding? She couldn't have children. And Curt didn't know it.

How didn't he know? Hadn't Amelia told him about the accident?

"I thought it was all over when Amelia and our baby died. That baby was the one special thing in my life. The only thing that was mine. I couldn't wait to be a dad, even though I knew my time with Amelia was through, I always intended to be there for my child."

"Of course you did." She held his hand where it rested on her belly and a tear ran down her cheek. It had been a long time since she'd thought about being a mother. She mourned the loss of that part of her, the inability to carry her own child—Curt's child.

Oh, God, how could she tell him?

"I know there was a possibility it wasn't biologically mine. I wasn't a fool. There was no reason to think Amelia did the sensible thing and used protection when she was fucking around. But she said it was."

And then the baby was gone, and he was alone.

She bit her lip. She couldn't tell him. Not yet, anyway.

"But now I get to have babies with you. Thank you, Jenna. For giving that back to me." And her heart broke just a little more.

18

Tears ran down her face until she could barely see the road in front of her. *Fuck.* She wiped furiously at her cheeks. She couldn't keep driving; she was going to cause an accident. She had to pull over. She saw an exit coming up and took it, ending up in a small town. She pulled into the parking lot of the first motel she came across.

"I think we better get a room, Daisy. I'm not up to driving to Haven. Not tonight." When she got there, she knew there'd be questions she didn't feel like answering right now, like why the hell she'd run from the man she loved.

She wasn't running away, she reassured herself. Yes, she'd taken off while he was away on a job. But she'd left him a note that told him where she was going. Just not why, exactly.

She'd lied to him, the one thing he'd asked her not to do, because she couldn't figure out how to tell him the truth.

"You're a wimp, Jenna. Leaving a note is such a cowardly thing to do."

She just needed some time to think.

And you couldn't do that in Dallas?

Curt had left two days ago on an out-of-town job, she'd had plenty of time to think. Thinking wasn't the problem. Talking was. How could she look at him while she explained that she could never have his child? How could she stand the disappointment on his face?

She swiped at her eyes, trying to calm down before she went into the office.

"Oh, Daisy, what have I done?"

Truth was, she missed Haven, and her friends so she'd left Curt a note telling him she was going back to Haven to pack up her stuff and that she needed some time to herself.

He was going to be furious.

After securing a room, she went back to the car and grabbed Daisy and her suitcase. Luckily, this motel allowed dogs to stay in the rooms. Although, as she looked around she could see there wasn't much a dog could do to make the place any worse.

Oh, well. It wasn't like she planned on staying longer than one night. She just needed time to regroup before she arrived in Haven. Maybe she'd manage to get some sleep. She snorted. She couldn't really see that happening.

She laid out some food for Daisy and put her bed on the floor, although she'd probably just sleep with her. She took a quick shower and climbed into some track pants and a T-shirt before laying back on the bed.

A RINGING WOKE HER. Feeling disorientated and still half asleep, she searched around for her phone. She held it up to her face, blinking to clear her vision. Melody.

With a yawn, she answered the call.

"Hello? Jenna?"

"Here," she replied, looking around with a bit of confusion.

Where was she? This wasn't Curt's bedroom. She stood and looked out the curtains. A parking lot. The motel. She was on her way to Haven. Away from Curt.

She dropped the curtain. It was getting dark; she must have slept for a few hours.

"Did I wake you?"

"Um, yeah. I haven't been sleeping that well and I laid down for a minute and fell asleep."

She didn't tell her where she was. She glanced over at Daisy then grabbed her leash. The poor dog was probably desperate. She wagged her tail excitedly.

"Are you okay? You sound funny."

"Actually, I'm not. I think I've been really stupid."

"Where are you? Has Curt hurt you? Are you somewhere safe? Do you need me to come get you?" With each question, Melody's voice rose, her agitation clear.

"Woah, okay, hold on. One question at a time. I'm all right. And, no, Curt certainly hasn't hurt me. I'm just a total wimp."

"What do you mean?"

"I took off," she said softly.

"What? Why?"

She bit down on her lip to hold back a sob. "Because I'm a coward."

"You're neither of those things," Mel defended her. "Although that doesn't mean you haven't done something stupid. What happened?"

It still amazed her how her friends had stood by her. Even knowing what her father had done.

Jenna explained everything. About her inability to have a child, Curt's excitement over the idea of a baby, and feeling home-sick for Haven.

"So while he was on an out-of-town job, I left a note telling him I was going to Haven for a bit to pack my stuff and spend some time with you guys."

"We've already packed up your stuff for you."

She sniffled. "I know, that's why I'm an idiot. I lied. Because I'm homesick, and I can't have babies, and I don't know how to tell him."

"Oh, Jenna, I take it back. You *are* an idiot."

"Well, thanks."

Melody sighed. "I'm not going to sugarcoat it; you know me, I tell it like it is."

"I know. I need to talk to him. But he'll try to convince me that it doesn't matter whether I can have babies or not. That he wants to be with me no matter what."

"Of course he would have. Because he loves you. If things were reversed, and he couldn't have kids, would you leave him?"

"No, but that's different."

"Why? Because he's lost a baby? Because he's a man? Just because you can't carry a baby doesn't mean you can't have children, Jenna." There was a disappointed note to Melody's voice.

And it made Jenna feel all the worse.

"You're right."

"Was it just an excuse so you could leave?" Melody asked. "It's okay if it was. I get it if you wanted to leave him but didn't know how to get out."

"No. No, it's not like that at all. I love Curt."

"But you also love living in Haven."

"Yes." She groaned. "What have I done?"

"You two really need to get your shit together."

"I know. You're right." And she was. Jenna had just needed someone to lay it out. A bit of tough love. "He's going to be so upset with me."

"So, make it up to him," Mel said pragmatically. "I find a blow job helps. Men will forgive anything for a blow job."

"Mel!" she protested, even though she was smiling.

"What? It's true. Women all over the world know this. I'm sure Curt is no different."

"This is more than just sex, Melody. This is forever we're talking about."

"I know," Melody said quietly, more gently. "And it's understandable you reacted the way you did. The two of you barely had time to breathe, let alone talk to each other, with everything else going on. It's been an emotional roller coaster and it's no wonder you needed some time out to think, but you need to talk to him. Go back, Jenna. And hey, you said he's out of town, right? So you can get back before he sees the note."

She could. But she'd still need to tell him. She needed to come clean with him. She couldn't play games like Amelia had.

"Have you always been this bossy?" she teased her friend.

"I like to think of it as assertive," Mel countered. "Where are you anyway?"

Daisy barked, and she frowned. What was wrong with her? Daisy hardly ever barked.

"I don't know. Some Podunk town off the highway. I think it had a name from the bible. I have to go, Daisy wants out. I'll talk to you soon, okay?" she said as she opened the door. She paused as she saw two large men standing there. Scruffy, and menacing looking, they glared back at her. Jenna's hand tightened on the door, prepared to shut it in their faces when the one to the right raised his hand.

"I wouldn't," he said, pointing a gun at her chest.

Terror held her frozen. Spots danced in front of her eyes and for a moment, she was back in Sudan, listening to Alana beg for her life. Her breath came in hard gasps, panic threatening to overwhelm her. Stomach churning, she stared at the two men.

No. No, this wasn't happening again. She dug her fingernails into her palms, the small bite of pain helping her push back the fear.

She wouldn't let herself be taken.

This time, she wasn't going without a fight.

"Drop the phone. Now."

Jenna swallowed, trying to moisten her dry mouth. Who were these guys?

"Drop it," the other man demanded. She let it slip from her numb fingers without turning it off, hoping Melody was still on the line.

"Who are you? What do you want?" she said loudly, aware of the wobble in her voice.

"Shut up," the one closest said, reaching for her. "Come quietly and you won't get hurt."

As he grabbed her arm, Daisy jumped with a snarl. Jenna took the opportunity to slam her fist into his throat. She quickly kneed him in the balls then followed with an elbow to the back of his neck as he bent over with a cry. Daisy snarled as she ripped into the other guy. He cried out in pain and as he dropped to the ground, Jenna took off.

"Daisy, come."

She could hear the dog running behind her as she headed to her car. *Fuck! No keys.* There was a ping against the car next to her, and she screamed, realizing one of them was shooting at her. Why was no one coming to help her? Was everyone else out? Or did they just not care about a woman and her dog being attacked?

Jenna ducked down, keeping low as she moved between cars. She had to make it to the hedge beyond the parking lot. That would give her and Daisy some cover. She grabbed hold of the dog's collar, keeping her close.

"Come on out, there's no hiding from us. Our employer just wants to chat with you."

Their employer? Who the hell's that?

She moved around another car, trying to slow her breathing. The last thing she wanted was to alert him to where she was.

"Hey, what's going on out here? What's all the noise about?" It was the old guy from the office. She didn't wait around to see what would happen; she took off in the direction of the hedge. Daisy raced silently beside her, and she thanked God for whomever had trained the dog. There was some yelling behind her, but she forced herself to ignore it. They weren't going to take her. Not again.

Once they were behind the hedge, she looked around. The street lighting wasn't great here, she'd chosen to stay in a crappy area of town, it seemed. About half a block down there appeared to be some sort of wrecking yard.

"Could be the best place to hide," she whispered quietly to Daisy. Or an ideal place to be tracked and gunned down. Damned if she knew what to do. What would Curt do?

Curt wouldn't even be in this position, he'd have disabled both men, taken their guns, and waited for the cops. Probably without breaking a sweat.

Well, she couldn't sit around thinking about it forever. She took off towards the junk yard, hoping like hell Mel knew to send help.

Oh, God, why had she left Curt?

SHE'D LEFT.

He stared down at the note as he sat in one of the armchairs in his living room. He'd come home from his job early to find her gone. In one hand, he held a glass of whiskey, in the other her note. He frowned. According to her note she'd gone to Haven to pack up her belongings.

Fucking bullshit.

She'd told him her friends were packing up her stuff. If she'd wanted to go and help them then why hadn't she said anything? Why the fuck would she just leave a note?

Had she left him?

His gut tightened. No. He wasn't losing Jenna. Whatever was going on, they could fix it. He'd make sure of it. He just wasn't certain what needed fixing. Fuck. He leaned his head back against the chair, closing his eyes. Actually, he had some idea of what might be the problem.

She missed Haven.

She'd tried to hide it, but he'd seen it in her voice, her face. He'd figured she'd just get over it. And now she'd gone there without him. What if she didn't want to come back?

Then you move there to be with her.

Could he do that? Leave everything?

And what exactly was he leaving? A crappy apartment? A job he loved, but he could still work from Haven. Or start his own company.

What mattered most was Jenna. Her happiness came first.

He ran his hand over his face. At least he knew where she was, and that she would be safe. If she couldn't be with him then she was safest in Haven where people would watch out for her.

Oh, but she was in a world of trouble when he caught up to her. She wasn't going to be able to sit down for a long time. In fact, the idea of spanking her ass each night for at least a week held a lot of appeal.

But first he needed to talk to her. He looked over at his phone. He could call her, but it wouldn't have the same impact as turning up on her doorstep. Then she wouldn't be able to refuse to speak to him. He quickly packed up his stuff then strode to the front door as the buzzer sounded. He stilled. Was she back?

He pressed down on the button. "Yeah?"

"Curt, it's Hunter, why the fuck aren't you answering your phone?"

"Got other things on my mind. I have to leave town for a few days." It occurred to him he should buzz Hunter in but he didn't have time to talk to him and explain. He needed to get to his woman and teach her a lesson about running away from him.

"Curt, Jenna's in trouble."

His stomach dropped. "I'll be right down." He stormed down the stairs, bag in hand. Hunter was waiting outside. Another car pulled up beside Hunter's truck. Gray stepped out, his hand holding a phone to his ear. He covered the speaker. "Have you told him?"

"Not yet. Just got here," Hunter snapped.

"Told me what? What's this about Jenna?" he asked urgently, his heart pounding.

"We think she's been attacked."

His heart missed a beat.

CURT DRUMMED his fingers against his thigh as he sat in the passenger side of Gray's car. He'd wanted to drive, but Gray had refused to let him. Hunter was following behind in his truck, Josh and Tiny riding with him. They'd both pulled up at his place while Gray was explaining everything. About an hour ago Melody had alerted Jake that Jenna was in trouble, after hearing a fight over the phone. Jake had placed a call to Travis who'd then contacted Gray.

"Why didn't Jake call me?"

"Said he didn't have your number and thought it would be quicker to talk to Travis than find it," Gray told him tensely. Gray's phone rang through the Bluetooth speaker.

"Hey, Connor, what do you have?" Gray asked.

"It's got to be Bethlehem," Connor replied. "It's the only town on the way to Haven with a biblical name. There are four hotels and three motels. I'm sending you the address for each. I've got the girls ringing each of them to see if Jenna checked in to one . . . wait a second . . . what's that?"

Someone spoke quietly in the background.

"Okay, we've got it. Jenna checked into the Silent Night Motel. Got the address and I'm sending it to all your phones. Cady's calling Haven's sheriff to let him know."

"Tell Lacey to call Travis as well," Gray said. "Good work."

"Travis?" he asked when Gray ended the call.

"He wants to be kept informed on what's going on. He's taken a liking to Jenna."

Curt couldn't blame him. She was damn near perfect. He just prayed like hell she was all right.

I'm coming for you, baby. Just stay safe.

JENNA WAS FREEZING. If she hadn't had Daisy to cuddle with to keep warm the cold might have sent her out of hiding and into her attackers' arms. Not that she'd seen or heard from either man again.

That didn't mean she was going to risk moving. She'd just wait until morning. Or until Curt came. Whichever came first.

I'll always come for you, Jenna.

He was coming. She knew he was. She just had to hold on. She snuggled in against Daisy, trying to ignore her shivering and the fact she really, really had to pee. Her stomach grumbled, and she swore under her breath. That's all she needed. For her hiding place to be discovered because her damn stomach wouldn't be quiet.

Was that a siren?

Should she get out and look? But what if it was going some-where else? Nope. She wasn't moving until Curt got here. She didn't trust anyone else. Well, maybe a few other people. *Please let Melody have heard me.* If she had and called Jake maybe they could figure out where she was. Maybe one of them would call Curt, and he'd come looking for her.

She'd hidden herself and Daisy in the back of an old car. It smelt terrible, the upholstery had seen better days, and there was a spring pressing into her hip. But she'd put up with worse. She'd been chained to the ground inside a dark hut for eight days. Compared to that this was a damn holiday.

Why do these things keep happening to me?

At least she had Daisy now. If it weren't for Daisy, she knew those guys would have taken her. God knew where she'd be by now. She had no idea who their boss was but she definitely knew she didn't want to chat with him.

WHEN THEY PULLED into the parking lot of the Silent Night Motel it was the middle of the night. Curt was prepared to wake the whole damn town if that's what it took to find Jenna. Instead, the recep-tion area was fully lit. They walked in to find a potbellied, older man taking a swig of whiskey from a bottle.

"We're closed," he snarled.

"We're looking for Jenna Jasons," Curt said. "What room is she in?"

The man seemed to pale. Then he stood and moved hastily backward. "Now, I don't want any more trouble."

"What do you mean *any more* trouble?" Curt stepped forward. "What trouble?"

The guy held up his hands. "Don't shoot me. I don't know nothin'."

"What the fuck?" Hunter asked.

"Curt. You got here quickly."

Curt turned to see Jake step through the door. He was in uniform and he looked tired. "Two guys turned up here a few hours ago and tried to kidnap Jenna. Apparently, she and Daisy fought them off. One of them took potshots at her."

"What? Is she all right?" His heart hammered hard. *Please don't say she's dead. Please let her be okay.*

"Don't know, no one can find her. I've been talking to the Sheriff of Bethlehem, he's got these guys locked up. One of them has a broken nose and swollen balls, the other had a few bites. Thought I'd go have a chat with them."

"We've got to find Jenna," Curt said urgently.

"She's probably somewhere close by," Gray suggested.

Curt nodded. She'd find a place to hide and wait for him to get to her. "We need to spread out and search for her."

"I've brought a few people with me," Jake told them. "Touch base with them and keep in contact."

When Curt walked outside, he saw Jake's idea of a few greatly differed from his.

"Damn, is there anyone left in that town?" Hunter asked, staring around as people handed out reflective vests, radios, and flashlights.

"Just the young and old, I'd say," Curt said.

"All right, everyone, listen up."

Curt looked over and saw Max Ferguson step forward. "We go in pairs. Each woman must be paired with a man, no complaints."

Curt spotted Melody, and she rushed over to him as Max gave a few more instructions about keeping safe and checking in with the coordinators who'd remain in the motel parking lot. No doubt they'd wake up the whole neighborhood, but he didn't care.

Melody threw herself at him. He took a step back, unprepared for the assault but as he felt her tremble he pulled her close. "I heard her on the phone, she said she had to go because Daisy was barking, but neither of us hung up. I heard her ask someone who they were then I heard her cry out. Oh, God."

He patted her back awkwardly. *God, I hope she doesn't start crying.*

"You did good, Melody. Really good. It's because of you we figured out she's missing. This is all thanks to you."

She pulled back to look up at him. "She was going back, Curt. She was going back to tell you she was sorry, that she should have talked to you. She loves you."

Something inside him nearly broke to hear that. She'd been coming back.

"It's all right, Melody," he told her, seeing she was waiting for an answer. "I'm not mad at her. We both need to work on our communication skills." He looked around him at everyone who'd come to help Jenna. "I can't believe all of these people came to help find her."

"Because she's one of us," Melody replied. "We take care of our own."

"Yeah. I can see that. So, is there room for one more idiot male in your town?"

Melody's eyes widened and then she grinned. "Hey, what's one more?"

～

"JENNA! JENNA!"

She mumbled under her breath. She'd been dozing, dreaming about Curt and she wasn't ready to wake up. In her dream, he'd wrapped his arms around her and held her tightly.

Daisy whined, and she tensed, coming fully awake, her heart racing. There was something she needed to be wary of, some reason she had to stay quiet. Her attackers.

That's right. She'd been shot at. She was hiding. Shoot, she had to stop waking up in strange places. It was really messing with her head.

"Jenna! Jenna!"

Daisy whined, her tail wagging. *That voice! It sounds like Curt.*

"Is that Curt, girl?"

Daisy licked her face and whined. For once she didn't even care about doggy breath.

"Jenna!"

"Curt!" she called back in a hoarse voice. She cleared her throat. That was pathetic. But then she didn't have to worry about how loud she was because Daisy started barking. Suddenly a flashlight beam landed on her. Then he was there, pulling open the door of the old car, which fell off its hinges as he yanked at it.

Daisy jumped out, climbing over him. "Easy, girl, let me get to Jenna."

He reached in and pulled her out. "Shit. You're freezing. Someone get me some blankets. She's freezing."

And then people surrounded her. Blankets were piled around her, and so many flashlights were aimed her way it was nearly blinding. Amazement filled her as she spotted many of her friends from Haven, as well as Curt's colleagues and friends. Everyone wanted to talk to her, check up on her, but not once did he let her go. Colin and Trace Richards took care of Daisy, and knowing her dog was in good hands, she leaned her head against Curt. She was so tired.

"Just hang on, baby," Curt murmured. "We're going to get you to the hospital soon."

"I don't need the hospital. Just a bed and you."

"I want you to get checked out, you're freezing cold."

She'd started to shiver, which she knew was a good sign. "Curt, the men who attacked me—"

"They're locked up. Jake is talking to them now."

"It's weird. They said their boss wanted to talk to me. I have no idea who their boss is."

She felt him climb into a car, where he sat with her on his lap. Warm air blasted her, and she sighed in contentment. She looked over as Gray slipped into the driver's seat.

"Hey, Gray."

"Hey, sweetheart."

"Are you taking us home?"

Gray looked over at Curt.

"We can go home soon, baby," Curt told her.

"I'm so sorry I left, Curt. I was an idiot. I should have talked to you."

"Yeah, you should have. But don't worry about that now. Just relax and lean against me."

19

Curt looked up from where he sat by Jenna's bed as the door to her room opened. She wasn't pleased when she realized he and Gray were taking her to the hospital, but she'd been too exhausted to put up much of a fight. They'd admitted her as a precaution, but other than being a bit run down and cold, she was all right.

Gray stepped in. "She okay?"

He nodded.

"Come out for a minute. I think you might want to hear this."

Curt stood and kissed the top of Jenna's head before he walked into the corridor. "What is it?" He didn't want to move far from her side.

"Jake got one of them to talk," Gray said, not bothering to explain who he was talking about.

"And? Did he say who hired him?"

"Didn't see the guy, just talked to him on the phone. Said he had a British accent."

"Jesus." Curt stilled. *Could it be him?*

"Said that they were hired to watch Jenna, and, if they saw an opportunity to grab her, they were to do it and then call him. He'd tell them where to bring her."

Could they use these guys to lead them to The Brit? But that would mean leaving Jenna.

"In return for a lighter sentence, this guy has agreed to place the call and say that he's got Jenna. This guy should give him an address, and then we can make a move on him."

"You called Travis?"

"Yep, he should be here in a couple of hours."

"I can't come. I can't leave Jenna."

Gray nodded and smiled. "I'd feel the same if it were Lacey lying in that bed."

"Just get him for me, all right? Did this guy say why he wanted Jenna?"

"Nope, but he seemed to be under the impression David Jasons was talking to the feds."

"Why the fuck would he think that?"

Gray looked grim. "My guess is someone might have set her up as bait."

"Hendricks? That bastard." It would be something that slime ball would do. "I'm going to kill him."

"Let's just hope he doesn't try to stick his nose into this."

Travis slammed Hendricks into the wall of the small room. "You bastard!"

"Get your hands off me! This is assault!" Hendricks looked over at Hunter, Gray, Jake, and then his partner, Marshall. "You're all my witnesses."

"Didn't see a thing," Gray said.

"Don't know what you're talking about," Jake added.

Hunter just grinned. It wasn't a pleasant smile.

Even Hendricks's partner looked away. "Marshall!"

His partner raised his head and stared from Travis to Hendricks nervously. "You set her up, Paul. She could have been killed."

"You're just lucky it's me here and not Curt, because then you'd be a dead man. In fact, I suggest you run and find a place to hide. I'm willing to bet that once he can pull himself away from Jenna's bedside he's going to come searching for you. You put her out there as bait, without her permission, and then you left her."

"Nothing was happening," Hendricks sniveled. "We couldn't watch her twenty-four seven."

"And you nearly got her killed." Travis shook him then pushed him away. "Get out of here. Quickly, little man. I don't have time to teach you a lesson."

"This is an FBI matter, you have no rights here—"

Travis turned and growled at him, getting a great deal of satisfaction from the way the man cowered back. "Go."

"Just go, Hendricks," Marshall said. "You're going to have a lot of explaining to do at headquarters. I'll handle things here."

Hendricks backed out after glaring at them all. Travis turned to Marshall. "I'll be running this show."

The younger man looked at him steadily. "This man is on the FBI's most wanted list."

"And if the FBI comes in guns blazing, it could scare him off," Gray pointed out calmly. "Why don't you let us do this? We know how to get in quietly and get out. After we have what we need, you can claim victory over capturing The Brit. If you think about it, there's no risk. It's all reward for you. If we fail, you can claim Hendricks fucked up by not having surveillance on Jenna."

Marshall thought that over. "All right. But I'm still coming with you."

"Fine." Travis glared at him. "But just know he's mine first."

He was going to make sure that bastard didn't spend another day breathing the same air as him.

JENNA WATCHED Curt as he slept. This was a new experience. Being able to watch him while he was so unguarded. God, she loved him so much.

Her stomach rumbled, and he opened his eyes, staring at her.

"How do you do that?" she asked.

"Do what?" He sat up and tugged at her blankets, covering her. She knew she'd worried him. She could see it in the way he fussed over her.

"Go from asleep to wide awake. It always takes me a while to get my bearings."

"I know, baby. It's kind of cute the way you wake up all disorientated. You're so helpless in those few seconds. Gives me a chance to take care of you."

"You always take care of me," she countered. "You came for me. I knew you would. That's why I found a safe place to hide after Daisy and I escaped. I waited for you. Where is Daisy?"

"Colin took her home with him. He'll take care of her until we come for her."

"She was amazing. If I hadn't had her I don't know what I would've done. I couldn't have fought off both of them. She leaped for one, and I kneed the other one in the balls, then we took off. They shot at us. I could have died." With him thinking she didn't want him. Tears filled her eyes. "I'm so sorry, Curt."

"Sh." He put his finger over her lips. "I know. Melody told me you were coming back. I know I don't make it easy for you to talk to me, but if you'd told me you needed to go back to Haven, I'd have done what I could to make it happen. I know I have a tendency to make assumptions or decisions for the both of us without talking to you."

"You mean everything to me. I don't want to lose you."

He leaned forward, his gaze fierce. "What makes you think you ever would?"

"Curt, I can't have children."

He stilled, closing up. Then he ran his hand over his face. "Fuck."

"I'm so sorry I didn't tell you. I always thought you knew. I thought Amelia would have told you."

"Amelia? What?"

"I was in a car accident when I was ten. I damaged my uterus. Curt, I'm so sorry. I can't give you children."

He grabbed hold of her hands, looking fierce. "Baby, I am so sorry that happened to you. That you can't have children. But if you think that means anything will change between us then you have another think coming."

"You want children. Four." Tears ran down her face.

He brushed them away with his cheeks. "I'm an asshole."

"What? No, you're not."

"I am. I never even asked you about children, I just assumed you wanted kids."

"I do. I mean, if I could have them."

His thumbs stilled. "You still want them?"

"Yes. Of course, I love kids."

"Baby." He gave a low laugh. "Just because you can't give birth to my child, doesn't mean we can't have kids. If you want them, then we'll look at other ways."

"Really?"

"Really. I love you. I want you. Kids are just a bonus. No matter what way they come to us. I'm here to stay. Whether we can have babies or not. I'm here forever, Jenna. And that's the way it's gonna be, got it?"

She smiled at him. "Got it."

He groaned. "Did it again, didn't I?"

"Yes. But you wouldn't be Curt if you weren't a bit dictatorial. Sometimes I even like when you order me around."

"Only sometimes, huh?" He leaned in and kissed her.

"When can I get out of here?" she asked as he pulled back. "I want to go home."

He took hold of her hand, rubbing his thumb over the back. "It's going to take me a while to sort things out in Dallas before I can move to Haven with you."

She tried to sit. Frowning, he gently pushed her back. "Lie down. What do you think you're doing?"

"I want to sit up. Curt, please."

"I'll get some pillows." He grabbed some spare pillows from the cupboard and propped her up.

"Curt, when I said home I meant your apartment in Dallas."

He sighed. "You're miserable in Dallas."

"I'm not miserable..." she trailed off at his firm look.

"We're going to have a long talk about holding things back from me. I know you miss Haven. It's why you haven't done anything about your house there or your job. You should have told me, Jenna."

The disappointment in his voice made her feel miserable.

"I didn't say anything because I figured I'd get past it. They say it takes six months to get used to a new place."

He raised an eyebrow. "So after six months you'd have said something?"

"Exactly. A lot has happened and I guess I just thought I needed some time. As long as I'm with you, it shouldn't matter where I live."

"And shouldn't the same apply to me?" he asked.

"What do you mean?"

"As long as I'm with you, Jenna. I don't care where I live."

"But you hate Haven. You didn't like the people, or the lack of privacy. You prefer the city."

He snorted. "I also want the woman I love to be happy. I think I can put up with a few nosy busybodies. And when I saw how everyone turned up to help look for you, I started to see the positive side of small town living. Amelia used to include everyone in our private business. It drove me insane to know that everybody else knew what was happening in our relationship, sometimes before I did."

"I'd never do that."

"I know, baby."

"I can live in the city."

"And I can live in Haven. You have a job you love, people who care about you, a place you belong. They'll just have to accept me as well. And I'll get used to the nosy bastards. Might have to punch a few more noses though."

She laughed.

He kissed her gently. "I love you, baby. But don't you ever scare me like that again, got it? No more trouble."

"Can't promise that, it does seem to like to follow me around."

"Yeah, well from now on, it has to go through me first."

As HE CREPT his way up through the forest towards the cabin hidden back from the road, he heard the gunshot. His heart raced. *Fuck, no.* He moved faster, nearly blowing his cover.

"Travis, stand back. Wait." Jake's voice in his ear barely penetrated the haze of anger. He hadn't come this far only to lose this guy.

He kicked the door in and entered, barely aware of the voices now swearing in his ear.

"No!" He stormed forward, part of him aware he should stop

and wait, search the cabin first. But he knew no one else was here. He saw the body on the ground, part of the head blown off, and the gun that lay inches from the man's hand.

"Bastard shot himself." Hunter came up behind him. "Damn. Didn't see that coming."

Travis stared down at the body, feeling numb. This was the man he'd searched for years for, and he'd taken his life just like that. He felt...devastated.

"You okay, man?" Gray smacked his back.

"Yeah. Yeah, I'm okay. Just need some fresh air." He left the cabin and sat on the steps outside. He'd wanted revenge on that bastard. Revenge for what he'd done to Carys. For murdering the only woman Travis had ever loved. And now that revenge had been ripped from his hands. *Fuck.*

EPILOGUE

"Jenna? You're awfully quiet. Everything okay?"

She had to stop her automatic reaction, which was to say she was fine. It would've been a lie. She was working on talking to Curt about her feelings rather than dismissing them as unimportant.

They'd been back in Haven for a week now. It had taken a fortnight for Curt to settle everything and finish up at Black-Gray, although he would still do some freelance work for them. He hadn't worked out exactly what he'd do now he lived in Haven, and that worried her. He'd moved here because of her. What if he wasn't happy? What if this had been a mistake?

She placed her hand over her stomach, trying to quell her fears. "I still feel guilty."

He paused. "I thought we'd talked about this."

They had and she'd listened to him as he'd told her all the reasons she shouldn't feel that way. It had helped for a while. "I know. But I can't help it. I lied to you. I caused so many problems. If those men who tried to kidnap me hadn't been caught, they could have shot someone, they could have hurt one of my friends who came to find me. It could have been avoided if I had just talked to you. And I feel so bad."

He pulled her over onto his lap where he sat on the couch in her living room. "Baby, you're not to blame for what those men did. If they didn't try to get you then, it would have happened another time. Or The Brit might still be out there, a threat. No one got hurt."

"I know. But I..."

He rubbed his hand over her back. "You still feel guilty."

She nodded.

"Guilt will eat you up alive. And it's the last thing I want for you. I know what it's like to live like that."

"What if moving here makes you unhappy? What if you hate it here? What if we've made a mistake?"

"Oh baby. You can't take everyone else's problems on as your own. You're going to eat yourself up." He ran his thumb over her lower lip then nipped it gently. "I should have known you'd feel this way. I haven't given you that spanking I owe you for not talking to me. I figured we'd both made mistakes and that we'd wipe the slate clean. That might have been a mistake if you're feeling so terrible."

"You're going to spank me to get rid of the guilt?"

Umm...maybe she shouldn't have said anything.

"Oh, I'm going to do more than that." He stood her up and slapped her ass. "Go put on something sexy. A skirt and corset or a tight dress. No panties. No bra."

Her heart raced. "Why?"

He narrowed his gaze. Whoops, probably not a good idea to question him when he was in Dom mode.

"Go."

She raced upstairs and quickly got dressed, putting on some make-up and doing her hair. When she came downstairs, he was waiting on the sofa. He swirled his finger around and she did a slow twirl.

"Did you obey me?"

"Yes, Sir." She was slightly shocked by the breathlessness in her voice.

"Lift your skirt. Show me."

Holy fuck. Face hot with embarrassment, she lifted the front of her skirt, giving him a small peek before dropping it down.

"No," he said slowly. "Lift it all the way up then leave it there until I give you permission to drop it."

She pulled her skirt up, wondering how it was possible for her cheeks to grow any hotter. Her skirt was tight and she had to wiggle slightly to get it up over her ass.

"Very good." Curt studied her bare pussy as she resisted the urge to cover herself. "Hands on your head. Turn slowly, show me that ass."

Her heart racing, she turned around.

"Stop there." He told her, sounding closer. Then he placed his hand on her ass and she jumped slightly. He chuckled. "Nervous, darlin'?"

Nervous? Was he kidding? She was going to jump out of her skin.

He gave her ass two heavy smacks. "I'm waiting for an answer. And I don't like to wait."

Yeah, like she didn't know that already.

"Y-yes," she quickly replied after two more spanks were applied to her vulnerable butt cheeks.

"Good," his voice was filled with satisfaction. "Wait here, right like this while I get ready."

Thank God all the drapes were pulled and the door locked or she wasn't certain she'd be able to stand there in such a vulnerable state. The minutes ticked by slowly until she heard him on the stairs again. Although the wait was worth it as he came into view. He wore dark jeans and a white linen shirt with the arms pushed up. With his hair slightly longer than usual and a five o'clock shadow on his cheeks, it wasn't hard to imagine him as a wicked pirate.

"Good girl," he told her, cupping a breast and running his thumb over her hard nipple. She was too big to go without a bra, but she'd chosen a sparkly top that had inbuilt support. Still, there was very little between her sensitive nipple and Curt's skillful fingers. He plucked at the nipple, pulling on it, easing back when it reached the point of pain. Jenna leaned into him, wanting more.

Curt ran his hand down her body to cup her mound. He pressed his thumb against her clit, rubbing it back and forth. Jenna bit down on her lip, hoping to stop the cries she could feel building inside her.

Suddenly, he stopped, leaving her feeling breathless and on fire. He pushed her hair back from her face. "You are so beautiful and damn sexy." Leaning in, he kissed her gently. "On your knees, baby. I need you to give me some relief. Spread those legs and put your hands on your thighs."

She eagerly dropped to her knees as he undid his fly then pushed his pants and boxers down, revealing his thick erection. She knew better than to touch without permission, so she waited as he took hold of his cock, running his hand up and down the long shaft.

Then he held it out to her.

"KEEP your hands on your thighs. Just use your mouth," Curt commanded, closing his eyes as her mouth wrapped around the head of his cock. He kept hold of the base, mostly so he wouldn't come too quickly. He wanted to savor the feel of her wrapping his dick in warm, wet heat. She ran her tongue over the head, across the slit and he shuddered. He squeezed his shaft tighter, his balls already aching with the need to come.

She sucked him in quick, taking him deep before slowly releasing him, running her tongue over his shaft. Part of him wanted to pick her up, throw her over his shoulder and carry her upstairs so he could fuck her all night long.

But that wasn't what she needed from him tonight. It wouldn't solve the guilt that was weighing her down. She needed to feel some sense of atonement. And if he was honest, he needed this too. Needed her. Needed that feeling of being in control. Of course, he could just punish her here, in the privacy of their home.

Their home. He liked the sound of that. Even if he knew it was going to take some getting used to.

But he was going to take her to Saxon's. Not only were there all sorts of wicked and depraved equipment that he could use on her, but it was time. She'd never played in a club and the longer they left it the more nervous she would become. The atmosphere, the people would just add to her excitement.

And her trepidation.

After all, he didn't want her to think he was a soft Dom.

He grinned wickedly right as he let go and came in her mouth. She sucked down every drop then licked him clean.

"Enough." He pulled her up, running his hand over her bare ass. Reaching between them, he slid two fingers through her slick heat, pushing them up inside her as he flicked her clit with his thumb.

"So wet. So ready."

As she clamped down around him, he pulled back, giving her a sharp smack on the ass. "No coming."

Her face was flushed, her breathing heavy as she stared up at him with dazed eyes.

"But-but—"

He had to work hard to keep his face stern. Damn, she was cute when she was frustrated.

He ran his finger down her nose. "If you're good I might give you permission to come at some stage tonight. But you'll have to be very, very good."

She stared at him in disbelief, her bottom lip dropping open. He tapped his finger against her chin. "Keep that mouth closed or I'll find something to fill it. I have a very nice ball gag that I've been saving for you."

Her eyes widened. So far, he hadn't used many toys. That was going to change tonight.

"You wouldn't."

He chuckled. "Darlin' you have no idea what's in store for you tonight."

DARLIN' you have no idea what's in store for you tonight.

Jenna looked out the truck window at the beautiful old house painted dark gray with white trim and a wide, wrap-around porch. If you were just driving past, you'd have no idea that it housed a BDSM club. The carpark was located around the back, the front lawn beautifully manicured. Curt maneuvered his truck around the back.

She swallowed heavily. She'd been to Saxons often and other than those first few times, she'd never been this nervous. Her hands were actually sweaty, she was slightly light-headed, her heart racing too fast, her breathing shallow and quick. Maybe it was because she was going to play for real tonight. Maybe it was because this would be her first time at a club with Curt.

"Jenna? Jenna, look at me." She startled as she heard Curt speak, turning to him. The parking lot was well lit and it wasn't hard to make out his face. His gaze narrowed as he studied her. "Shit, you're freaking out."

Reaching over, he grasped hold of her hands in his. "Listen to me, Jenna. Big, slow breaths. Come on, breathe in. Then out. In again."

She followed his directions and her heart rate slowly returned to normal, the dizziness fading. Curt rubbed his thumbs over the backs of her hands.

"Better now, baby?"

Jesus, how embarrassing. She couldn't believe she'd had a panic attack because Curt was going to spank her ass in front of a room full of people. Actually, when she put it like that, she could believe it.

"Sorry," she told him. "Bit nervous."

He snorted. "A bit? More like you're in a full panic. We're going home." He turned on the truck.

"What? No." She reached over and grasped hold of his thigh with her hand, squeezing. Damn, the man was rock hard with muscle. "I'm acting like an idiot."

"You're terrified. A little bit of fear is good, but scared to death is not. That is the last thing I want. If the idea of going inside makes you panic, how do you think you'll react once we get started? I'm not here to force you to do things you don't want to do."

"I thought you Doms liked to push boundaries."

"Yeah, we like to push them. We don't like to bulldoze our way through them."

"Curt, please, I'm ready for this. It's just…"

"Just what?"

"I'm not sure what's making me so nervous. It could be that I've never done anything but watch, or that I know people here and they're going to see me…you know…"

"Get your butt spanked."

Yeah, that.

"Or that I don't know what's going to happen." She looked over at him. "I trust you, though. And I want to do this. With you. Please, Curt."

He was quiet for a long moment and she held her breath,

certain he was going to drive them home. Then he turned off the truck, turning to her slightly. She let out a deep breath.

"All right, we'll go in. Nervousness is okay. Any panic and we'll pull back and try another time. I expect you to talk to me."

"I will, Sir."

He ran his thumb down her cheek. "We don't have to do anything more than watch or some fun play. It's only been five weeks since those guys tried to take you."

She blinked away some tears. She'd never had someone take care of her or put her first the way Curt did. She shook her head. Time to be brave.

"I want this." But it was more than that. "I need it."

"Yeah, I think you do. Remember, you can always use your safeword. Say yellow if things are going too fast or you need to pause and talk."

She nodded. "No ball gag, then?"

He shook his head and relief filled her.

He opened the door then leaned in. "Not tonight anyway."

CURT ALMOST FELT a sense of coming home once he walked into the dungeon at Saxons. Not that he'd played here before. The other day when he'd come to speak to Saxon about becoming a member was the first time he'd ever been inside.

But he knew from speaking to Saxon that he ran a tight ship. Subs were closely watched. The Doms he used to monitor play were experienced and vetted by Saxon. The waitresses were all subs who usually had other jobs but enjoyed special privileges as Saxons subs, as he called them. They got their membership for free and they had the personal protection of Saxon, who spoke to each Dom they wished to play with and handled any negotiations necessary.

Underneath that annoying, sardonic exterior, Saxon was

extremely careful and protective of what he considered to be his. Almost made Curt like...no, that wasn't right, he didn't like the guy. But he could almost admire him.

As they walked in, he saw the way the Doms in the club turned to stare at his sub, he reached back and pulled her close, taking hold of her hand.

Mine.

He knew he was probably acting too possessive, but he hadn't realized how hard it would be to have everyone staring at her with hunger. Fuck, how had she gone so long without one of these Doms convincing her to play with them? They wanted her.

And why wouldn't they? She was gorgeous and delightfully open as she gazed around. Her eyes widened as a sub cried out in pleasure, her Dom using a vibrator on her pussy. The sub was strapped down to an examination table, her feet fastened in the stirrups and spread wide, her arms pinned at her sides as wide leather straps ran over her body, holding her down.

The Dom pulled the vibrator back and his sub cried out, sobbing.

"Please, please, Sir."

"Archer likes to make them beg," Saxon said from beside him. Curt felt Jenna jump, she obviously hadn't seen the other man approach. "He'll have her sobbing by the time he relents and lets her come."

Saxon moved around so he stood in front of them. "You're playing tonight?"

"We are," Curt said firmly, tensing himself for any argument from Saxon. He'd realized by now how protective the town was of Jenna. It both pleased him and pissed him off a little. Something else to get used to. But Saxon just grinned. There was a gleam in his eyes as he stared down at Jenna. "It's about time. I thought I was going to have to interfere. Permission to speak to your sub?"

Satisfaction filled him. His sub. He heard Jenna gasp a little, probably shocked that Saxon would ask him for permission to speak to her.

"Go ahead," he said with a nod, looking down at Jenna, who appeared wide-eyed and a little apprehensive.

Saxon studied Jenna for a moment. "Nervous, pet?"

She looked up at Curt, as though for permission to answer. That feeling of satisfaction grew and he gave her a short nod.

"Yes, Sir."

Saxon grinned. "Good. A bit of nerves is expected." He turned to Curt. "I'm sure you'll be watching for anything else."

Curt stiffened slightly.

Saxon held up his hands as though in surrender. "No insult implied. The reports from your old club all said you were an experienced Dom. No red flags. But we all know our Jenna has been through a lot lately, I'd be remiss if I didn't look out for her. I just wanted to make certain that Jenna was ready for this."

"I am," she said quietly but with steely determination. "I want this. I'm fine. We both are."

Saxon gave her a wink. "Good. Enjoy yourselves. Let me know if there is anything you need."

Curt squeezed her hand and turned so he faced her. "Look at me."

As she looked up, he cupped her face and leaned in to kiss her. "Thank you for your trust in me. And your faith."

"I've always trusted you," she whispered. "I love you."

He ran his thumb over her lower lip. "I love you."

"Does that mean I get to come tonight?"

He threw back his head and laughed. "No promises, my darlin'."

THEY WALKED SLOWLY around the dungeon. She didn't know if Curt was searching for a particular piece of equipment or whether he wanted to look at each of the scenes. In one corner, a naked woman she didn't know was bent over a low metal pole. Her wrists and ankles were shackled to the floor, her legs spread far apart, her ass and pussy on display. She shuddered at the idea of being tied down like that. Curt slipped an arm around her waist.

"Easy, baby. Remember, you're here with me. Nothing happens that you can't control with a safeword. This isn't Sudan. You're safe."

"Can we move on?"

"Not yet. Just watch."

The sub's Dom, a large man who wore just a pair of tight, dark pants was currently smearing lube over an anal plug. He knelt behind his sub and she half-expected him to shove it into her asshole. Instead, he ran his finger between the sub's ankles and the metal cuffs.

"All right, sweetheart?" he asked in a low, rumbly voice.

The woman couldn't turn enough to see him, but she visibly relaxed at his voice, the tension in her body fading.

"Yes, Sir."

He ran his hand over her ass gently. "You tell me if that changes."

"Yes, Sir."

Jenna felt her tension fade at his caring. He pulled apart her ass cheeks and slowly pushed the plug into her ass. Her head thrashed back and forth, her cries of pleasure making Jenna's whole body tighten.

Curt tugged her along with a chuckle. She glanced back as she reluctantly followed him. She'd wanted to watch until the end.

"Feeling a bit voyeuristic, are we?" he murmured in her ear.

She blushed. "They're at a club, don't they want people watching?"

"Yes. But we have more to look at." He lightly smacked her ass. "And I want to play with you tonight."

Her breath caught. They moved further around the room, stopping at a suspension scene. The female sub had been wrapped in rope then pulled into the air. She now hung facedown, her breasts hung down, her legs were spread wide. A Domme, dressed in tight leathers, her dark hair flowing down her back, suckled and licked at the sub's nipples while a tall, thin Dom had his face buried between the sub's legs. The Domme pulled away then grabbed something from her pocket. Jenna's breath caught as she saw it was a long chain that connected two nipple clamps. The Domme pulled at the subs nipples, then attached each clamp. The sub screamed and Jenna winced in sympathy. Once the clamps were attached, she saw the small weight attached to the chain, so that the clamps would pull at the sub's nipples.

Curt moved behind her, drawing down her top so that both of her breasts were exposed. She stiffened slightly, resisting the urge to look around and see if anyone had noticed. Curt pinched her nipple. "Attention on me."

Oh, the majority of her attention was exactly on what he was doing. He cupped her breasts, rubbing his thumbs over her tight nipples. She jumped slightly as she heard the sub in front of her scream, realizing that she'd come.

Curt stepped back, dropping his hands from her breasts. Disappointment filled her. She quickly pulled up her top and followed him. He turned back, frowning, his face growing cold. What was it? She stilled in worry.

"Did I tell you to put your top back?"

"No, but I..." she trailed off as his brows lowered, that warning look sending shivers through her.

He pointed over at an empty spanking bench. "Get yourself over that bench. Now."

Eyes wide, she hurried to obey him. She knelt then bent over the bench, turning her head so her cheek rested on the cool, padded top. She blinked back tears. Had she disappointed him?

Why had she pulled her top up? It wasn't like the majority of people in here had their boobs, and more, showing.

"Sir, can I help?" a female voice asked. Jenna stiffened. Who was that? Why were they speaking to Curt? Worry and insecurity whirled inside her, making her feel ill.

"I left my bag at reception, could you retrieve it please," he spoke in a low voice. "It has the name Curt Nolan on it."

"Yes, Sir, straight away."

She let out the breath she'd been holding.

"Spread your legs," he ordered.

She attempted to part them but her skirt was too tight. Curt pushed it up over her ass. Oh hell, could she do this?

"Easy, darlin'," he told her patting her ass lightly. "Just a small punishment for a small infraction. But you need to learn to obey your Dom. When I give an order, I expect it to be obeyed to the letter. Your job isn't to worry about what others think or see. It's to worry about me. What I want. What I expect, understand?"

"Yes, Sir. I'm so sorry."

"Here you are, Sir," a female voice said.

"Thank you," Curt replied to the waitress. She heard him unzip his bag. She'd seen the big black bag when he'd carried it in from his truck but she had no idea what was inside. Did she dare look?

"Don't move, Jenna," he ordered. "You're getting ten spanks. Five with my hand. Five with the paddle. Move, and you'll get more. With what you have coming soon, you're going to want these to be as few as possible."

Oh, fuck.

Before she could reply, his hand landed on her ass with a loud smack. Holy shit. That was harder than anything she'd experienced from him before. And he was going to hit her with a paddle? The next four smacks followed quickly. Tears filled her eyes, but they had more to do with the fact that she'd disappointed him than from the pain, although that wasn't insubstantial.

The paddle landed next. And shit! If she'd thought his hand was hard, then the paddle was next level. The burn filled her, making her cry out as it seared her skin. Before she could even process what had happened, the paddle landed again and again. Five heavy smacks that stole her breath. By the time she'd realized he'd stopped, tears were streaming down her face and her breath was coming in sharp sobs.

Curt ran his hand up and down her back. "Easy, baby. All done now. You were such a good girl, you took your punishment so well. I'm proud of you. Now, just stay there a minute longer," he told her when she went to move.

She cringed, wondering if anyone was looking. Crap, being naked and vulnerable in front of others was even harder than expected.

Curt leaned in and kissed away her tears. Then he crouched so they were eye-level and he studied her.

"I'm s-sorry for d-disappointing you."

"Sh." He ran his hand through her hair. "You're still learning, which is why your punishment was so light."

That was light?

"I was just h-having trouble w-with..."

"Being on display? Being naked in front of others?"

"Y-yes."

"I know. That's why you're not allowed to pull your top up until I give permission."

She closed her eyes. Jesus, help her.

"Jenna, look at me."

She opened her eyes, expecting to see him looking angry or upset. But there was a kind patience in his eyes. "I know this is hard. And it makes me happier than you can know that you're obeying me right now. That you're letting me push you." He pushed a strand of hair off her face. "You have no reason to be embarrassed. You're beautiful and I want to show you off. I'm not going to leave you, I'll stay right beside you the whole time, all right?"

She nodded. "All right. I'm sorry, Curt."

"Hey, once a punishment is given then that's it. Slate wiped clean, okay?" He smiled at her then stood. "Come on, let me help you up." He helped her stand then gathered her into his chest, rubbing his hand up and down her back. Then pulled her skirt down. "Feeling better, now?"

She nodded. "Yeah, except well, ouch." Her skirt rubbed against her newly reddened butt cheeks.

He grinned. "A punishment spanking is meant to hurt, darlin'. Come on. Let's walk."

And so she followed him around with her boobs on display and her ass cheeks on fire. They watched a few more scenes until Curt finally stopped in front of an empty piece of equipment.

A swing.

She swallowed heavily. Heavy chains were attached to a thick frame. The main part of the swing was made from black leather and would provide plenty of support. Two separate straps hung from the front of the frame that had loops at the bottom for your feet. They were more of a support rather than a restraint.

Curt placed his bag down. "Strip off."

Her hands trembling, she pulled off her top and skirt. It was actually a relief to get rid of the skirt, each time she moved, it rubbed against her sensitive butt cheeks. Speaking of her butt, how was she going to take any more punishment? She watched as he pulled some things from his bag. Lube, a butt plug, nipple clamps, a butterfly vibrator with straps and a riding crop.

Holy shit.

He turned to her, moving closer and cupping her face between his hands. "Scared?"

"A little."

He grinned. "A little is expected. Remember, you have your safeword." He lightly kissed her. Then he turned back and grabbed the butterfly vibrator and kneeling in front of her. "Hold onto my shoulders and step into this." She held onto him for balance as she stepped into the straps. He pulled them up, adjusting the butterfly over her and pulling the straps tight. Good. "Now, up you go."

He lifted her, settling her in the sling. Her ass hung off the end, but it wasn't uncomfortable, in fact she was well-supported. It was almost relaxing.

Almost.

Curt slipped her feet into the loops so her legs were spread wide, once more putting her on full display. That seemed to be the theme of the night.

"I'm not going to tie your hands but I expect you to hold onto the straps above you and not let go."

She nodded, wide-eyed as he tested the butterfly vibrator, switching it on with a remote he held. Immediately, it buzzed against her sensitive clit and she let out a cry of pleasure.

"Good," he muttered, turning it off.

She let out a shuddering breath, noticing that they were attracting a crowd. Oh God. Curt moved back and she saw he held the nipple clamps.

Trepidation filled her as she stared at the clamps.

He switched on the butterfly vibrator and she arched up as her clit started to throb. "Remember, no coming."

Fuck. This was going to be hard. Curt leaned in and suckled on one nipple then nipped at it, pulling on it. He drew back and placed the clamp around her engorged nipple.

"Ah," she cried out at the bite of pain that soon morphed into a deep throbbing. Oh God, she was going to come. She whimpered, her head thrashing from side to side as he gave her other nipple the same treatment. Too much, it was too much. She had to come.

Suddenly, the butterfly switched off and she let out a long, loud groan. Curt chuckled from beside her. "Easy, darlin', we're just beginning."

"I'm never going to survive."

Leaning down, he gave her a surprisingly gentle kiss. "But you will, because I need you. Always."

She sighed. Damn, how did he know exactly what to say? She blamed his sweet words for her inattention. And it wasn't until something hard pressed against her asshole that she realized she really should have being paying attention.

Her eyes widened as he started to press the anal plug inside her.

"Cur...ah, Sir!"

"Good save," he said. "You're going to take this plug. You've taken it before. Relax. That's it. You love having your ass plugged, don't you baby?"

Fuck, those words shouldn't turn her on but as her clit throbbed, and her pussy grew even more wet there was no denying that they did.

When the plug was fully seated inside her, Curt turned on the vibrator. She nearly came then and there. It was only his hard slap to her pussy that stopped the impending orgasm. She cried out, stunned by the heavy smack on her sensitive clit.

Then he started smacking her ass. Heavy, hard smacks that were fast then slow. She clenched her hands around the chains of the sling, needing something to hold onto but also scared that otherwise she'd be tempted to reach down and what? Push him away? Pull him closer? She wasn't entirely sure.

The sharp pain of his spanking kept her from falling over the edge into bliss. Just. But it was a hard fight. Tears ran down her face, her whole body shaking from the mix of pleasure and pain.

Then the vibrator stopped and Curt pulled back, moving around so he stood behind her. He leaned down.

"Look at everyone watching you, darlin'. Look at them all admiring what belongs to me."

She stared out at the crowd and saw the way they watched, riveted. Some of the tension she hadn't realized she still carried left her.

Curt reached down and pulled lightly at the nipple clamps. She cried out, arching her back. "Poor baby," he crooned. "I bet you need to come, don't you?"

"Yes, please, Sir."

He massaged her shoulders, rubbing away some knots. Then he pulled her hands away from where she still clung to the chains, clicking his tongue as he saw her red palms, the indentations from the chains. "You're holding onto the straps too tightly. You're going to hurt yourself."

"You just clamped my nipples and spanked me," she said with disbelief.

"That's different. That was on purpose." He placed her hands down by her sides.

"Not ideal, but I don't want your hands above your head. You keep them there, though, hear me?"

She nodded, her eyes widening as he picked up the crop. Oh hell.

CURT COULD TELL that Jenna was worried, but he was keeping a close eye on her. If that trepidation turned to true fear he would slow things down. But she was doing so well, if he stopped now he would be doing her a disservice. She was brave. Strong and beautiful and his. And he was so damn proud of her. He swung the crop, taking care to get the fleshiest part of her ass. She gasped, cried out. Two more strikes and he switched on the butterfly vibrator. She arched back with a scream. Another few strikes. Damn that was beautiful. The next few landed and he knew he couldn't wait much longer. He needed her.

But first he had to make certain of something. He moved to stand next to her head, pushing some strands of hair off her face. "Jenna, do you still feel guilty?"

"What?" she almost slurred her words. She was close to subspace. He turned off the vibrating butterfly.

"This is punishment for not talking to me, for keeping things from me. But once I've finished, there is no more guilt. No more worry. Understand? But that doesn't mean you'll do it again, will you?"

She shook her head, staring up at him with wide, blue eyes. "No. Never. I'm yours."

He kissed her. Hard. "You are. Five more."

He moved between her legs, smacking the crop down hard and fast, wanting this over, needing to be inside her. Then he placed the crop down and undid his pants. He drew them and his boxers off then grasped her around the hips and swung her toward him, slowly pushing his way into her pussy. She was wet and ready for him.

"Curt. Curt."

He didn't correct her. He liked hearing his name from her lips.

"Please, please," she cried out. Damn, she looked gorgeous. Her eyes were wide and glazed, her face flushed, a light sheen of sweat covered her skin.

"I love you, Jenna Jasons. You're mine. Now and always." He drew out then in. Faster and faster. Then he switched on the vibrator, needing to feel her come with him, around him. "Come, baby. Come now."

It only took a few seconds before she let out a scream and came. He tried to hold off, wanting to make it last, but all too soon he crashed over as well.

Fuck yeah.

"WOAH, THERE." Curt grabbed the door as it swung back, nearly hitting the person who was trying to maneuver her way through on crutches. He gave Melody a firm look. "What do you think you're doing? Why didn't you ask someone to hold the door for you?"

"I'm fine. I can get through the damned door," she snapped. The plaster on her foot was bright pink today, not the deep emerald green he'd last seen.

He looked around, expecting to see Brye. "Who's taking you home?"

"I'm getting myself home."

"No, you're not," he told her sternly. "The doctor said you're not to drive. Who's supposed to be picking you up and why aren't they here already?"

"For a guy who thought everyone was too nosy in this town, you've sure become as meddlesome and bossy as they rest of the men around here."

"Why, thank you, I do believe that's the nicest thing you've ever said to me."

She scowled at him. "It wasn't a compliment."

"If you hadn't been fooling around on that dirt bike and doing moves you weren't supposed to be doing, you wouldn't have broken your foot."

She rolled her eyes. "Like I haven't thought of that."

"I think someone needs a spanking."

Her jaw dropped.

"I might suggest that to Brye. Hey, Brye," he called out as the other man approached.

"Don't you dare," Melody hissed.

He smiled, enjoying himself. He'd definitely misjudged this town. The men really did look out for the women, and those same women gave them a run for their money. And he liked being a part of that. It gave him a sense of belonging. Of family.

"Melody, I told you to wait in the waiting room until I came for you," Brye scolded with a frown.

Melody sighed then she gave Curt a wary look. "Sorry."

Curt winked at her then walked into the clinic to find his wife standing by the reception desk, smiling at something Hannah was telling her. She turned with a smile. "Hey, you."

"Hey, baby." He took her into his arms and kissed her.

"Bags are in the truck, and we're ready to go," he said.

"I'm going to miss you." Hannah pouted.

"We're only going to the city for a few days," Jenna said with a smile.

Hannah smiled. "I hope the meeting with the adoption agency goes well."

"So do we." Jenna gave him a look filled with such hope he knew that if the adoption thing didn't work out they'd find another way to make their wish come true.

They made their way out to his truck, and he helped her into the passenger side, brushing a kiss across her lips before climbing into the driver's seat.

Jenna slipped her hand into his as they drove through Haven. He waved at people then slowed to let two older women cross the street.

"I called my mother and let her know we're coming to visit." Jenna's mother had moved into a smaller house, close to her sister. While she didn't have the life she once had, she seemed to be getting stronger as a person. She was even talking about getting a part-time job. Hendricks had lost his job with the FBI and disappeared to God knew where. If Curt hadn't been so happy he might have thought about going after the bastard. Travis was still moping over the fact The Brit had killed himself, but Curt was relieved he was no longer a threat to Jenna. Marshall was ecstatic as he'd ended up getting a promotion after claiming responsibility for finding the fugitive.

"You got a letter today, baby."

"I did?"

He reached into his pocket and handed it over, unsure if now was the right time. But if her father wanted to see her then they had time this weekend.

"It's from Dad, isn't it?"

"Think so. Want me to pull over?"

"No, I can do this. I can't believe he finally contacted me."

Jenna had been sending him letters each week, but so far nothing had come back. She opened the letter and cleared her throat.

DEAR JENNA,

Thank you for your letters, darling. I read and appreciated each one. They're the only bright things in my otherwise bleak world.

SHE MADE A STRANGLED NOISE, and he pulled off the road and turned off the truck. Undoing both seatbelts, he pulled her across and onto his lap. She let out a deep breath. He leaned over her shoulder to read the rest of the letter aloud.

NOT THAT I don't deserve to be here. I do. I did those terrible things. Although not for the reasons many might believe. I got into financial trouble, darling. Deep trouble. I owed some bad people a lot of money. Doug knew about my problem and offered me a solution. It was supposed to be a one-time thing. Little did I know, in my naivety, that once you're in, you're in forever. I was so ashamed of myself. I hated what I'd done. But I couldn't stop. And the one time I tried to get out you paid the price.

SHE LOOKED UP AT HIM. "My kidnapping."

He nodded, his jaw clenched in anger. That bastard.

I TOLD him I'd go back to doing what he wanted. There was no way I wanted to risk him hurting you, Jenna. I love you more than life and I'm sorry.

Take care of your mother.

Love, Dad

SHE FOLDED up with the letter with shaking hands. "Well, that's that. He's truly guilty."

He hugged her tightly. "Want to go back home? We can postpone the meeting with the adoption agency."

She straightened her shoulders and glanced up at him, blinking back a few tears. "No. I'm not going to let what he did ruin everything else for me. It's time to move on."

She attempted to move from his lap, but he grabbed her, kissing her. Once she was back in her seat and buckled in, he started the truck again. They were silent for a few minutes as he drove.

"Are you sure you're okay?" he asked.

She took a deep breath in. That last bit of unease was gone. She had some sense of closure. "Yeah, I really am." She smiled at him.

"Good." He smiled back. "You know, I think we only really need to stay one night in the city."

"But don't you want to see everyone?" she asked, looking surprised.

"Yeah, but there's that meeting on Thursday night about the new housing complex going in that I want to attend, and then Saxon has got a poker game arranged for Friday night, and Duncan needs my help chopping down some trees."

JENNA SMILED as she listened to Curt explain all the reasons he was eager to get back to Haven. But she knew what the real reason was. The town had grown on him, he fit right in, and, after a few months, people had started to forgive him for his introduction to the place. Well, except for Logan Ferguson, but everyone knew he liked to hold a grudge. Curt had found a place for himself. He'd even been talking about starting his own security company in Haven.

Yep, Curt had finally discovered there was no place quite like home.

READ on for some excerpts from Laylah Roberts other books.

Made in the USA
Columbia, SC
31 August 2023

22330036R00176